Dear Reader,

Welcome to Parable, Montana, and the third story in my Big Sky series!

Sheriff Boone Taylor has been staying under the radar, doing his job but letting the rest of his life slide—much to the annoyance of his neighbor, cosmetics executive turned chicken farmer Tara Kendall. When she looks out over her otherwise lovely view of the countryside, her eyes invariably find the "eyesore" Boone calls home.

Now, suddenly, children arrive on the doorstep—Boone's two little boys, who have been living with his sister since soon after his wife Corrie's death, and the twin preteen stepdaughters Tara loves and constantly misses, since her ex-husband allows her little or no time with them.

Big Sky River is a book about two wonderful, heart-bruised people who have nearly stopped believing in love, even though it's all around them, like the mountains and rivers and famed

Big Sky, finding their way to each other and pooling their broken dreams to make a new one together—the kind that lasts.

So here's a hearty welcome to Parable, whether you've been here before or this is your first visit. Sit back, join in and be prepared to smile—and maybe even shed a tear or two.

You're going to like it here.

Best,

Praise for the novels of #1 *New York Times* bestselling author Linda Lael Miller

"Miller's name is synonymous with the finest in western romance."
—*RT Book Reviews*

"This is a delightful addition to Miller's Big Sky series. This author has a way with a phrase that is nigh-on poetic, and all of the snappy little interactions between the main and secondary characters make this story especially entertaining."
—*RT Book Reviews* on *Big Sky Mountain*

"After reading this book your heart will be so full of Christmas cheer you'll want to stuff a copy in the stocking of every romance fan you know!"
—*USATODAY.com Happy Ever After* on *A Lawman's Christmas*

"Miller once again tells a memorable tale."
—*RT Book Reviews* on *A Creed in Stone Creek*

LINDA LAEL MILLER

DOUBLEDAY LARGE PRINT HOME LIBRARY EDITION

This Large Print Edition, prepared especially for Doubleday Large Print Home Library, contains the complete, unabridged text of the original Publisher's Edition.

ISBN 978-1-62090-749-8

BIG SKY RIVER

This edition published by arrangement with Harlequin Books S.A.

Printed in U.S.A.

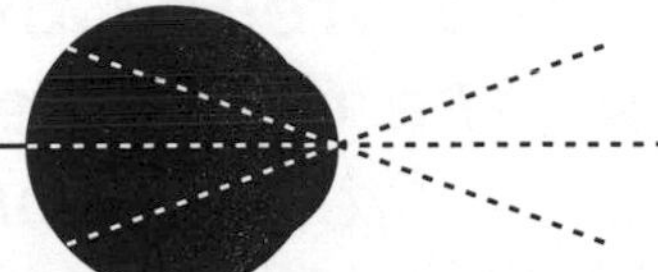

This Large Print Book carries the Seal of Approval of N.A.V.H.

Also available from
Linda Lael Miller
and Harlequin HQN

The Parable series
Big Sky Mountain
Big Sky Country

McKettricks of Texas
An Outlaw's Christmas
A Lawman's Christmas
McKettricks of Texas: Austin
McKettricks of Texas: Garrett
McKettricks of Texas: Tate

The Creed Cowboys
The Creed Legacy
Creed's Honor
A Creed in Stone Creek

The Stone Creek series
The Bridegroom
The Rustler
A Wanted Man
The Man from Stone Creek

The McKettricks

A McKettrick Christmas

McKettrick's Heart

McKettrick's Pride

McKettrick's Luck

McKettrick's Choice

The Mojo Sheepshanks series

Deadly Deceptions

Deadly Gamble

The Montana Creeds

A Creed Country Christmas

Montana Creeds: Tyler

Montana Creeds: Dylan

Montana Creeds: Logan

For Sadie—third time's
the charm, sweet dog.
Send me another just like you.

BIG SKY
River

CHAPTER ONE

Sheriff Boone Taylor, enjoying a rare off-duty day, drew back his battered fishing rod and cast the fly-hook far out over the rushing, sun-spangled waters of Big Sky River. It ran the width of Parable County, Montana, that river, curving alongside the town of Parable itself like the crook of an elbow. Then it extended westward through the middle of the neighboring community of Three Trees and from there straight on to the Pacific.

He didn't just love this wild, sprawling country, he reflected with quiet contentment. He *was* Montana, from the wide sky arching overhead to the rocky ground under the well-worn soles of his boots. That scenery was, to his mind, his soul made visible.

A nibble at the hook, far out in the river, followed by a fierce breaking-away, told Boone he'd snagged—and already lost—a good-sized fish. He smiled—he'd have released the catch anyway, since there were plenty of trout in his cracker-box-sized freezer—and reeled in his line to make sure the hook was still there. He found that it wasn't, tied on a new one. For him, fishing was a form of meditation, a rare luxury in his busy life, a peaceful and quiet time that offered solace and soothed the many bruised and broken places inside him, while shoring up the strong ones.

He cast out his line again, and adjusted the brim of his baseball cap so it blocked some of the midmorning glare blazing in his eyes. He'd forgotten his sunglasses back at the house—if that junk heap of a double-wide trailer could be called a "house"—and he wasn't inclined to backtrack to fetch them.

So he squinted, and toughed it out. For Boone, toughing things out was a way of life.

When his cell phone jangled in the pocket of his lightweight cotton shirt, worn unbuttoned over an old T-shirt, he muttered under his breath, grappling for the device. He'd have preferred to ignore it and stay inaccessible for a little while longer. As sheriff, though, he didn't have that option. He was basically on call, 24/7, like it or not.

He checked the number, recognized it as Molly's, and frowned slightly as he pressed the answer bar. She and her husband, Bob, had been raising Boone's two young sons, Griffin and Fletcher, since the dark days following the death of their mother and Boone's wife, Corrie, a few years before. A call from his only sibling was usually benign—Molly kept him up-to-date on how the boys were doing—but there was always the possibility that the news was bad, that something had happened to one or both of them. Boone had reason to be paranoid, after all he'd been through, and when it came to his kids, he definitely was.

"Molly?" he barked into the receiver. "What's up?"

"Hello, Boone," Molly replied, and sure enough, there was a dampness to her response, as though she'd been crying, or was about to, anyhow. And she sounded bone weary, too. She sniffled and put him out of his misery, at least temporarily. "The boys are both fine," she said. "It's about Bob. He broke his right knee this morning—on the golf course, of all places—and the docs in Emergency say he'll need surgery right away. Maybe even a total replacement."

"Are you crying?" Boone asked, his tone verging on a challenge as he processed the flow of information she'd just let loose. He hated it when women cried, especially ones he happened to love, and couldn't help out in any real way.

"Yes," Molly answered, rallying a little. "I am. After the surgery comes rehab, and then more recovery—weeks and weeks of it."

Boone didn't even reel in his line; he

just dropped the pole on the rocky bank of the river and watched with a certain detached interest as it began to bounce around, an indication that he'd gotten another bite. "Molly, I'm sorry," he murmured.

Bob was the love of Molly's life, the father of their three children, and a backup dad to Griff and Fletch, as well. Things were going to be rough for him and for the rest of the family, and there wasn't a damn thing Boone could do to make it better.

"Talk to me, Molly," he urged gruffly, when she didn't reply right away. He could envision her, struggling to put on a brave front, as clearly as if they'd been standing in the same room.

The pole was being pulled into the river by then; he stepped on it to keep it from going in and fumbled to cut the line with his pocketknife while Molly was still regathering her composure, keeping the phone pinned between his shoulder and his ear so his hands stayed free. Except for the boys and her and Bob's kids, Molly was all the blood kin

Boone had left, and he owed her everything.

"It's—" Molly paused, drew a shaky breath "—it's just that the kids have summer jobs, and I'm going to have my hands full taking care of Bob. . . ."

Belatedly, the implications sank in. Molly couldn't be expected to look after her husband *and* Griffin and Fletcher, too. She was telling her thickheaded brother, as gently as she could, that he had to step up now, and raise his own kids. The prospect filled him with a tangled combination of exuberance and pure terror.

Boone pulled himself together, silently acknowledged that the situation could have been a lot worse. Bob's injury was bad, no getting around it, but he could be fixed. He wasn't seriously ill, the way Corrie had been.

Visions of his late wife, wasted and fragile after a long and doomed battle with breast cancer, unfurled in his mind like scenes from a very sad movie.

"Okay," he managed to say. "I'll be there as soon as I can. Are you at home, or at the hospital?"

"Hospital," Molly answered, almost in a whisper. "I'll probably be back at the house before you get here, though."

Boone nodded in response, then spoke. "Hang on, sis," he said. "I'm as good as on my way."

"Griffin and Fletcher don't know yet," she told him quickly. "About what's happened to Bob, I mean, or that you'll be coming to take them back to Parable with you. They're with the neighbor, Mrs. Mills. I want to be there when they find out, Boone."

Translation: *If you get to the boys before I do, don't say anything about what's going on. You'll probably bungle it.*

"Good idea," Boone conceded, smiling a little. Molly was still the same bossy big sister she'd always been—thank God.

Molly sucked in another breath, sounded calmer when she went on, though she had to be truly shaken up. "I know this is all pretty sudden—"

"I'll deal with it," Boone said, picking up the fishing pole, reeling in the severed line and starting toward his truck, a rusted-out beater parked up the bank a ways, alongside a dirt road. He knew he ought to replace the rig, but most of the time he drove a squad car, and, besides, he hated the idea of going into debt.

"See you soon," Molly said, and Boone knew even without seeing her that she was tearing up again.

Boone was breathless from the steep climb by the time he reached the road and his truck, even though he was in good physical shape. His palm sweated where he gripped the cell phone, and he tossed the fishing pole into the back of the pickup with the other hand. It clattered against the corrugated metal. "Soon," he confirmed.

They said their goodbyes, and the call ended.

By then, reality was connecting the dots to form an image in his brain, one of spending a whole summer, if not longer, with two little boys who basically regarded him as an acquaintance rather than a father. And it was a natural reaction on their part; he'd essentially abdicated his parental role after Corrie had died, packing off the kids—small and baffled—to Missoula to stay with Molly and Bob and their older cousins. In the beginning, Boone had meant for the arrangement to be temporary—all of them had—but one thing led to another, and pretty soon, the distance between him and the children became emotional as well as physical. While his closest friends had been needling him to man up and bring Griffin and Fletcher home practically since the day after Corrie's funeral, and he missed those boys with an ache that resembled the insistent, pulsing throb of a bad tooth, he'd always told himself he needed just a little more time. Just until after the election, and then until he'd gotten into the swing of a new job, since being sheriff was a lot more demanding than being a deputy, like before, *then* until he could replace the double-wide with a decent house.

Until, until, until.

Now, it was put up or shut up. Molly would need all her personal resources, physical, spiritual and emotional, to steer Bob and her own children through the weeks ahead.

He sat there in the truck for a few moments, with the engine running and the phone still in his hand, picturing the long and winding highway between Parable and Missoula, and finally speed-dialed his best friend, Hutch Carmody.

"Yo, Sheriff Taylor," Hutch greeted him cheerfully. "What can I do you out of?"

Married to his longtime love, the former Kendra Shepherd, with a five-year-old stepdaughter, Madison, and a new baby due to join the outfit in a month or so, Hutch seemed to be in a nonstop good mood these days.

It was probably the regular sex, Boone figured, too distracted to be envious but still subliminally aware that he'd been living like a monk since Corrie had died.

"I need to borrow a rig," he said straight out. "I've got to get to Missoula quick, and this old pile of scrap metal might not make it there and back."

Hutch got serious, right here, right now. "Sure," he said. "What's going on? Are the kids okay?"

Though they'd only visited Parable a few times since they'd gone to live with

Molly and Bob, Griffin and Fletcher looked up to Hutch, probably wished *he* was their dad, instead of Boone.

"The boys are fine," Boone answered. "But Molly just called, and she says Bob blew a knee on the golf course and he's about to have surgery. Obviously, she's got all she can do to look after her own crew right now, so I'm on my way up there to bring the kids home with me."

Hutch swore in a mild exclamation of sympathy for the world of hurt he figured Bob was in, and then said, "I'm sorry to hear that—about Bob, I mean. Want me to come along, ride shotgun and maybe provide a little moral support?"

"I appreciate the offer, Hutch," Boone replied, sincerely grateful for the man's no-nonsense, unshakable friendship. "But I think I need some alone-time with the kids, so I can try to explain what's happening on the drive back from Missoula."

Griffin was seven years old and Fletcher was only five. Boone could "explain" until he was blue in the face, but they weren't going to understand why they were suddenly being jerked out of the only home and the only family they really knew. Griffin, being a little older, remembered his mother vaguely, remembered when the four of them had been a unit. The younger boy, Fletcher, had no memories of Corrie, though, and certainly didn't regard Boone as his dad. It was *Bob* who'd raised him and his brother, taken them to T-ball games, to the dentist, to Sunday school.

"Not a problem," Hutch agreed readily. "The truck is gassed up and ready to roll. Do you want me to drop it off at your place? One of the hands could follow me over in another rig and—"

"I'll stop by the ranch and pick it up instead," Boone broke in, not wanting to put his friend to any more trouble than he already had. "See you in about fifteen minutes."

"Okay," Hutch responded, sighing the word, and the call was over.

Boone stayed a hair under the speed limit, though just barely, the whole way to the Carmody ranch, called Whisper Creek, where he found Hutch waiting beside the fancy extended-cab truck he'd purchased the year before, when he and Kendra were falling in love for the second time. Or maybe just realizing that they'd never actually fallen *out* of it in the first place.

Now, Hutch was hatless, with his head tilted a little to one side the way he did when he was pondering some enigma, and his hands were wedged backward into the hip pockets of his worn jeans. Kendra, a breathtakingly beautiful blonde, stood beside him, pregnant into the next county.

"Have you had anything to eat?" Kendra called to Boone, the instant he'd stopped his pickup. Dust roiled around her from under the truck's wheels, but she was a rancher's wife now, and unfazed by the small stuff.

Boone got out of the truck and walked toward them. He kissed Kendra's cheek and tried to smile, though he couldn't quite bring it off. "What is it with women and food?" he asked. "A man could be lying flat as a squashed penny on the railroad track, and some female would come along first thing, wanting to feed him something."

Hutch chuckled at that, but the quiet concern in his gaze made Boone's throat pull tight like the top of an old-time tobacco sack. "It's a long stretch to Missoula," Hutch observed, quietly affable. "You might get hungry along the way."

"I'll make sandwiches," Kendra said, and turned to duck-waddle toward the ranch house. Compared with Boone's double-wide, the place looked like a palace, with its clapboard siding and shining windows, and for the first time in his life, Boone wished he had a fine house like that to bring his children home to.

"Don't—" Boone protested, but it was too late. Kendra was already opening the screen door, stepping into the kitchen beyond.

"Let her build you a lunch, Boone," Hutch urged, his voice as quiet as his manner. Since the wedding, he'd been downright Zen-like. "She'll be quick about it, and she wants to help whatever way she can. We all do."

Boone nodded, cleared his throat, looked away. Hutch's dog, a black mutt named Leviticus, trotted over to nose Boone's hand, his way of saying howdy. Kendra's golden retriever, Daisy, was there, too, watchful and wagging her tail.

Boone ruffled both dogs' ears, straightened, looked Hutch in the eye again. Neither of them spoke, but it didn't matter, because they'd been friends for so long that words weren't always necessary.

Boone was worried about bringing the boys back to his place for anything longer than a holiday weekend, and Hutch knew that. He clearly cared and sympathized, but at the same time, he was pleased. There was no need to give voice to the obvious.

Kendra returned almost right away, moving pretty quickly for somebody who could be accused of smuggling pumpkins. She carried a bulging brown paper bag in one hand, holding it out to Boone when she got close enough. "Turkey on rye," she said. "With pickles.

I threw in a couple of hard-boiled eggs and an apple, too."

He took the bag, muttered his thanks, climbed into Hutch's truck and reached through the open window to hand over the keys to the rust-bucket he'd driven up in. Some swap that was, he thought ruefully. His old buddy was definitely getting the shitty end of *this* stick.

"Give Molly and Bob our best!" Kendra called after him, as Boone started up the engine and shifted into Reverse. "If there's anything we can do—"

Boone cut her off with a nod, raised a hand in farewell and drove away.

After a brief stop in Parable, to get some cash from an ATM, he'd keep the pedal to the metal all the way to Missoula. Once there, he and Molly would explain things, together.

God only knew how his sons would take the news—they were always tentative and quiet on visits to Parable, like exiles to a strange new planet, and visibly relieved when it was time to go back to the city.

One thing at a time, Boone reminded himself.

* * *

Tara Kendall stood in front of her chicken coop, surrounded by dozens of cackling hens, and second-guessed her decision to leave a high-paying, mega-glamorous job in New York and reinvent herself, *Green Acres*–style, for roughly the three thousandth time since she'd set foot in Parable, Montana, a couple years before.

She missed her small circle of friends back East, and her twelve-year-old twin stepdaughters, Elle and Erin. She also missed *things,* like sidewalk cafés and quirky shops, Yellow Cab taxis and shady benches in Central Park, along with elements that were harder to define, like the special energy of the place, the pure *purpose* flowing through the crowded streets like some unseen river.

She did not, however, miss the stress of trying to keep her career going in the midst of a major economic downturn, with her ex-husband, Dr. James Lennox, constantly complaining that she'd stolen his daughters' love from him when they divorced, along with a chunk of his investments and real estate assets.

Tara didn't regret the settlement terms for a moment—she'd forked over plenty of her own money during their rocky marriage, helping to get James's private practice off the ground after he left the staff of a major clinic to go out on his own—and as for the twins' affection, she'd gotten that by *being there* for Elle and Erin, as their father so often hadn't, not by scheming against James or undermining him to his children.

Even if Tara had wanted to do something as reprehensible as coming between James and the twins, there wouldn't have been any need, because the girls were formidably bright. They'd figured out things for themselves—their father's serial affairs included. Since he'd never seemed to have time for them, they'd naturally been resentful when they found out, quite by accident, that their dad had bent his busy schedule numerous times to take various girlfriends on romantic weekend getaways.

Tara's golden retriever, Lucy, napping on the shady porch that ran the full length of Tara's farmhouse, raised her head, ears perked. In the next instant, the cordless receiver for the inside phone rang on the wicker table set between two colorfully cushioned rocking chairs.

Hurrying up the front steps, Tara grabbed the phone and said, "Hello?"

"Do you *ever* answer your cell?" her former husband demanded tersely.

"It's charging," Tara said calmly. James loved to argue—maybe he should have become a lawyer instead of a doctor—and *Tara* loved to deprive him of the satisfaction of getting a rise out of her. Then, as another possibility dawned on her, she suppressed a gasp. "Elle and Erin are all right, aren't they?"

James remained irritable. "Oh, they're *fine,*" he said scathingly. "They've just chased off the fourth nanny in three weeks, and the agency refuses to send anyone else."

Tara bit back a smile, thinking of the mischievous pair. They were pranksters, and they got into plenty of trouble, but they were good kids, too, tenderhearted and generous. "At twelve, they're probably getting too old for nannies," she ventured. James never called to chat, hadn't done that even when they were married, standing in the same room or lying in the same bed. No, Dr. Lennox always had an agenda, and she was getting a flicker of what it might be this time.

"Surely you're not suggesting that I let them run wild, all day every day, for the whole summer, while I'm in the office, or in surgery?" James's voice still had an edge to it, but there was an undercurrent of something else—desperation, maybe. Possibly even panic.

"Of course not," Tara replied, plunking down in one of the porch rocking chairs, Lucy curling up at her feet. "Day camp might be an option, if you want to keep them busy, or you could hire a companion—"

"Day camp would mean delivering my daughters somewhere every morning and picking them up again every afternoon, and *I don't have time for that,* Tara." There it was again, the note of patient sarcasm, the tone that seemed to imply that her IQ was somewhere in the single digits and sure to plunge even lower. "I'm a busy man."

Too busy to care for your own children, Tara thought but, of course, didn't say. "What do you want?" she asked instead.

He huffed out a breath, evidently offended by her blunt question. "If that attitude isn't typical of you, I don't know what is—"

"James," Tara broke in. "You *want* something. You wouldn't call if you didn't. Cut to the chase and tell me what that something is, please."

He sighed in a long-suffering way. *Poor, misunderstood James. Always so put-upon, a victim of his own nobility.* "I've met someone," he said.

Now there's *a news flash,* Tara thought. James was *always* meeting someone—a female someone, of course. And he was sure that each new mistress was The One, his destiny, harbinger of a love that had been written in the stars instants after the Big Bang.

"Her name is Bethany," he went on, sounding uncharacteristically meek all of a sudden. James was a gifted surgeon with a high success rate; modesty was not in his nature. "She's special."

Tara refrained from comment. She and James were divorced, and she quite frankly didn't care whom he dated, "special" or not. She *did* care very much, however, about Elle and Erin, and the fact that they always came last with James, after the career and the golf tournaments and the girlfriend du jour. Their own mother, James's first wife, Susan, had contracted a bacterial infection when they were just toddlers, and died suddenly. It was Tara who had rocked the little girls to sleep, told them stories, bandaged their skinned elbows and knees—to the twins, she was Mom, even in her current absentee status.

"Are you still there?" James asked, and the edge was back in his voice. He even ventured a note of condescension.

"I'm here," Tara said, after swallowing hard, and waited. Lucy sat up, rested her muzzle on Tara's blue-jeaned thigh, and watched her mistress's face for cues.

"The girls are doing everything they can to run Bethany off," James said, after a few beats of anxious silence. "We need some—some *space,* Bethany and I, I mean—just the two of us, without—"

"Without your children getting underfoot," Tara finished for him after a long pause descended, leaving his sentence unfinished, but she kept her tone moderate. By then she knew for sure why James had called, and she already wanted to blurt out a yes, not to please him, but because she'd missed Elle and Erin so badly for so long. Losing daily contact with them had been like a rupture of the soul.

James let the remark pass, which was as unlike him as asking for help or giving some hapless intern, or wife, the benefit of a doubt. "I was thinking—well—that you might enjoy a visit from the twins. School's out until fall, and a few weeks in the country—maybe even a month or two—would probably be good for them."

Tara sat up very straight, all but holding her breath. She had no parental rights whatsoever where James's children were concerned; he'd reminded her of that often enough.

"A visit?" she dared. The notion filled her with two giant and diametrically opposed emotions—on the one hand, she was fairly bursting with joy. On the other, she couldn't help thinking of the desolation she'd feel when Elle and Erin returned to their father, as they inevitably would. Coping with the loss, for the second time, would be difficult and painful.

"Yes." James stopped, cleared his throat. "You'll do it? You'll let the twins come out there for a while?"

"I'd like that," Tara said carefully. She was afraid to show too much enthusiasm, even now, when she knew she had the upper hand, because showing her love for the kids was dangerous with James. He was jealous of their devotion to her, and he'd always enjoyed bursting her bubbles, even when they were newlyweds and ostensibly still happy. "When would they arrive?"

"I was thinking I could put them on a plane tomorrow," James admitted. He was back in the role of supplicant, and Tara could tell he hated it. All the more reason to be cautious—there *would* be a backlash, in five minutes or five years. "Would that work for you?"

Tara's heartbeat picked up speed, and she laid the splayed fingers of her free hand to her chest, gripping the phone very tightly in the other. "Tomorrow?"

"Is that too soon?" James sounded vaguely disapproving. Of course he'd made himself the hero of the piece, at least in his own mind. The self-sacrificing father thinking only of his daughters' highest good.

What a load of bull.

Not that she could afford to point that out.

"No," Tara said, perhaps too quickly. "No, tomorrow would be fine. Elle and Erin can fly into Missoula, and I'll be there waiting to pick them up."

"Excellent," James said, with obvious relief. Not "thank you." Not "I knew I could count on you." Just "Excellent," brisk praise for doing the right thing—which was always whatever he wanted at the moment.

That was when Elle and Erin erupted into loud cheers in the background, and the sound made Tara's eyes burn and brought a lump of happy anticipation to her throat. "Text me the details," she said to James, trying not to sound too pleased, still not completely certain the whole thing wasn't a setup of some kind, calculated to raise her hopes and then dash them to bits.

"I will," James promised, trying in vain to shush the girls, who were now whooping like a war party dancing around a campfire and gathering momentum. "And, Tara? Thanks."

Thanks.

There it was. Would wonders never cease?

Tara couldn't remember the last time James had thanked her for anything. Even while they were still married, still in love, before things had gone permanently sour between them, he'd been more inclined to criticize than appreciate her.

Back then, it seemed she was always five pounds too heavy, or her hair was too long, or too short, or she was too ambitious, or too lazy.

Tara put the brakes on that train of

thought, since it led nowhere. “You’re welcome,” she said, carefully cool.

“Well, then,” James said, clearly at a loss now that he’d gotten his way, fresh out of chitchat. “I’ll text the information to your cell as soon as I’ve booked the flights.”

“Great,” Tara said. She was about to ask to speak to the girls when James abruptly disconnected.

The call was over.

Of course Tara could have dialed the penthouse number, and chatted with Elle and Erin, who probably would have pounced on the phone, but she’d be seeing them in person the next day, and the three of them would have plenty of time to catch up.

Besides, she had things to do—starting with a shower and a change of clothes, so she could head into town to stock up on the kinds of things kids ate, like cold cereal and milk, along with those they tended to resist, like fresh vegetables.

She needed to get the spare room aired out, put sheets on the unmade twin beds, outfit the guest bathroom with soap and shampoo, toothbrushes and paste, in case they forgot to pack those things, tissues and extra toilet paper.

Lucy followed her into the house, wagging her plumy tail. Something was up, and like any self-respecting dog, she was game for whatever might happen next.

The inside of the farmhouse was cool, because there were fans blowing and most of the blinds were drawn against the brightest part of the day. The effect had been faintly gloomy, before James's call.

How quickly things could change, though.

After tomorrow, Tara was thinking, she and Lucy wouldn't be alone in the spacious old house—the twins would fill the place with noise and laughter and music, along with duffel bags and backpacks and vivid descriptions of the horrors wrought by the last few nannies in a long line of post-divorce babysitters, housekeepers and even a butler or two.

She smiled as she and Lucy bounded

up the creaky staircase to the second floor, along the hallway to her bedroom. Most of the house was still under renovation, but this room was finished, having been a priority. White lace curtains graced the tall windows, and the huge "garden" tub was set into the gleaming plank floor, directly across from the fireplace.

The closet had been a small bedroom when Tara had purchased the farm, but she'd had it transformed into every woman's dream storage area soon after moving in, to contain her big-city wardrobe and vast collection of shoes. It was silly, really, keeping all these supersophisticated clothes when the social scene in Parable called for little more than jeans and sweaters in winter and jeans and tank tops the rest of the time, but, like her books and vintage record albums, Tara hadn't been able to give them up.

Parting with Elle and Erin had been sacrifice enough to last a lifetime—she'd forced herself to leave them, and New York, in the hope that they'd be able to move on, and for the sake of her own sanity. Now, they were coming to Parable, to stay with her, and she was filled with frightened joy.

She selected a red print sundress and white sandals from the closet and passed up the tub for the room just beyond, where the shower stall and the other fixtures were housed.

Lucy padded after her in a casual, just-us-girls way, and sat down on a fluffy rug to wait out this most curious of human endeavors, a shower, her yellow-gold head tilted to one side in an attitude of patient amazement.

Minutes later, Tara was out of the shower, toweling herself dry and putting on her clothes. She gave her long brown hair a quick brushing, caught it up at the back of her head with a plastic squeeze clip and jammed her feet into the sandals. Her makeup consisted of a swipe of lip gloss and a light coat of mascara.

Lucy trailed after her as she crossed the wider expanse of her bedroom and paused at one particular window, for reasons she couldn't have explained, to look over at Boone Taylor's place just across the field and a narrow finger of Big Sky River.

She sighed, shook her head. The view would have been perfect if it wasn't for that ugly old trailer of Boone's, and the overgrown yard surrounding it. At least the toilet-turned-planter and other examples of extreme bad taste were gone, removed the summer before with some help from Hutch Carmody and several of his ranch hands, but that had been the extent of the sheriff's home improvement campaign, it seemed.

She turned away, refusing to succumb to irritation. The girls were as good as on their way. Soon, she'd be able to see them, hug them, laugh with them.

"Come on, Lucy," she said. "Let's head for town."

Downstairs, she took her cell phone off the charger, and she and the dog stepped out onto the back porch, walked toward the detached garage where she kept her sporty red Mercedes, purchased, like the farm itself, on a whimsical and reckless what-the-hell burst of impulse, and hoisted up the door manually.

Fresh doubt assailed her as she squinted at the car.

It was a two-seater, after all, completely unsuitable for hauling herself, two children and a golden retriever from place to place.

"Yikes," she said, as something of an afterthought, frowning a little as she opened the passenger-side door of the low-slung vehicle so Lucy could jump in. Before she rounded the front end and slid behind the steering wheel, Tara was thumbing the keypad in a familiar sequence.

Her friend answered with a melodic, "Hello."

"Joslyn?" Tara said. "I think I need to borrow a car."

CHAPTER TWO

Like traffic lights, ATMs were few and far between in Parable, which was why Boone figured he shouldn't have been surprised to run into his snarky—if undeniably *hot*—neighbor, Tara Kendall, right outside Cattleman's First National Bank. He was just turning away from the machine, traveling cash in hand, his mind already in Missoula with his boys and the others, when Tara whipped her jazzy sports car into the space next to his borrowed truck. She wore a dress the same cherry-red as her ride, and her golden retriever, a littermate to Kendra's dog, Daisy, rode beside her, seat belt in place.

Tara's smile was as blindingly bright as the ones in those ads for tooth-whitening strips—she'd probably recognized the big extended-cab pickup he was driving as belonging to Hutch and Kendra, and expected to meet up with one or both of them—but the dazzle faded quickly when she realized that this was a case of mistaken identity.

Her expression said it all. No Hutch, no Kendra. Just the backwoods redneck sheriff who wrecked her view of the countryside with his double-wide trailer and all-around lack of DIY motivation.

The top was down on the sports car and Boone could see that, like its mistress, the dog was wearing sunglasses, probably expensive ones, a fact that struck Boone as just too damn cute to be endured. Didn't the woman know this was *Montana,* not L.A. or New York?

Getting out of the spiffy roadster, Tara let her shades slip down off the bridge of her perfect little nose and looked him over in one long, dismissive sweep of her gold-flecked blue eyes, moving from his baseball cap to the ratty old boots on his feet.

"Casual day at the office, Sheriff?" she asked, singsonging the words.

Boone set his hands on his hips and leveled his gaze at her, pleased to see a pinkish flush blossom under those model-perfect cheekbones of hers. He and Tara had gotten off on the wrong foot when she had moved onto the land adjoining his, and she'd made it plain, right from the get-go, that she considered him a hopeless hick, a prime candidate for a fifteen-minute segment on *The Jerry Springer Show.* She'd come right out and *said* his place was an eyesore—in the kindest possible way, of course.

In his opinion, Tara was not only a city slicker, out of touch with ordinary reality, but a snob to boot. Too bad she had that perfect body and that head of shiny hair. Without those, it would have been easier to dislike her.

"Hello to you, too, neighbor," Boone said, in a dry drawl when he was darned good and ready to speak up. “How about this weather?”

She frowned at him, making a production of ferreting through her shoulder bag and bringing out her wallet. Behind her, in the passenger seat, the dog yawned without displacing its aviator glasses, as though bored. The lenses were mirrored.

“If you’re finished at the machine—?” Tara said, with a little rolling motion of one manicured hand. For a chicken rancher, she was stylin’.

Boone stepped aside to let her pass. “You shouldn’t do that, you know,” he heard himself telling her. It wasn’t as if she’d welcome any advice from him, after all, no matter how good it might be.

“Do what?” She had the faintest sprinkling of freckles across her nose, he noticed, oddly disconcerted by the discovery.

“Get your wallet out between the car and the ATM,” Boone answered, in sheriff mode even if he *was* dressed like a homeless person. He was in a hurry to get to Missoula, that was all. Hadn’t wanted to take the time to change clothes. "It's not safe."

Tara paused and, sunglasses jammed up into her bangs now, batted her thick lashes at him in a mockery of naïveté. "Surely nothing bad could happen with the *sheriff of all Parable County* right here to protect me," she replied, going all sugary. She had the ATM card out of her wallet by then, and looked ready to muscle past him to get to the electronic wonder set into the bank's brick wall.

"Have it your way," Boone said tersely. Why wasn't he back in Hutch's flashy truck by now, headed out of town? He wanted to see his boys, do what he could do for Molly and her three kids, maybe stop by the hospital and find out how Bob was holding up. But it was as if roots had poked right through the bottoms of his boots and the layer of concrete beneath them to break ground, wind down deep, and finally twist themselves into a hell of a tangle, and that pissed him off more than Tara's snooty attitude ever had.

"Thank you," she said, a little less sweetly, brushing by him and shoving her bank card into the slot before jabbing at a sequence of buttons on the number pad. "I will."

Boone rolled his eyes. Sighed. "People get robbed at ATMs all the time," he pointed out, chafing under the self-imposed delay. It would take a couple hours to reach Missoula, who knew how long to sort things out and load up the kids, and then two *more* hours to make it home again. And that was if they didn't stop along the way for supper.

Tara took the card out of the machine, collected a stack of bills from the appropriate opening, and started the process all over again. Who needed that much cash?

Maybe it was a habit from living in New York.

Her back—and a fine little back it was, partly bared by that skimpy sundress of hers—was turned to him the whole time, and she smelled like sundried laundry and wildflowers. "In Parable?" she retorted. "Who would *dare* to commit a crime in your town, Boone Taylor?"

He waited until she'd completed the

second transaction and turned around, nearly bumping into him. She was waving all those twenties around like the host on some TV game show, just *asking* for trouble. "I do my best," he told her, enjoying the flash of flustered annoyance that lit her eyes and pulsed in her cheeks, "but Parable isn't immune to crime, and there are some risks nobody but a damn fool will take."

She arched her eyebrows, shoved her sunglasses back into place with an eloquent gesture of the middle finger on her right hand. "Are you calling me a damn fool?" she asked, in a tone about as companionable as a room full of pissed-off porcupines.

"No," Boone said evenly. *I'm calling you a spoiled city girl with a very high opinion of yourself,* he thought but didn't say. "I'm only suggesting that you might want to be a little more careful in the future, that's all. Like I said before, Parable is a good town, but strangers do pass through here, in broad daylight as well as after dark, and we might even have a few closet outlaws in our midst."

Tara blinked up at him. "Are you through?" she asked politely.

He spread his hands and smirked a little, deliberately. "I tried," he said. He could have added, *"Don't come crying to me if you get mugged,"* but of course she'd have every right to do just that, since he was the law.

She went around him, sort of stalked back toward her car. It was amusing to watch the slight sway of her hips under that gauzy dress as she moved.

"Thanks so much," she said tersely, opening the driver's side door and plunking down behind the wheel. Only then did she bother to stick the cash in her wallet and drop that back into her bag.

The dog looked from her to Boone with the casual interest of a spectator at a slow tennis match.

Boone swept off his baseball cap and bowed deeply. "Anytime, your ladyship," he said.

Tara pursed her lips, looked back over one satin-smooth shoulder to make sure no one was behind her, and ground the car's transmission into Reverse. Her mouth was moving, but he couldn't hear what she said over the roar of the engine, which was probably just as well.

It would serve her right, though, he thought, if he cited her for reckless driving. He didn't have the time—or a case, for that matter—but he savored the fantasy as he got back into Hutch's truck.

Boone Taylor was just plain irritating, Tara thought, as she and Lucy drove away from the bank. Unfortunately, he was also a certified hunk with the infuriating ability to wake up all five of her senses and a few she hadn't discovered yet. How did he *do* that?

She stayed on a low simmer all the time she was running errands—buying groceries, taking them home and putting them all away, filling the pantry and the fridge and part of the freezer. Boone had disrupted her whole afternoon, and wasn't *that* just perfect, when she should have been enjoying the anticipation of her stepdaughters' arrival?

To sustain her momentum, she prepared the guest quarters, scrubbing down the clean but dusty bathroom, opening the windows, vacuuming and fluffing pillows and cushions, swapping out the sheets, even though the first ones hadn't been slept in. Tara hadn't had company in a while, and she wanted the linens to be clothesline-fresh for the twins.

Throughout this flurry of activity, Lucy stayed right with her, supervising from the threshold, occasionally giving a little yip of encouragement or swishing her tail back and forth.

"Everything is done," Tara told the dog when it was, straightening after smoothing each of the white chenille bedspreads one final time and glancing at the little clock on the nightstand between them. "And it isn't even time to feed the chickens."

Lucy uttered a conversational little whine, keeping up her end of the conversation.

Tara thought about her family-unfriendly car again, and Joslyn's generous offer to lend her the clunky station wagon her housekeeper, Opal, shared with Shea, Joslyn and her husband Slade's eighteen-year-old stepdaughter.

Borrowing the vehicle would be too much of an imposition, she decided, as she and Lucy headed down to the kitchen via the back staircase. It was time to head over to Three Trees, cruise past both auto dealerships, and pick out a big-girl car. Something practical, like a minivan or a four-door sedan, spacious but easy on gas.

Within minutes, she and Lucy were back on the road, this time with the car's top up so they wouldn't arrive all windblown, like a pair of bad credit risks.

Molly and Bob lived in a modest two-story colonial on a shady side street in the best part of Missoula. The grass in the yard was greener than green and neatly trimmed, possibly with fingernail scissors. Flowers grew everywhere, in riotous tumbles of color, and the picket fence was so pristinely white that it looked as if the paint might still be wet.

Boone stopped the truck in front, and though not usually into comparisons since he wasn't the materialistic type, he couldn't help being struck by the contrast between his sister's place and his own.

He sighed and shoved open the driver's side door, keys in hand. He'd been wishing he'd taken the time to shower and put on something besides fishing clothes ever since the run-in with Tara Kendall outside the bank in Parable, if only to prove to the world in general that he did his laundry and even ironed a shirt once in a while. Now, faced with the obvious differences, he felt like a seedy drifter, lacking only a cardboard begging sign to complete the look.

The screen door opened and Molly stepped out onto the porch, waving and offering up a trembling little smile. Her long, dark hair was pulled back into a messy ponytail, and she wore jeans, one of Bob's shirts and a pair of sneakers that looked a little the worse for wear. Mom-shoes.

"Bob's been admitted," she said right away, coming down the porch steps and meeting him at the front gate, opening the latch before Boone could reach for it. "He's getting a new knee in the morning."

"Maybe I'll stop by and say hello to him on the way out of town," Boone offered, feeling clumsy.

"He's pretty out of it," Molly answered. "The pain was bad."

Boone put a hand on his sister's shoulder, leaned in to kiss her forehead lightly. "What happened, anyhow?" he asked. Bob was the athletic type, strong and active.

Molly winced a little, remembering. "One of the regulars brought his nephew along today—he's never played before—but he has one heck of a backswing. Caught Bob square in the knee."

Now it was Boone who winced. "Owww," he said.

"Owww, indeed," Molly verified. "The nephew feels terrible, of course."

"He should," Boone said.

That was when Molly made a little sound of frustration and worry, and hugged him close, and Boone hugged her back, his chin propped on top of her head.

"I'm sorry, sis," he told her. The phrase sounded so lame.

Molly sniffled and drew back, smiling

up at him. "Come on inside. I just made iced tea, and the kids will be back soon. My crew went to pick up some pizza—late lunch, early dinner whatever—and Griffin and Fletcher went with them." Her eyes misted over. "I've told them about the operation and rehab and how they'll be going back to Parable with you, but I'm not sure they really understand."

Boone nodded and followed his sister up the porch steps and on into the house. While it wasn't a mansion, the colonial was impressive in size and furnished with a kind of casual elegance that would be impossible to pull off in a thirdhand double-wide.

"I imagine they'll have plenty of questions," he said as they passed beneath the glittering crystal droplets dangling from the chandelier in the entryway. An antique grandfather clock ticked ponderously against one wall, measuring out what time remained to any of them, like a heartbeat. Life was fragile, anything could happen.

Molly glanced back at him over one shoulder, nodded. "I told them they'd be coming back here in a couple of months," she replied. "After their uncle Bob has some time to heal."

Boone didn't comment. Despite his trepidation—he definitely considered himself parentally challenged—a part of him, long ignored but intractable, remained stone-certain that Griffin and Fletcher belonged with him, their father, on the little spread beside the river. Home, be it ever so humble.

This wasn't the time to discuss that, though. Molly loved her nephews like they were her own, and with so many things to cope with, she didn't need anything more to worry about.

And worry she would. With all that roiling in Boone's mind, he and Molly passed along the wide hallway that opened onto a big dining room with floor-to-ceiling windows on one side overlooking the side yard, where a small stone fountain stood spilling rainbow-colored water and surrounded by thriving rosebushes. The scene resembled a clip from HGTV.

They'd reached the sunlit kitchen when Molly spoke again, employing her being-brave voice, the one she'd used during the hard days after their parents had died. She'd been just nineteen then, to Boone's fifteen, but she'd managed to step up and take charge of the household.

"Griff is excited—already has his bags packed," she told Boone, as she opened the refrigerator door and reached in for the pitcher of tea. Bright yellow lemon slices floated among the tinkling ice cubes, and there were probably a few sprigs of mint in there, too. Molly believed in small gracious touches like that. "Fletcher, though—" She stopped, shook her head. "He's less enthusiastic."

Boone suppressed a sigh, baseball cap in hand, looking around him. The kitchen was almost as big as his whole double-wide, with granite surfaces everywhere, real wood cabinets with gleaming glass doors, top-of-the-line appliances that, unlike the hodgepodge at his place, actually matched each other. There was even a real brick fireplace, and the table, with its intricately mosaicked top, looked long enough to accommodate a serious crowd.

Back at the double-wide, more than three people at a meal meant someone had to eat in the yard, or on the back steps, balancing a throwaway plate on their lap.

Molly smiled somewhat wistfully, as if she'd guessed what he was thinking, and gestured for Boone to sit down. Then she poured two tall glasses of iced tea and joined him, placing the pitcher in the middle of the table. Sure enough, there were little green leaves floating in the brew.

"Fletcher will adjust," Molly went on gently. Her perception was nothing new; she'd always been able to read him, even when he put on a poker face. She was the big sister, and she'd been a rock after the motorcycle wreck that killed their mom and dad. Somehow, she'd seen to it that they could stay in the farmhouse they'd grown up in, putting off going to college herself until Boone had finished high school. She'd waitressed at the Butter Biscuit Café and clipped coupons and generally made do, all to prevent the state or the county from stepping in and separating them, shuffling Boone into foster care.

In the aftermath of the tragedy, the whole community of Parable had helped, the way small towns do, with folks sharing produce from their gardens, eggs from their chicken coops, milk from their cows, clothes from their closets, all without any hint of charity. Boone had done odd jobs after school and on weekends, but the main burden of responsibility had always been Molly's.

Oh, there'd been some life insurance money, which she'd hoarded carefully, determined that they would both get an education, and the farm, never a big moneymaker even in the best of times, had at least been paid for. Their mom had been a checker at the supermarket, and their dad had worked at the now-closed sawmill, and somehow, latter-day hippies though they were, they'd whittled down the mortgage over the years.

The motorcycle had been their only extravagance—they'd both loved the thing.

When Boone was ready for college, he and Molly had divided the old place down the middle, with the house on Molly's share, at Boone's insistence. She'd sold her portion to distant cousins right away and, later on, those cousins had sold the property to Tara Kendall, the lady chicken rancher. Thus freed, Molly had studied business in college and eventually met and married Bob and given birth to three great kids.

And if all that hadn't been enough, she'd stepped up when Corrie got sick, too, making regular visits to Parable to help with the kids, just babies then, cook meals, keep the double-wide fit for human habitation, and even drive her sister-in-law back and forth for medical treatments. Boone, young and working long hours as a sheriff's deputy for next-to-no money, had been among the walking wounded, mostly just putting one foot in front of the other and bargaining with God.

Take me, not her.

But God hadn't listened. It was as if He'd stopped taking Boone's calls, putting him on hold.

Now, poignantly mindful of all that had gone before, Boone felt his eyes start to burn. He took a long drink of iced tea, swallowed and said, "Where were we?"

Molly's smile was fragile but totally genuine. She looked exhausted. "I was telling you that your younger son isn't as excited about going home with you as his older brother is."

A car pulled up outside, doors slammed. Youthful voices came in through the open windows that made the curtains dance against the sills.

"Yeah," Boone said. "I'll deal with that. You just think about yourself, and Bob, and your own kids."

Right on cue, Molly's trio of offspring, two girls and a boy, rattled into the house. Ted, the oldest, had a driver's license, and he carried a stack of pizza boxes in his big, basketball-player's hands, while the girls, Jessica and Catherine, twelve and thirteen respectively, shambled in after him, bickering between themselves.

Griffin and Fletcher, who had accompanied them, were still outside.

When Jessica and Cate spotted Boone, their faces lit up and their braces gleamed as they smiled wide. They were pretty, like their mother, while Ted looked like a younger version of Bob, a boy growing into a man.

"Uncle Boone!" Jessica crowed.

He stood up, and just in time, too, because his nieces promptly flung themselves into his arms. He kissed them both on top of the head, an arm around each one, and nodded to his more reserved nephew.

Ted nodded back, and set aside the pizza boxes on one of the granite countertops. "I guess Mom told you about Dad being injured," he said, with such an effort at manly self-possession that Boone ached for him.

"She told me," Boone confirmed.

His nieces clung to him, and suddenly there were tears in their eyes.

"It's awful, what happened to Dad," said Jessica. "It must hurt like crazy."

"He's being taken care of," Molly put in quietly.

Boone again squeezed both girls, released them. After a pause, he asked, "What's keeping those boys of mine?"

"They're admiring your truck," Ted put in, grinning now.

Boone didn't explain that he'd borrowed the rig from his best friend; it just didn't matter. He wondered, though, if Griff and Fletch were avoiding him, putting off the unexpected reunion as long as they could.

Then the screen door creaked on its hinges and Boone braced himself.

Molly cleared her throat. "Kids," she said quietly, addressing her brood. "Wash up and we'll have pizza."

"We're still going to visit Dad tonight, right?" Cate asked worriedly.

"Yes," Molly answered, as Boone's young sons crossed the threshold and let the screen door slam behind them.

Ted, Jessica and Cate all left the room. Boone wondered if they were always so obedient and, if so, what was the magic formula so he could try it out on his own kids?

Meanwhile, Griff, the older of the pair, straightened his spine and offered a tentative smile. "Hello, Dad," he said.

Fletcher, the little one, huddled close to his brother, their scrawny shoulders touching. "I don't want to go to stupid Parable," the boy said. He looked scared and sad and obstinate all at once, and his resemblance to his late mother made Boone's breath snag painfully in the back of his throat. "I want to stay here!"

Boone walked over to them but left a foot or two of personal space.

"Uncle Bob broke his knee," Griffin said, in case word hadn't gotten around. "Ted says they're going to give him a plastic one."

Boone nodded solemnly, waiting. He didn't want to crowd these kids, or rush them, either, but he was chafing to load up whatever stuff they wanted to take along and head for Parable.

"I'm ready to go anytime," Griff announced.

"Not me," Fletch glowered, folding his skinny arms and digging in the heels of his sneakers.

Boone crouched so he could look both boys in the eye. "It's important to everybody, including your Uncle Bob, that you guys go along with the plan.

That shouldn't be too hard for a couple of tough Montana cowboys, right?"

Griff nodded, ready to roll, prepared to be as tough as necessary.

Fletcher, on the other hand, rolled out his lower lip, his eyes stormy, and warned, "I wet the bed almost every night."

Boone recognized the tactic and maintained a serious expression. "Is that so?" he asked. "Guess that's something we'll have to work on."

Fletcher nodded vigorously, but he kept right on scowling. He had Boone's dark hair and eyes, as Griffin did, but he was Corrie's boy, all right.

"He smells like pee every morning," Griffin commented helpfully.

In a sidelong glance at Molly, who was getting out plates and silverware and unboxing the pizza, Boone saw her smile, though she didn't say anything.

"Shut up, Griff," Fletcher said, reaching out to give his brother an angry shove.

"Whoa, now," Boone said, still sitting on his haunches, putting a hand to each of their small chests to prevent a brawl.

"We're all riding for the same outfit, and that means we ought to get along."

His sons glared at each other, and Fletcher stuck out his tongue.

They were probably too young to catch the cowboy reference.

Boone sighed and rose to his full height, knees popping a little.

"Pizza time!" Molly announced, as Ted, Jessica and Cate reappeared, traveling in a ragtag little herd.

For a family in what amounted to a crisis, if not a calamity, they all put away plenty of pizza, but the talk was light. Every once in a while, somebody spoke up to remind everybody else that Bob would be fine, at least in the long run. New knee, good to go.

It was dark outside by the time the meal was over.

Boone did the cleanup, since Molly refused to let him reimburse her for the pizza.

Fletcher had been cajoled into letting Jessica and Cate help him pack, and Ted had loaded the suitcases in the back of Hutch's truck.

Both boys needed booster seats, being under the requisite height of four foot nine dictated by law, and transferring those from Bob and Molly's car and rigging them up just right took a few minutes with Molly helping and Fletcher sobbing on the sidewalk, periodically wailing that he didn't want to go, couldn't he please say, he wouldn't wet the bed anymore, he promised. He swore he'd be good.

Boone's heart cracked down the middle and fell apart. He hugged Molly goodbye—knowing she and the kids were anxious to get over to the hospital and visit Bob—shook his nephew's hand and nodded farewell to his nieces.

"Tell Bob I'm thinking about him," Boone said.

Molly briefly bit her lower lip, then replied, "I will." Her gaze was on Griffin and Fletcher now, as if drinking them in, memorizing them. Her eyes filled with tears, though she quickly blinked them away.

Boone lifted a hand to say goodbye and got into the truck.

Molly stepped onto the running board before he could pull away, and spoke softly to the silent little boys in the backseat. "You guys be good, okay?" she said, in a choked, faint voice. "I'm counting on you."

Turning his head, Boone saw both boys nod in response to their aunt's parting words. They looked nervous, like miniature prisoners headed for the clink.

Molly smiled over at Boone, giving him the all-too-familiar *you can do this* look she'd always used when she thought he needed motivation or encouragement. "We'll keep you posted," she promised. And then she stepped down off the running board and stood on the sidewalk, chin up, shoulders straight.

Boone, who'd already used his quota of words for the day, nodded again and buzzed up the windows, bracing himself for the drive home.

It was going to be a long night.

Tara called Joslyn from the front seat of her previously owned but spacious SUV, watching as one of the car-lot people drove her cherished convertible around a corner and out of sight. She felt a pang when it disappeared, headed for wherever trade-ins went to await a new owner.

"I just wanted to let you know that I won't be needing to borrow the station wagon, after all," she said into the phone, studying the unfamiliar dashboard now. Lucy was in back, buckled up and ready to cruise.

"Okay," Joslyn said, her tone thoughtful. "Mind telling me what's going on?"

Still parked in the dealer's lot, with hundreds of plastic pennants snapping overhead, Tara bit her lip. "It's a long story," she said after a moment's hesitation. "Short version—Elle and Erin, my ex-husband's twelve-year-old twins, are arriving tomorrow. Since we couldn't all fit in the Mercedes—"

"Elle and Erin," Joslyn repeated. She and Kendra Carmody were Tara's best friends, and yet she'd never told either of them about the twins, mostly because talking about Elle and Erin would have been too painful. All Kendra and Joslyn knew was that there had been an ugly divorce.

"I'll tell you the whole story later," Tara said, eyeing the passing traffic and hoping she wouldn't feel as though she were driving an army tank all the way back to Parable. "It's time to get home and feed the chickens."

"Right," Joslyn said. "Exactly when is 'later' going to be?"

"Tonight?" Tara suggested. "You and Kendra could stop by my place for lemonade or tea or something?"

Once, she would have offered white wine instead, but Kendra was expecting, and Joslyn, the mother of a one-year-old son, was making noises about getting pregnant again, soon.

"I can make it," Joslyn replied, clearly intrigued. "I'll give Kendra a call—what time would be good?"

"Six?" Tara said, uncertain. She lived alone, while both her friends had husbands, and, in Joslyn's case, kids, as well. They'd have to take family matters, like supper, into consideration.

"Make it seven and we're good," Joslyn said. "See you then."

They ended the call with lighthearted goodbyes, and Tara turned in the driver's seat to look back at Lucy. The dog wore a blue bandanna and her sunglasses dangled from a loose cord around her neck. "Hold on," she said. "One test-drive doesn't make me an expert at handling the big rigs."

Lucy yawned and relaxed visibly, though she couldn't lie down with the seat belt fastened around her. As always, she was ready to go with the flow.

They drove back to Parable and then home to the farm, blessedly without incident. There, Tara was met by a flock of testy chickens, probably suffering from low blood sugar. She rushed inside and up the stairs, Lucy right behind her, and exchanged her sundress and sandals for coveralls and ugly boots, the proper attire for feeding poultry and other such chores, and returned to the yard.

Lucy, who was alternately curious about the birds and terrified of their squawking, kept her distance, waiting patiently in the shade of the overgrown lilac bush that had once disguised a privy.

"Dog," Tara said, gathering handfuls

of chicken feed from a dented basin and flinging the kernels in every direction, “we are definitely not in New York anymore.”

CHAPTER THREE

Both the boys were sound asleep in their safety seats when Boone finally pulled up in his own rutted driveway around eight that night, shut off the truck engine and gazed bleakly into his immediate future. A concrete plan for the long term would have been good, a to-do list of specific actions guaranteed to carry Griffin and Fletcher from where they were right now—confused and scared—right on through to healthy, productive manhood.

Boone sighed. *One step at a time,* he reminded himself silently. *Just put one foot in front of the other and keep on keeping on.* For now, he only had to think about getting his sons inside and bedded down for the night. After that, he'd take a quick shower and call to let Molly know that he and the kids had arrived home safely. Then, if it wasn't too late, he'd give Hutch a ring, too, and tell him his truck was still in one piece, offer to drop it off at Whisper Creek before he went on to work in the morning.

Work. Inconvenient as it was, Boone was still sheriff, with a whole county full of good people depending on him, and a few bad apples to keep an eye on, too, and that meant he'd be in his office first thing tomorrow, with his boys tagging along, since he had yet to make any kind of child-care arrangements.

Just then, things seemed patently overwhelming. *One step,* he reiterated to himself, *and then another.*

Glad to be out of a moving vehicle and standing on his own two feet, Boone opened one of the rear doors and woke Griffin first with a gentle prod to the shoulder. The boy yawned and blinked his eyes and then grinned at Boone in the dim glow of the interior lights. "Are we there?" the kid asked, sounding hopeful.

Boone's heart caught. "We're there," he confirmed with a nod, then unfastened Fletcher from the safety seat. Griffin scrambled out of the truck on his own, but the little guy didn't even wake up. He just stirred slightly, his arms loose around Boone's neck, his head resting on his shoulder.

For all Boone's trepidation about getting the dad thing right, it felt good to be holding that boy. Real good.

They started toward the double-wide, slogging through tall grass. The trailer was pretty sorry-looking in broad daylight, and darkness made it look even worse, like a gloomy hulk, lurking and waiting to pounce. Why hadn't he thought to leave a light burning before he took off for Missoula in such an all-fired hurry?

"I bet Fletch peed his pants," Griffin said sagely, trekking along beside

Boone with his small suitcase in one hand. "He stinks."

Sure enough, the seat of Fletcher's impossibly small Wranglers felt soggy against Boone's forearm, and there was a smell, but it wasn't a big deal to a man who'd spent whole nights guarding some drunken miscreant at the county jail.

Boone spoke quietly to Griffin, man-to-man. "Let's not rag on him about that, okay? He's still pretty little, and there's a lot to get used to—for both of you."

Griffin nodded. "Okay," he agreed solemnly.

They climbed the steps to the rickety porch, Boone going first, and once he'd gotten the door open and stepped inside, he flipped the light switch.

They were in the kitchen, but in that first moment Boone almost didn't recognize the room. The dishes he'd left piled in the sink had been done up and put away. The linoleum floor didn't exactly shine, being so worn, with the tar showing through in some places, but it glowed a little, just the same.

The effect was almost homey.

"Do we sleep where we did when we visited before?" Griffin asked. He sounded like a very small man, visiting a foreign country and eager to fit into the culture without breaking any taboos.

Still carrying Fletcher, who was beginning to wriggle around a bit now, Boone nodded a distracted yes and, having spotted the note propped between the sugar shaker and the jar of powdered coffee creamer in the middle of the table, zeroed in on it.

Griffin marched off to inspect the cubbyhole he and Fletcher would be staying in while Boone picked up the note. It was written in Opal Dennison's distinctive, loopy handwriting, and he smiled as he read it. Although she kept house for Slade and Joslyn Barlow, Opal was definitely a free agent, working where she wanted to work, *when* she wanted to work.

Hutch called and said your boys were coming home for a spell, and you'd all probably get in tonight, so I let myself in and spruced the place

up a mite. There's food in the refrigerator and I put clean sheets on the beds and some fresh towels in the bathroom. I'll be over first thing tomorrow morning to look after those kids while you're working, and don't even think about telling me you can manage on your own, Boone Taylor, because I didn't just fall off the turnip truck.

She'd signed the message with a large *O.*

Boone set the slip of paper back on the table and carried a now-wakeful Fletch into the one and only bathroom. He set the boy on the lid of the toilet seat and started water running into the tub, which, thanks to Opal, was well scrubbed. Boone always showered, and that seemed like a self-cleaning type of operation, so he rarely bothered with the tub.

Fletch, realizing where he was, and with whom, rubbed both eyes with small grubby fists and immediately started to cry again.

"Hey," Boone said quietly, turning to crouch in front of him the way he'd done earlier, in Molly's kitchen. "Everything's going to be all right, Fletcher. After a bath and a good night's sleep, you'll feel a whole lot better about stuff, I promise."

He'd told the boys, during the first part of the drive back from Missoula, that their uncle Bob, hurt the way he was, would need lots of care from their aunt Molly and the cousins, so that was why they were going back to Parable to bunk in with him for a while. It was the best way they could help, he'd explained.

Griff hadn't said anything at all in response to his father's short and halting discourse. He'd just looked out the window and kept his thoughts to himself, which, in some ways, concerned Boone more than Fletcher's intermittent outbursts. The littlest boy had exclaimed fiercely that he wanted to go back and help take care of Uncle Bob *for real,* and would Boone just turn around the truck right now, because Missoula was home, not Parable. When Boone had replied that he couldn't do that, Fletch had cried as if his heart had been broken—and maybe it had.

After quite a while, during which Boone felt three kinds of useless and just kept driving because he knew the kid would have resisted any kind of fatherly move, like stopping the truck and taking him into his arms for a few minutes, Fletcher's sobs gradually turned to hiccups. That went on for a long time, too, like the crying, before he finally fell into a fitful sleep, exhausted by the singular despair of being five years old with no control over his own fate.

Now, in this run-down bathroom, with the finish peeling away from the sides of a tub hardly big enough to accommodate a garden gnome, and the door off the cupboard under the sink letting the goosenecked pipe and bedraggled cleaning supplies show, Boone waited, still sitting on his haunches, for Fletcher's response to the tentative promise he'd made moments before.

It wasn't long in coming. "Everything *won't* be all right," Fletcher argued. "You're not my dad—I don't care what Griff says—*Uncle Bob* is my dad—and

I'm not staying here, because I *hate* you!"

This was a scared kid talking, Boone reflected, but the words hurt just the same, like a hard punch to the gut.

"I can see why you'd feel that way," he answered calmly, reasonably, catching a glimpse of Griffin out of the corner of his eye. The boy huddled in the bathroom doorway, looking on worriedly, so small in his jeans and striped T-shirt, with his shoulders hunched slightly forward, putting Boone in mind of a fledgling bird not quite trusting its wings. "But we're going to have to make the best of things, you and Griff and me."

Fletcher glared rebelliously at Boone and slowly shook his head from side to side.

"Dad?" Griff interceded softly. "I can help Fletcher with his bath, get him ready for bed and everything, if you want me to."

Boone sighed as he rose to his full height. "Maybe that would be a good idea," he said, shoving a hand through his hair, which was probably creased from wearing the baseball cap all day. He was still in the clothes he'd put on to go fishing early that morning, too, and he felt sweaty and tired and sad.

"He's got pajamas in the suitcase," Griffin said helpfully. "You could get them out—they're the ones with the cartoon train on the front. . . ."

Boone smiled down at his older son and executed an affable if lazy salute. "Check," he said, starting down the short hallway to follow through on the errand assigned. As he walked away, he could hear Griff talking quietly to his little brother, telling him he'd like living here, if he'd just give it a chance.

Griffin was clearly having none of it.

Boone went outside, retrieved the suitcases and brought them in, opening the smaller one after setting both bags on the built-in bed that took up most of the nook of a bedroom reserved for the boys. Back in Missoula, they shared a room four times that size, with twin beds and comforters that matched the curtains and even a modest flat-screen TV on the wall.

He sighed again, bent over the suitcase and rooted through for the pajamas Griff had described. He found them, plus a couple toothbrushes in plastic cases, each one labeled with a name.

He took the lot back to the bathroom and rapped lightly on the now-closed door. "Pajama delivery," he said, in the jocular tone of a room-service person.

There was some splashing in the background, and Griff opened the bathroom door far enough to reach for the things Boone was holding, grinning sympathetically.

"Thanks, Dad," Griff said in a hushed voice.

Boone nodded in acknowledgment, turned away and wandered back into the kitchen, where he picked up the receiver from the wall phone and called Molly and Bob's home number.

Molly answered right away. "Boone?" she said.

"Yep," Boone replied. "We got home just fine."

"Good," Molly responded. "How are

they doing? Griffin and Fletcher, I mean?"

"As well as can be expected, I guess," Boone said, as another wave of weariness swept over him. "How's Bob?"

"He's probably asleep by now," Molly answered. "He goes into surgery at six tomorrow morning." She paused, though not long enough for Boone to wedge in a reply. "Are they in bed already? Griffin and Fletcher, I mean? Did they brush their teeth? Say their prayers?"

"Fletch is in the tub, mother hen," Boone told his frazzled sister, with a smile in his voice. "We'll get around to the rest of it later."

Molly gasped, instantly horrified. "Fletcher is in the tub *by himself?*"

Boone frowned as it came home to him, yet again, how much he didn't know about bringing up kids. "Griff is with him," he said.

"Oh," said Molly, clearly relieved.

"So things are pretty much okay on your end?" Boone asked. He was out of practice as a father, and every part of him ached, from the heart out. Bob was in for some serious pain and a long, rigorous recovery, and Molly, Ted, Jessica and Cate had no choice but to go along for the ride.

"We're doing all right," she said. "Not great, but all right."

"You'll let me know if there's anything you need?"

"You know I will," Molly answered. She paused a beat before going on. "Can we stay in touch by text and email for a while? I'm not sure I'm going to have enough energy for the telephone right at first, and I'm afraid every time I hear the boys' voices, I'll burst into tears and scare the heck out of them. I already miss them so much."

Boone's reply came out sounding hoarse. "Do whatever works best for you," he said. "I'll look after the boys, Molly. I'll figure all this fathering stuff out. In the meantime, try to stop worrying about us, okay? Take care of *yourself,* or you'll be no good to Bob and the kids. In other words, get some rest."

"I'll try," she said, and he knew she was smiling, although she was probably dead on her feet after the day she'd put in. "You're a good brother, Boone. And I love you."

"Flattery will get you everywhere," Boone answered. "And I love you, too. I'll text or email tomorrow."

"Me, too," Molly said. "Bob will be out of surgery around noon."

They said their goodbyes and rang off.

Boone glanced at the wall clock, decided it was still early enough to call Hutch and punched in the numbers for his friend's landline.

Hutch answered on the second ring. "Back home?" he asked, instead of saying hello. Thanks to caller ID, people tended to skip the preliminaries these days and launch right into the conversation at hand.

"Yep," Boone answered.

"How are Molly and Bob?"

"About as well as can be expected," Boone said truthfully. "Bob's having surgery in the morning."

Hutch sighed. "That's a hassle," he said.

Boone chuckled ruefully. "Amen to that, old buddy," he said, remembering how Hutch and Slade had stood by him during Corrie's illness and after her death, notwithstanding that the two of them, half brothers though they were, hadn't gotten along at the time. Hutch had resented Slade for being living proof that dear old Dad slept around, and Slade, the unacknowledged son, born of an affair that still scandalized some folks even now, must have felt like an outsider, looking in. He was the prodigal who hadn't actually gone anywhere.

"We're a phone call away if you need us," Hutch said.

"Thanks," Boone replied. Yet another inadequate word. "Listen, about the truck—I'd like to run it through the car wash and fill the tank before I bring it back to you, unless you need it right away."

"Never mind all that," Hutch answered. "We've got plenty of rigs around here. Just bring it by when you can, and we'll make the switch."

Boone grinned. Folks probably hadn't even noticed that Hutch was driving an old junker instead of his pricey new truck; for years, he'd used any rattletrap ranch pickup that would run to get where he was going, provided it wasn't already in use. He had land and plenty of money, Hutch did, but he'd never given two hoots and a holler about appearances, and that hadn't changed. "I guess the old beater didn't quit on you," he said.

"I kept it going, but it took some spit, duct tape and elbow grease," Hutch joked. "You ought to spring for something a little more dependable, now that you're going to be hauling a couple of kids around most everywhere you go."

"That's a distinct possibility," Boone admitted. "They like riding in the squad car, but that'll probably wear thin sooner or later."

Hutch laughed. "I'm thinking sooner," he said.

"Dad?" The voice was Griff's.

Boone turned, saw his boys standing side by side just inside the kitchen, both of them pajama-clad, with their teeth gleaming so white they must have already brushed. Fletcher stood as close to his brother as he could without climbing right up on his shoulders.

Another pang struck Boone, partly sorrow but mostly love.

"Gotta go," he told Hutch, probably sounding a touch more confident than he really felt. "My boys are about to turn in, and I've had a hell of a day myself."

Hutch said goodbye and they both hung up.

Griff's expression was earnest. "Fletcher wants to know if we can sleep with you tonight," he said bravely. "He says he won't pee the bed if you let us."

Boone wanted to grin at the proffered bargain, but he didn't. "Fletcher's gone mute all of a sudden?" he asked, though not unkindly. "He can't speak for himself?"

"It's more like he *won't,*" Griff said seriously.

"Yeah," Boone agreed. "It's more like that."

"Can we? Sleep with you?" It was Griff who asked, but the answer seemed important to both of them. Fletcher's eyes looked enormous in his small face.

"I don't see why not," Boone replied

offhandedly. He didn't want them to make a habit of bunking in with him, but this was their first night home, after all, and Fletcher was pretty shaken up. Griff might have been, too, but if so, he was hiding it better.

Both of them looked relieved. Evidently, Fletcher didn't think his dad was a *complete* monster.

"Go on," Boone said, his voice gone gruff again. "Hit the sack. I'll be with you in a minute or two."

Griff nodded, and the two of them turned and scampered for Boone's room, which was only slightly bigger than their own, landing on the mattress with a ruckus audible from the kitchen. In the trailer, which wasn't nearly as well made as some of its modern counterparts, sound carried.

Boone shook his head, smiled and waited for them to settle down a little before he went to tuck them in and get out a pair of sweatpants to put on after his shower. He found them crowded together on the side of that bed that had once been Corrie's, with the covers pulled up to their noses and their eyes round.

"Guys?" Boone said huskily. "I love you, like it or not."

"I like it," Griff said.

"I don't," Fletcher clarified. He was a man who knew his own mind.

Boone laughed and went off to take his shower.

When he returned to the bedroom half an hour later, both boys were sleeping, Fletcher spooned close against his brother's back.

Boone switched out the light but lingered in the doorway for a few moments, just looking at them. *Corrie,* he said silently, *help me get this right. Please.*

After that, he crawled into his side of the bed, closed his eyes and thought what a strange and unfair thing it was that something bad had to happen to Bob and Molly and their kids for something so good to happen to him.

Griffin and Fletcher were home with him, where they belonged. Tired as he was, as sorry as he felt for Bob and Molly and the kids, something inside him soared in celebration because, finally, he had his kids back.

Soon, he fell into a sound sleep and didn't wake up until the wee small hours, when he rolled over into a wet spot in the middle of the bed.

James's text didn't come in until late that night, long after Kendra and Joslyn had paid their visit to Tara, consumed their lemonade and heard the whole story, from the day Tara met James to that day's phone call.

Kendra, with pregnancy hormones running amok in her system and her empathy meter hitting the red zone, had teared up as she reached across the table to squeeze Tara's hand. "It must have been the hardest thing in the world to leave those children," she'd said. "I can't even *imagine* being separated from Madison."

Madison, a precocious, copper-haired five-year-old, was the biological daughter of Kendra's late ex-husband, Jeffrey Chamberlain, and the classic Other Woman he'd fooled around with while he and Kendra were still married.

That hadn't stopped Kendra from adopting the child as her very own and loving her completely; in fact, Madison had the distinction of being adopted *twice.* Soon after Kendra and Hutch were married, Madison had officially become a Carmody, too.

Moved by Kendra's understanding, Tara had cried then, too, letting down the last of her guard, she supposed, and nodded in agreement. "It's been worse than hard," she admitted.

Joslyn had seemed a little miffed in the beginning, because Tara had kept such a secret from her two closest friends for all this time, but she got over that fast, knowing that Tara had barely been able to *think* about parting with the children she'd loved as much as if they'd been born to her, let alone talk about it, even with the people she trusted most.

The evening ended around nine that night.

Tara saw her friends to their cars, waved them out of sight as they drove away, and then went back into the house to check her cell phone for the umpteenth time.

No message from James.

Sleeping was impossible—had her famously temperamental ex changed his mind about sending Elle and Erin to her? Had he ever intended to put them on a westward-bound airplane at all? It would be like him to set up Tara for a disappointment like this. He was a man with a score to settle, in his own opinion at least, and he could be ruthless at times.

No, her sensible side argued, as she locked doors and put away the pitcher of lemonade in the refrigerator. This visit from the children wasn't something James was doing for Tara's sake, certainly, or even for that of his daughters. The whole thing was all about *him,* what *he* wanted. And that was some "alone-time"—read: lots of impromptu sex—with this Bethany person. The deal was simple enough: if he didn't send the twins to Tara in Montana, he wouldn't get that.

Calmer now, Tara fed Lucy, let her outside, let her back in again. She watched the news on her small kitchen TV, the only set in the house, and shut it off when, after fifteen minutes or so, the programming looped back around to the beginning.

Tara retreated to her study, keeping her cell phone close at hand, and logged on to her computer to check her email. Nothing from James, nothing from the twins. She frowned, worried in spite of all her best reasoning.

Lucy, curled up on the hooked rug in front of the bookcase, gave a little whimper of shared concern. She was just one big fur-covered heart, that dog.

Finally, the phone made a familiar *ting* sound, signaling an incoming message.

Tara fumbled for the device, holding her breath, and peered at the screen. **Sorry it took so long to get back to you,** James had texted, **but Bethany managed to book the kids' flights, and here's the info.** The name of the airline followed, along with departure and arrival times.

There was nothing about the return trip, and Tara tried not to read anything into that. She couldn't afford to hope for further miracles, because the let-down would be crushing. This was a *visit,* not a homecoming, she reminded herself firmly, and Elle and Erin *would* be going back to New York.

For now, though, it was enough to know that James hadn't pulled out the proverbial rug from under her as she'd feared he would, and this wonderful *gift* of a thing was actually going to happen. She was about to see them again, Elle and Erin, the daughters of her heart if not her body, the very next morning. They'd arrive in Missoula at eleven-fifteen and come out through the security gate a few minutes later, and she would hug them and hug them, and then she would bring them home with her and treasure every moment spent in their company.

Tears of joy and relief filled Tara's eyes, and her hand trembled so that she nearly dropped the phone before she managed to text back, **I'll be there to meet them and make sure they call you right away. Thank you, James.**

He didn't respond, being James.

Problem solved, on to the next challenge.

Elle and Erin were as good as on their way, and that was all that mattered to Tara.

She swiveled around her office chair, phone still in hand, and saw that Lucy was sitting up now, watching her, totally alert to every nuance.

Tara laughed and reached out to ruffle the dog's silky ears. "You're going to love the twins," she said, knowing it was true, "and they're going to love you right back."

Lucy seemed to take her at her word, wagging her tail and donning a dog grin.

It took a long time to get to sleep that night—every time Tara closed her eyes, she thought of something fun she and the girls and Lucy could do together, or something she wanted to remember to tell them, or ask them, and then she was wide-awake again.

She got up once for a drink of water and found herself at the bedroom window once more, looking across the narrow, moon-streaked finger of Big Sky

River. There was a light on in Boone's trailer. What was he doing up at this hour?

Of course she knew it was none of her business what Boone Taylor was doing over there in his ramshackle double-wide in the middle of the night, but something kept her at the window just the same, and for a long time.

When the light eventually blinked out, Tara went back to bed, and this time, she slept.

As good as her word, Opal was on Boone's doorstep bright and early that first morning after the boys came home, wearing one of her flowery homemade dresses, clutching her big faux patent-leather purse to her ample bosom and grinning wide.

Yawning, still clad in the backup sweatpants he'd put on after Fletcher's bed-wetting episode, though he'd pulled on a T-shirt to answer the door, Boone let her in. Opening the door always reminded him that the inside of the double-wide was a kind of vacuum—there was a faint *whoosh,* more feeling than sound, whenever anybody came or went. It was a little like living in a refrigerator, except warm.

"Is there coffee?" Opal immediately wanted to know. Her eyes were bright with purpose, like her smile.

"Not yet," Boone said, yawning again, smoothing down his sleep-rumpled hair with a motion of one hand. The boys were still out of commission, this time in their own bed. The three of them had had to vacate his, of course, and he'd washed and dried the sheets during the night, and crashed on the couch while he was waiting for the last cycle to finish.

Opal made a tsk-tsk sound. "I declare," she fussed good-naturedly, heading resolutely for the coffeemaker. "How do you get through a single day on your own?"

When Boone noticed her purple high-top sneakers, he couldn't help grinning. Then he remembered that Bob was under the knife at that very moment, and a lot of hard things would happen before his good and inherently decent brother-in-law got back to normal, that

Molly and the kids would suffer, too, by extension.

"I depend on the kindness of strangers," Boone said cheerfully. He knew Opal's question hadn't really required an answer—she'd merely been reminding him that he needed a wife.

Opal thought every single man in the world needed a wife.

As for how he managed, well, he got through his days the way most everybody else did, he reckoned—by showing up and doing his best with what he had.

"I'm no stranger, Boone Taylor," Opal objected sweetly, starting the coffee brewing. "I'm your second mama. I just *happen* to be *black,* that's all."

He chuckled and once again shoved a hand through his hair, wondered if he ought to wake up the boys or let them sleep for a while longer. They'd met Opal before, on their brief visits to Parable, and he knew they liked her a lot. They liked Hutch and Kendra, too, and Slade and Joslyn. *He* was the one they tended to be skittish around.

He sobered, remembering. "Molly's

husband shattered his knee yesterday," he said very quietly.

Opal immediately stepped away from the counter and crossed the sagging floor of that tiny kitchen to put her arms around Boone, gave him a hard motherly squeeze and then stepped back to look up at him through the lenses of her old-fashioned glasses. The frames resembled a pair of jaunty wings, and they were studded with tiny rhinestones.

"Bless your heart, honey, I know all about that," she said. "Hutch told me. I won't pretend I'm not glad the boys are back home, but I am so sorry it had to happen like this." She paused then, squared her broad shoulders and shook a finger under his nose. "Times like now, prayer's the ticket. It makes everything easier."

No prayers had made Corrie's passing easier, not one whit, for her or for him, but he didn't say that. Boone numbered himself among the former believers of the world, the disgruntled and doubtful ones, but that didn't mean he could go around raining on Opal's parade, so he kept his opinion to himself. After all, Opal was a churchgoing woman, and she *did* seem to get a lot of prayers answered. There was a rumor floating around that she might just marry up with the new pastor, Dr. Walter Beaumont, the two of them joining forces against the devil. They'd been seen fishing together and sharing a pancake special over at the Butter Biscuit Café, and just the other day, Slade had said he and Joslyn were on the lookout for another housekeeper.

"I guess so," Boone finally said, because he knew his old friend was waiting for an answer to her brief but inspirational message. "You're an angel, Opal. Moving was a shock to my boys, sudden as it was, and they're worried about their uncle, of course. It'll make them feel better having you here."

She smiled and patted his cheek. "Let me just get breakfast on the stove," she said. "There'll be coffee in a few minutes, and you look like a man who needs some sustenance, pronto."

Boone nodded gratefully and went off to grab a shower and get dressed in his usual go-to-work getup of jeans, a cotton shirt cut Western-style and a decent pair of boots. He'd put on his badge and his service revolver later, he decided. Most of the time, he didn't need either one, since everybody in Parable County knew who he was and no one was likely to behave in a way that would require shooting them.

When he got back to the kitchen, Opal handed him the promised cup of coffee, and he inhaled the rich scent of it before he took a sip, savoring it as he took in the sight of his boys, sitting at the table in their cartoon pajamas, their feet bare and their eyes still puffy from sleeping hard and deep.

"Are you mad at me?" Fletcher asked, right out of the chute, leveling a look at Boone. A blush pulsed in his freckled cheeks, and his voice dropped to a near whisper, as though Opal and Griff weren't right there to hear every word. "For wetting the bed, I mean?"

Boone shook his head. "Nope," he said, taking another sip of his coffee before going on. "Stuff happens."

Fletcher looked relieved, but he was

still holding a grudge, too. That much was abundantly clear. “I want to go back to Missoula,” he reminded his father.

Boone let that one pass, since stubbornness ran in the family.

CHAPTER FOUR

Elle and Erin had both grown a head taller since Tara had last seen them, more than a year before, on the most recent of her rare and brief visits to New York, and they'd both had haircuts. Gone were the long blond locks she'd brushed and braided so many times—now they sported short, breezy styles that framed their faces. And they were almost the same height as she was.

Although the girls were actually fraternal twins, and there were some marked differences between them if one knew what to look for, the resemblance was striking enough to convince most people they were identical.

Elle, the elder by four minutes, was the confident one, the ringleader. Erin, who wore glasses despite her father's repeated attempts to sell her on contact lenses, was shy and formidably bright. Tara suspected the glasses served as a kind of shield for the girl, something to hide behind when she was scared or simply wanted time to observe and assimilate whatever might be going on around her.

When the pair spotted Tara, waiting with a big smile and her arms already opened wide, they rushed her, backpacks bouncing between their skinny shoulder blades, cheeks flushed, eyes glowing with delight.

"Mom!" Elle cried jubilantly, as the three of them tangled in a group hug, at once laughing and teary-eyed.

Since the divorce, James had expressly forbidden the twins to address Tara as "Mom," and she thought of correcting Elle, but she didn't have the heart to do it and, besides, her ex wasn't there to object. He was thousands of miles away, just the way she liked him best.

"It's wonderful to see you two," Tara said, when the hubbub had died down a little and they were headed for baggage claim, a zigzag trio with their arms linked at the elbows.

"It's wonderful to *be* here," Erin answered, adjusting her wire-rims.

Tara felt a little stab of love as she shifted, putting an arm around each of their tiny waists. They wore the narrowest of jeans, sandals and long-sleeved T-shirts, Elle's blue, Erin's pink. "We're going to have a great time," she told them. "You'll like Parable, and the farm, too."

Erin's eyes grew big and very blue. "We were so scared Dad would change his mind and make us go to summer camp instead of coming out here to stay with you."

Elle nodded her agreement as they all strolled purposefully through the small airport, moving aside now and then so they didn't block foot traffic. "And summer camp started *weeks* ago," she added. "The day after school let out. So everybody's already chosen their friends. We would have been, like, *geeks.*"

Tara laughed. "Geeks?" she countered. "Never."

"Elle likes to be in on all the action," Erin said, wisely tolerant of her sister.

They reached the baggage claim area and waited with the other arriving travelers, until a buzzer squawked and the first bags lurched into view.

Erin and Elle had two large suitcases each, color coordinated like their T-shirts, with busy geometric patterns.

Tara, after getting one luggage cart, went back for a second after her stepdaughters pointed out their bags. By the time she got back, a man in a cowboy hat had lifted one pair of suitcases onto the cart. He repeated the process, tugged at the brim of his hat and, without a word, picked up his own bag, and walked away.

"That was a *cowboy,*" Erin breathed, impressed. "A *real* one, I think."

Tara grinned and nodded. "The genuine article," she agreed.

"How do you know?" Elle asked them

both, ever practical. "Maybe he was just a guy in boots and a hat."

"I know he's a cowboy," Tara replied, "because he stepped up and helped with the suitcases without being asked."

Elle pondered that, looking only partially convinced, and Erin gave her sister a light prod in the ribs. "Cowboys do polite stuff," she informed Elle. "Like lifting suitcases and opening doors."

"Not *just* cowboys," Elle retorted. "Tony—" she glanced at Tara, no doubt figuring her stepmother was out of the loop, having been gone for a couple years "—he's the doorman in our building. He does the same things."

"But he doesn't wear boots and a hat," Erin said in the tone of one bringing home a salient point. "Not one like the cowboy had on, anyway."

"He'd look silly if he did," Elle said. "Right in the middle of Manhattan."

"I've seen cowboy hats in Manhattan, though," Erin reasoned. She was the diplomat of the pair, Elle the pragmatist.

Tara, enjoying the exchange, reveling in the presence of her beloved stepdaughters, didn't comment. She simply led the way outside, pushing one cart while Erin managed the other, and silently counted her blessings, two of them in particular.

Sunshine shimmered in the twins' hair, and there was a cool breeze out.

Life is good, Tara thought, rolling her cart through the crosswalk.

Elle swung around her backpack in front of her as they walked, rummaged through it, extracted an expensive cell phone and switched it on before pressing a sequence of icons. By the time they'd found the SUV, she was finished with whatever she was doing and popping the device into a jeans pocket.

"There," she said. "The paternal unit has been duly informed of our whereabouts."

Tara smiled again—not that she actually *stopped* smiling since the moment she had spotted Elle and Erin in the flow of incoming passengers—and opened the hatch on the SUV with a button on her key fob.

This time, there was no cowboy to step up and load the baggage into the back of the rig, but working together, they jostled the luggage inside. Then the twins flipped a coin to see who would sit in front with Tara and who would sit in back.

Erin won the toss, crowed a little and climbed in across the console from Tara.

"I thought you had a dog," Elle remarked from the back as she buckled herself in for the ride home.

"Lucy's waiting impatiently back at the farm," Tara told the girls, starting the engine, preparing to back out of her parking space. "She likes to ride in cars, but she's still a puppy, really, and I think this trip would have been a little too long for her."

"What happened to the red car?" Erin wanted to know. "The one you sent us pictures of?"

Tara might have sighed in memory of her zippy little convertible, if she'd been alone, or in a less ebullient mood. "I traded it in," she replied.

"We wouldn't all fit in a sports car, goon-face," Elle pointed out, affably disdainful.

"I *know* that, ding-dong," Erin answered, without a trace of hostility.

"No name-calling," Tara said lightly. The way the girls said "goon-face" and "ding-dong" sounded almost affectionate, but it was the principle of the thing.

Erin bent to lift her backpack off the floorboard and ferret through it for her own phone, an exact duplicate of Elle's, except for the case. "You texted Dad that we got here okay, right?" she asked Elle without looking back.

"He'd be the paternal unit I mentioned, goon—" Elle paused, and her tone took on a note of mischievous acquiescence. "I mean, *Erin,*" she said sweetly.

Tara concentrated on maneuvering the SUV through the exit lane and onto the road, still smiling. *Talk about a goon-face,* she thought, having caught a glimpse of herself in the wide-range rearview mirror. She couldn't seem to stop grinning.

Erin sat with her head tilted slightly forward so her short hair curtained her face, working the virtual keyboard on her phone with all the deft expertise of any contemporary child. Presently, she gave a little whoop of delight and announced, most likely for her sister's benefit, "Savannah got her ears pierced!"

"No way," Elle said. "Her mom told her she had to wait until she was fifteen. I was there when she said it."

"Savannah's not with her mom," Erin answered airily. "She's with her *dad* and her stepmom at their place on Cape Cod and her stepmom took her to some place at the mall. It stings a little, she says, but she has gold posts and looks at least five years older than she did fifteen minutes ago."

Amused, Tara marveled at the perfection of her own happiness as she drove away from the airport, headed in the direction of Parable. The twins' front-seat/backseat conversation might have seemed pretty mundane to anybody else, but she'd been starved for the small things, like the way the twins bantered.

"Maybe we could get *our* ears pierced," Elle ventured.

Duh, Tara thought, finally picking up on the stepmom correlation. She wondered if the text exchange with Savannah had been a ruse. It was possible that the sisters had rehearsed this entire scenario on the flight out, or even before that, hoping Tara would fall in with their plan. "Not without express permission from your father, you can't," she said.

Both girls groaned tragically.

"He'll never let us," Erin said. "Not even when we're fifteen. He says it's too 'come-hither,' whatever that means."

"His call," Tara said, with bright finality, busy thinking of ways to skirt the probable next question, which would be something along the lines of, *What does* come-hither *mean, anyway?* "Are you hungry?"

"Why do grown-ups always ask that?" Erin reflected.

"We were in first class," Elle added. "Every time the flight attendants came down the aisle, they shoved food at us. I may explode."

"Okay," Tara said. "Well, then. We'll just head straight for home."

"I want to meet your dog," Erin said, sounding both solemn and formal. "Dad won't let us have one in the penthouse. He says the rugs are too expensive for wholesale ruination."

"For the time being," Tara replied, watching the highway ahead as it unrolled like a gray ribbon, twisting toward the mountain-spiked blue horizon, "you can share mine."

"Like Dad ever bought anything wholesale," Elle scoffed quietly.

Erin rolled her eyes at Tara, but allowed the remark to pass unchallenged. Then, looking more serious, she smiled over at Tara. "Thanks," she said. "That's nice of you, offering to let your dog be ours, too, at least for a little while." She considered. "What about horses? Do you have any of those?"

"Just chickens," Tara replied. "Sorry."

"Chickens?" Elle asked, interested.

Tara had told her about the hens and roosters via email, but a conversational opening was a conversational opening.

"How many?"

"Dozens," Tara answered. Since she'd never been able to bring herself to kill one for the stew pot or the frying pan, the birds were proliferating.

"That's a lot of eggs," Elle said.

"And drumsticks," Erin added. "Yum."

"Southern fried," Elle dreamed aloud. "With mashed potatoes and gravy."

Tara bit her lower lip, and both girls instantly picked up on her hesitation.

"What?" they asked in chorus.

Tara merely shook her head, signaling to change lanes. She liked fried chicken as well as the next person, but when she indulged, which wasn't often, she generally bought a few choice pieces from the deli section at the supermarket or ordered it at the Butter Biscuit Café. She was basically an impostor, since she lied by omission and let people *think* she was a country type like them. If Boone Taylor ever found out about this fraud, God forbid, he'd smirk and make snide comments.

Something about *city slickers trying to go country,* probably.

"They have names," she explained lamely, after a few moments of fast thinking. "The chickens, I mean. They're like—pets." To her mind, the Tuesday night special at the Butter Biscuit was one thing, and plunging a fork into Doris or Harriet or Clementine was quite another. She *had* considered serving Boris up with dumplings a time or two when she'd wanted to sleep in past sunrise and he'd crowed anyway, but nothing had ever come of the idea.

The girls were quiet for a while. Then they burst out giggling.

Tara thought she caught a note of relief in their amusement, though, and she relaxed.

After that, everybody lapsed into benign silence—Erin continued to text, chuckling to herself every once in a while, and Elle plugged a pair of earbuds into her phone and settled back to listen to music.

Eventually, both girls fell asleep—they'd gotten up early to catch their flight and changed planes not once but twice along the way, after all, and who knew how much rest they'd gotten the night before. They would have been excited about the trip ahead then, but now they didn't have to rush.

It wasn't until Tara had driven through Parable proper and turned onto the bumpy dirt road that led to her farm that Elle and Erin awakened, blinking and sleepy and curious.

Chickens scattered everywhere as Tara parked the SUV, and even over the squawking and flapping of wings she could hear Lucy barking a welcome from just inside the front door.

She smiled.

"Let's get the bags later," she said as the girls leaped out of the vehicle and turned in circles, looking around them, taking in everything in great, visual gulps. "Lucy might turn inside out if she has to stay shut up alone for another minute."

Erin hurried through the gate in the white picket fence surrounding Tara's front yard, partly to get away from the chickens, Tara figured, and Elle followed.

Reaching the porch, Tara opened the screen door, turned her key in the lock and cautiously stepped back, grinning a warning at the twins, who were still on the walk.

"Heads up," she warned. "Here comes Lucy!"

Lucy shot through the opening like a

fur-covered missile, paused only briefly to nuzzle Tara in one knee, and bounded toward the girls before Tara could catch hold of her collar and gently restrain her.

"She won't hurt you," she said, but the assurance proved unnecessary, because Elle and Erin were as pleased to make Lucy's acquaintance as she was theirs. The three of them went into a rollicking huddle, like long-lost friends finally reunited.

Lucy yipped and yelped exuberantly and broke away to run in circles around the now-crouching twins, her ears tucked back in that funny way, simply unable to contain herself in the face of such joy.

Elle and Erin laughed at her antics, rising back to their feet, dusting bits of lawn grass off their jeans. Glancing warily back, in tandem, to make sure the chickens were still on the far side of the picket fence.

"I think it's safe to say Lucy likes you," Tara observed.

"Silly dog," Erin said, with such fondness that Tara's throat constricted. "Silly, *wonderful* dog."

Inside, Tara gave the twins a quick tour of the downstairs, Lucy following everywhere they went, panting with the lingering excitement of having guests—these humans were just full of delightful surprises, she seemed to be thinking—and then they all trooped up the back stairs, along the hallway and into their room.

Tara had worked hard renovating that old house, and she was proud of it, but she knew a moment's trepidation while she waited for the girls' reactions to their very modest quarters.

They lived in a very pricey penthouse, after all, with ten rooms and a spectacular view of the most exciting city in the world.

"This is cool," Elle finally said, one hand resting on Lucy's golden head as she looked around.

"Like being at camp," Erin added cheerfully, tossing her backpack onto one of the twin beds. "Except fewer bunks."

"Goon-face," Elle said benevolently,

"it's not like camp at all. The look is called 'shabby chic,' for your information."

Tara pretended she hadn't heard the term "goon-face," pointed out the door to the guest bathroom, and suggested the girls get themselves settled in while she went downstairs and made a pitcher of lemonade.

They were flipping a coin for the first shower, evidently their go-to way of making minor decisions, Lucy watching them in fascinated adoration, when Tara left the room and returned to the kitchen, humming under her breath. Fifteen minutes later, she was sitting on the front porch, contentedly rocking in her favorite wicker chair and waiting to serve the lemonade, when Opal drove up in her tanklike station wagon, causing the previously calm chickens to squawk wildly and kick up clouds of fresh dust.

Lucy, probably still enthralled with the goings-on upstairs, wasn't there to bark a greeting.

"Hello, there!" Opal sang, waving as she got out of the car.

Two small boys scrambled from

booster seats in the back, and Tara, who had seen the children a few times, usually at a distance, thought she would have recognized them even without previous encounters. Both of them looked like Boone in miniature, which meant they'd be heartbreakers for sure when they got older, though hopefully not arrogant ones, like their father.

"Ms. Kendall," Opal said, as the boys came to stand on either side of her, looking warily at the mob of clucking, pecking chickens surrounding them, "this is Griffin." She laid a hand on the older boy's shoulder, then did the same with the younger one. "And this is Fletcher."

Fletcher frowned at the chickens and moved closer to Opal. "Do those things bite?" he asked.

"No," Opal assured him. "They just make a lot of noise."

"Chickens don't even have teeth," Griffin informed his brother scornfully. "So how could they bite?"

Tara met the visitors at the front gate, swinging it open, hugging Opal and then solemnly shaking hands with each of the boys in turn. “I’m very glad to meet you both,” she said. “And I know Elle and Erin will be, too.”

“Who’s that?” Fletcher said, wrinkling his nose.

“Thought we’d just stop by and say hello,” Opal explained, overriding the question. “We won’t stay long.”

“Nonsense,” Tara answered. “I’m glad you’re here. I just made lemonade, and I think I could rustle up a few cookies if I tried.” She smiled at the boys, wanting them to feel welcome. Lord knew, they must have had problems enough, being Boone Taylor’s sons. “Elle and Erin are my stepdaughters. They’re visiting from New York.”

“Oh,” said Fletcher, mildly disgusted. *Girls,* his expression said.

“Cookies?” Griffin asked hopefully.

Fletcher made a face. “I don’t like lemonade,” he said. “It’s too sour.”

“Hush, now,” Opal told him. “Don’t you be rude, Fletcher Taylor.”

“Yeah,” Griffin agreed. “Don’t be so *rude,* poop-head.”

“That will be enough of that ornery talk,” Opal decreed good-naturedly.

Nothing seemed to fluster the woman—she was the eye of the hurricane, the port in the storm, generous competence personified.

Without comment, Tara led them all inside, through the house to the kitchen, Opal checking everything out as they went and making approving noises.

"You have sure done wonders with this old house," she said as they reached their destination. "Back when Boone's folks lived here, it was a sight, let me tell you." Both the boys looked up at her curiously, and she was quick to add, "Not that it wasn't clean, mind you. Polly Taylor kept it up real nice, but Leroy used to park his motorcycle in the living room when the weather was bad, to protect the paint job, he said. Leroy didn't trust that old barn not to fall right in on top of his pride and joy once the snow came and made the roof sag."

Tara smiled to herself, thinking that the proverbial apple didn't fall far from the tree, given the shape Boone's own place was in, but of course she wouldn't have said it out loud with Griffin and Fletcher right there to hear.

Opal had just taken a seat at the table, with a somewhat weary sigh, when Lucy came racing down the back stairway, barking her brains out, having finally clued in that, wonder of wonders, there was *more company.* Elle, freshly showered and barefoot, wearing white shorts and a yellow top, was right behind her.

Griffin and Fletcher glanced at her, then immediately gave themselves up, laughing, to Lucy's face-licking hello.

Tara made introductions, over the tumult, and Elle nodded to the boys and extended a hand to Opal. "How do you do?" she said, sounding very grown-up.

Opal beamed a smile at the child. "I do just fine," she replied. "How about you?"

"I'm good," Elle said, sounding unusually shy.

"Boys," Opal said, "quiet down a little now. I declare, I can't hear myself think over the racket."

"The *dog's* the one making all the noise," Fletcher protested.

Opal sighed again. “Well, take her outside, then,” she said, the soul of patience.

“Let’s check out the yard,” Elle suggested, leading the mass exodus through the back door, Lucy bringing up the tail-wagging rear.

“Phew,” Opal said when she and Tara were alone in the newly quiet kitchen. “I’m not used to kids that age anymore. Joslyn and Slade’s little one, Trace, being just a baby and all.” She leaned forward a tad and added confidentially, “Poor little fellas. They’re missing their aunt and uncle something fierce.”

Absorbing that, Tara washed her hands at the sink, took glasses from the cupboard and lined them up on the counter, added ice to two of them, then got the lemonade pitcher from the fridge and poured for Opal and herself. “Will they be visiting long?” she asked, remembering yesterday’s interlude with Boone by the ATM at Cattleman’s Bank.

“I do believe they’re here to stay this time,” Opal said quietly. There was a still a glint of sympathy in her eyes, but something else, too, something Tara couldn't quite read. "Griffin—that's the bigger boy, you know—he's just thrilled to be back with his daddy, though he tries not to let on too much. Fletcher, on the other hand, well, he's likely to try hitchhiking back to Missoula first chance he gets if we don't keep an eye on him right along."

Tara felt a twinge of sadness, for the children and maybe even for Boone. A little.

"Did something happen?" she asked carefully. Either Joslyn or Kendra had mentioned Boone's children the night before, during their visit, but Tara had been thinking about Elle and Erin at the time, and how much she'd missed them, and hadn't gotten the gist of it.

Opal sighed and gave a little nod. "Sure did," she replied. "Molly—that's Boone's sister—she and her husband, Bob, have been looking after Griffin and Fletcher pretty much since their mama, Corrie, died. Now, Bob's gone and had an accident on the golf course, which is the bad news. The *good* news is that those boys are back here where they belong. Bob and Molly were real good to them, but *Boone's* their daddy."

Tara had known some of Boone's story, that he was a widower anyway, and that he had two children, but she'd been hazy on the details, telling herself that the less she knew about her redneck neighbor, the better off she'd be. Before she'd come up with a response to Opal's words, though, Erin came down the back stairs, her hair damp from her shower and curling madly in all directions. She wore a pink sundress and, like her twin, she was barefoot.

Tara made more introductions, and Erin responded politely before looking around the quiet kitchen. "Where are Lucy and Elle?" she asked.

"Outside," Tara answered, with another smile. Her face was starting to hurt, but she couldn't help it. She was just too happy to maintain a normal expression for very long.

Erin excused herself and hurried through the back door.

"Maybe I ought to find out what they're doing out there," Tara fretted.

She was a little rusty at mothering, she realized; back in New York, she'd never have let Elle and Erin out of her sight unless they were in the company of one or more trusted adults.

"They're just fine," Opal said with pleasant certainty, and Tara believed her. Settled back into the chair she'd half risen from on the spur of the moment.

"Are you working for Sheriff Taylor now?" Tara asked when the conversation lagged, albeit in a comfortable, kick-off-your-shoes-and-sit-awhile kind of way.

"No," Opal said, shaking her head slowly. "I'm just helping out for a little while. Boone wasn't expecting to get the kids back when he did, and I figured he might be in over his head at first."

"Oh," Tara said, nodding and taking a sip from her frosty glass of lemonade. When it came to Boone Taylor, irritation had sustained her for a long time. It was odd to find herself feeling a little sorry for the man, but kind of satisfying, too, because she knew it would annoy him plenty, rooster-proud as he was.

The kids came back inside then, all four of them, with Lucy in the lead.

They were only passing through, it turned out, on their way to the front porch, where they could keep an eye on the chickens and Griffin could point out his dad's place, across that slice of river that separated it from Tara's property.

Leaving Opal to sip her lemonade in peace, Tara piled a plate high with cookies, filled four more glasses from the pitcher and carried the refreshments out front on a tray.

Griffin was standing at the end of the porch, one arm extended toward the double-wide on the other side of the water, pointing an index finger.

"You live *there?*" Elle asked, sounding amazed though not quite disdainful. "That's an actual house?"

Tara closed her eyes for an instant, cleared her throat loudly and made a rattling fuss of setting down the tray on the low porch table.

"Yes, it's a *house,*" Griffin replied tersely, offended.

"It's really a trailer," Fletcher interjected, in a helpful tone. "It had wheels, once."

"Lemonade and cookies!" Tara sang out.

"What's wrong with it?" Griffin asked, frowning at Elle. So much for diverting the conversation away from the trailer next door.

"Nothing, squirt," Elle replied cheerfully. "Give me a break, here, will you? I didn't mean any harm—I'm from New York City and we don't *have* trailers there, that's all."

Tara passed out lemonade, and the children each accepted a glass, though they barely seemed to see her.

"We lived in a *house* in Missoula," Fletcher said, gripping his lemonade tightly in small hands. "It was bigger than this one and *way* nicer."

"Well, *excuse* me," Elle said, with lighthearted indignation.

Erin was perched in the porch swing, her feet curled beneath her on the floral cushion. She smiled angelically and commented, “That’s what you get for making snotty remarks, sister-dear.”

“Suppose we all start over?” Tara suggested.

The tension seemed to abate a little, and she was just congratulating herself on the success of her front-porch peacekeeping mission when she saw a car turn in out by the mailbox.

Specifically, a sheriff’s department squad car.

Boone.

Tara froze, irritated with herself for being surprised and, admit it, a tad electrified, too. *Get a grip,* she thought. *The man lives next door. He probably saw Opal’s car here as he was passing by and decided to stop in, knowing his boys would be with her.*

The cruiser caused another chicken riot, which resulted in clouds of feather-speckled dust and a cacophony of fowl complaints. Boone opened the door, a wry half grin resting easy on his sexy mouth, and set his hat on his head as he got out.

Tara almost expected to hear the twangy theme from *The Good, the Bad and the Ugly* as he shut the car door and ambled, in that loose-jointed way of men who are damnably comfortable in their own skin, toward the front gate.

Out of the corner of her eye, Tara saw Griffin's little-boy chest swell with a pride that clearly said, *That's my dad.*

"Another cowboy," Erin said, in a fascinated whisper.

"With a *gun,*" Elle added, sounding as awed as her sister.

For some ridiculous and incomprehensible reason, Tara's heart was racing, and her breathing was so shallow that hyperventilation seemed a very real possibility. She swallowed and smiled, raising one hand to shield her eyes from the afternoon sun.

And the dazzle of a cowboy sheriff with a killer smile.

Boone gave the brim of his hat a cordial tug and worked the latch on the gate. He looked tall enough to step right over the top of it, but he passed through it like a normal human being. Lucy, that traitor, scrambled to her feet and trotted down the porch steps toward him, toenails clicking, tail swinging like a big feather. The dog didn't even bark.

Boone chuckled and bent to pat Lucy's head, then lifted his deep brown eyes to take in the greeting committee clustered under the shade of the sloping porch roof.

It was the oddest thing, Tara reflected, then and long after, how time seemed to stop in that instant, as if the whole galaxy had paused, drawn in a collective breath and then started up again.

"Hey, Dad," Griffin called, breaking the silence.

"Hey," Boone responded gruffly, and though he was speaking to the child, his gaze was fixed on Tara. He looked confused, maybe even a little alarmed.

Was she just imagining it, or had he felt the cosmic shift, too?

Impossible, she decided as Opal stepped out onto the porch to join them.

"Are we disturbing the peace, Sheriff?" she teased, grinning.

Boone stopped in the middle of the walk, folded his muscular arms, and tilted his head ever-so-slightly to one side. A grin quirked one corner of his mouth as he pretended to consider the question. "Well," he finally drawled, still looking at Tara, "*one* of you is surely doing that, but I don't expect I'll be filing charges anytime soon."

CHAPTER FIVE

Tara invited Boone to join the gathering on her porch and have some lemonade. At least, he *thought* she had—he couldn't be sure of that or much of anything else, standing there on her front walk the way he was, struck stone-cold stupid by the mere sight of her. And had he *really* just make that lame joke about how she was disturbing the peace?

Tara was definitely disturbing *his* peace, but Opal, all four of the kids and the dog seemed calm enough.

After an internal struggle that seemed to take half of forever, Boone gathered the wits to look away from Tara's slightly flushed face and say to his sons, "I guess we ought to go on home now."

"Supper's waiting for you in the refrigerator," Opal said, looking from Boone to Tara and back again, an impish little smile forming at one corner of her mouth. "All you've got to do is heat it up—I wrote the temperature on the foil. I'll be at your place in the morning, around the same time I got there today."

Finally free from whatever had held them in statue formation, Griffin and Fletcher both started toward Boone, Griffin with a sort of restrained eagerness, Fletcher dragging his sneakered feet. His lower lip stuck out a little, too, and a lonely place deep in Boone's heart flinched at the sight—the kid looked so small and so skinny, all knees and freckles, elbows and attitude.

Was it possible to love somebody the way he loved these kids and survive?

"Thanks for making supper and for offering to babysit again, Opal," Boone said, finding his voice, still keenly aware of Tara and wishing he could ignore her, block her out of his awareness somehow, "but I've signed the boys up for the day-camp program over at the community center, and they're expected first thing tomorrow."

Fletcher looked at him then, further rebellion gathering in that pug-nosed little face like thunderclouds in a glowering sky. There was a tantrum brewing, for sure.

"Day camp?" Griffin asked seriously, not exactly balking, but not as friendly as before, either. "Or day *care?*"

"Day care," Fletcher said ominously, "is for *babies.*"

"Like *babysitting,*" agreed Griffin.

Boone suppressed a sigh, resettled his hat. No matter what he said, no matter how good his intentions, it was always wrong. "We can discuss all that later," he said, his voice quiet and even, "at home. Right now, just get in the car, okay?"

"It won't be legal," Griffin pointed out sagely, sizing up the cruiser. "Me and Fletcher need booster seats."

Shit, Boone thought. Was *every* conversation going to turn into a verbal tug of war? He wasn't used to getting all this guff—he was the head honcho at work, after all, and there'd been no one at home to differ with him, either. Until now, that is.

"I'll bring the boys over in a few minutes, and we can switch out the car seats then," Opal offered, unruffled even though there might as well have been fiery arrows flying through the air, given the tinderbox mood. "Right now, Boone Taylor, I think you could do with some lemonade and a chance to sit in the shade for a spell. Might cool you off a bit."

Boone didn't refuse outright—once Opal Dennison made up her mind, it would take an edict from God to change it—but he didn't accept the backhanded invitation, either. He needed to establish some distance between himself and Tara Kendall, get some perspective. All this time, he'd thought of her one way and now, all of a sudden, he was thinking about her in another. It was disconcerting. "I'll see you at my place, then," he told Opal, turning to walk away.

"Wait!" called a girlish voice.

He looked back over one shoulder and saw one of the blonde girls—twins, he reckoned, since they looked so much alike—coming down the porch steps.

"You're a cowboy, right?" the child asked. She was a winsome little thing, gawky and knobby-kneed, wearing a pink dress and peering up at him through the lenses of her too-adult wire-rimmed glasses. She took in his hat, his Western shirt, his jeans and boots. "At least, you *look* like one."

Boone waited, mildly confounded by the observation. Around Parable, Montana, *every* man was a cowboy.

The girl busted loose with a beaming smile. "We've got bags in the back of Tara's car," she said. "And they're real heavy."

"Erin—" Tara began, but then all the air seemed to go out of her, like a balloon that had been blown up but never tied off at the bottom.

"I'd better carry them in while I'm here, then," Boone heard himself say. Although he hadn't owned a horse or entered a rodeo in years, he was a Westerner to the core.

Next thing he knew, he was hauling suitcases from the back of that SUV, inside the house and right upstairs to a small, airy bedroom, with Erin leading the way, annoyed with himself for wondering where Tara slept. It took two trips to complete the job, and the backs of Boone's ears burned the whole time, not because he was expending any particular effort, but because he had an audience, and he wasn't accustomed to that. The porch crowd had dispersed and then reassembled in the small foyer, watching him like they'd never seen a man carrying luggage before.

"Thank you, Mr.—?" the girl with glasses began, when he came down the stairs for the second time.

"Taylor," Opal supplied, with a verbal smack to her own forehead. "Where are my manners? This is Sheriff Boone Taylor, Erin. Erin and her sister, Elle, are visiting from New York."

Boone nodded and tugged again at his hat brim, chagrined to realize he hadn't taken it off when he had stepped inside the house. His mother had probably rolled over in her grave.

"Do you have horses?" Erin asked eagerly.

He didn't dare look in Tara's direction again, because he knew he'd feel like he'd just shoved one end of a screwdriver into an electrical outlet if he did, but he was aware that she was standing nearby, all right. All over his body, tiny nerves jumped and crackled under his hide, as if fixing to break right through to the surface.

"No," he said. "Sorry. No horses."

Erin looked disappointed, and he didn't risk a glance at his boys.

After the bellman episode, Boone made his escape. Strode out of there with only slightly more dignity than an alley cat with a burr stuck in its tail. He went down the porch steps and across the yard, swinging one leg over the gate in the picket fence, wading through a million chatty chickens to get back to the squad car.

His neck was hot as he executed a casual, salutelike wave at the audience, who had gathered on the porch, watching him intently. The whole scenario made him wonder if he'd grown an extra ear in the middle of his forehead.

Befuddled, he drove home, parked the county car in the overgrown yard, and went into the double-wide, tossing his hat aside as he entered and making straight for the kitchen sink, where he started the faucet running and splashed his head and neck with cold water until his skin cooled down and the front of his shirt was soaked.

What the *hell* was the matter with him, anyhow? All this time he'd managed to coexist with Tara Kendall, gall him though she sometimes did, with her little digs about the way his place looked, but now, for some crazy reason, she had him good and rattled.

By the time Opal drove up in her station wagon fifteen or twenty minutes later, bringing the kids with her, Boone had calmed down enough to safely lock away his service revolver, take off his badge and pull on a dry T-shirt, but he still felt oddly *stranded,* and restless, too, like a dog trapped on a median between six lanes of traffic going both ways.

Opal came inside with Griffin and Fletcher, both of whom immediately hightailed it for the living room to turn on the seldom-used TV, shook her head and frowned when Boone offered her cash for looking after the kids all day, not to mention cooking and cleaning, too. "I'm your *friend,* Boone Taylor," she said, hands-on-her-hips indignant.

"I know you are," Boone replied, still holding the twenties he'd just pulled from his wallet, "and that's why I won't take advantage of you."

Opal set her jaw and again shook her head, scowling at him as fiercely as if he'd just suggested switching out the communion wine at church for home-made whiskey. "I do not have a clue, Boone Taylor, why you can't accept a simple kindness from somebody who cares about you and just leave it at that."

"Put it in the collection plate," he persisted, gently prying open one of her hands and pressing the money into it. "Or give it to some charity."

She hesitated for a long time.

"I could do that, I suppose," Opal

eventually allowed. "The foreign mission fund has been running a little low lately. The economy, you know."

Inwardly, Boone sighed with relief, though there was a lingering prickle of disquiet, too. Her earlier remark had struck close to the bone, since it *was* hard for him to accept help, from his closest friends or from Molly and Bob. "That's a fine idea," he said, speaking moderately so he wouldn't give away too much of what he was feeling.

Whatever the hell it was.

Opal squinted at him, looking suspicious, but finally opened the maw of her enormous purse and dropped the bills inside. "You're sure you don't need me to look after Griffin and Fletcher for a few more days? I wouldn't mind at all—they're a pleasure to be around, you know."

Yeah, Boone reflected ruefully, remembering Fletcher's scowl. *A real pleasure.*

"I'm sure," he said, with a little too much certainty. Like everybody else in Parable, he was fond of Opal, so he added gently, "They'll be just fine at day camp. They might even learn something."

"I don't know," Opal fretted, clearly unconvinced. "That's a good program the center has going there and all that, but I believe most of the other children are younger than yours."

He heard the silent echo of his younger son's words back there at Tara's place. *Day care is for babies.*

"Can't hurt to try," Boone said, to himself as much as Opal.

Opal headed away from him then, with a sigh and another shake of her head, moving toward the living room doorway, where she paused to say goodbye to Griffin and Fletcher. Both of them thanked her politely, which restored some of Boone's faith in the youth of America—in his line of work, that ebbed and flowed.

Most of the kids in and around Parable were good, but he'd ended his workday a little under an hour ago by ordering down a half-dozen snarky teenagers off the rickety old water tower outside of town, and they hadn't been too happy about it.

Setting aside the memory of their grumbling, Boone followed Opal outside to take the boys' car seats out of her station wagon and set them on what passed for a porch, to be installed in the cruiser later. He waved as she drove away.

Fletcher was waiting for him in the kitchen when he got back inside, matchstick arms folded, feet set a little apart, chin jutting forward. "There's nothing on TV," he said. There was a more-than-vague accusation in his tone, as though he figured Boone was personally responsible for network programing.

Boone sighed. "Life is hard," he replied.

Fletcher stood his ground. "Are you putting us in day care?" the kid asked, reminding Boone less of Corrie now and more of himself. Back in the day, when his high school classmates garnered titles like, "Most Likely to Succeed" or some such, the line under his yearbook photo had read, "Most Cussed." "Because day care is—"

"Not just for babies," Boone interrupted his son's statement quietly, mirroring Fletcher's stance by folding his own arms and digging in his heels a little. When he went on, though, he tried for a more diplomatic tone. "You have to be somewhere, buddy. I can't take you and your brother to work with me. Not all the time, anyway. And you can't stay here alone."

"Aunt Molly never made us go to day care," Fletcher pointed out. "Not once."

Boone didn't want to strong-arm the boy, physically or emotionally, but he couldn't afford to come off as a pushover, either. If he set that kind of wimpy precedent, he knew he'd come to regret it, immediately if not sooner. "Do you know what 'nonnegotiable' means?"

"No," Fletcher admitted, but only after he'd considered the matter for a moment or two, trying to stretch his five-year-old mind around the concept.

Griffin meandered into the kitchen then, stood a step or two behind his brother. "It means, dumb-face," he told Fletcher, "that rules are rules. Dad makes them, and we have to do what he says because he's a grown-up and we're kids."

Boone was impressed—his elder son was only seven, after all, but he understood the ins and outs of parental authority well enough, it seemed. "Don't call your brother 'dumb-face,'" he said, as a mild aside. Then he shifted his gaze back to Fletcher. "Otherwise, Griff has it right. Somebody has to head up this outfit, and I'm that somebody."

"Yeah," Griffin said, probably just glad to be right about something.

Fletcher remained clearly skeptical, but at least he didn't argue. "They have a dog," he announced. "Those girls over at Ms. Kendall's chicken farm, I mean. Can we get a dog?"

The request was one Boone could say yes to, and he almost leaped at the chance, he wanted so badly to be on better terms with the kid, but then his common sense kicked in, and he hesitated. He was a deliberate man, and he did not make snap decisions unless there was a lethal weapon involved.

"We'll give that idea some thought," he said, in compromise. Then, rolling his shoulders to release some of the tension that had collected there—he figured the tightness in his muscles and his gut still had more to do with Tara Kendall than setting boundaries with his boys—he walked over and pulled open the refrigerator door, bent to peer inside. "Let's see what Opal whipped up for supper."

"It's a Mexican meatball casserole," Griffin said helpfully.

Boone smiled as he pulled a baking dish—not his own, so Opal must have brought it with her when she drove over that morning—and peeled back a corner of the foil covering. He spotted tomato sauce and a sprinkling of grated cheddar cheese, and his mouth watered at the prospect of a woman-cooked meal. "Yep," he said. "Whatever that is."

"I'm not sure I like that stuff," Fletcher said. He might have been angling to become the poster boy for Childhood Obstinacy. If so, he was not only in the running, he was out there in the lead.

"Too bad," Boone told him, his tone firm but affable. "This is what we're having, dude. It's a take-it-or-leave-it kind of deal." He shut the fridge door and carried the dish over to the stove. Helpful to the end, Opal had indeed scrawled baking instructions and a temperature setting on the foil using a marker. He turned on the oven at 350 degrees and took three plates from the cupboard to set the table.

None of his dishes matched, but thanks to Opal, they were clean.

"Supper's on in half an hour," he told the boys, feeling oddly domestic. "Talk among yourselves, watch TV, swing from the rafters, whatever."

Fletcher looked a little disgruntled, since the argument had petered out on him before he was ready to let it go, but he followed his brother back into the front room, where the TV was blaring zippy cartoon music—probably a chase scene, by the sounds of it.

Boone's cell phone chimed, indicating a text message, so he picked up the device off the kitchen counter to read it.

Molly had written, **How's it going?**

Boone smiled and tapped in a reply. **It's going. The boys are okay. What's happening on your end?**

Bob came through surgery just fine, Molly answered, with typical speed. **Sorry I took so long to let you know, but today it was one thing after another.** A smiley face followed. **Say something that will cheer me up.**

Boone thought for several seconds, then wrote, **The boys want a dog. Is that cheerful?**

They'd love a dog, Molly replied, adding a whole row of smiley faces this time. **Are you going to get them one?**

Probably, Boone texted, starting over twice because he kept putting in the wrong letters. He was a little slower on the draw than his sister when it came to typing on a tiny screen—or a big one, for that matter. Molly, an electronic wiz, used perfect punctuation and never ran words together. **I'd like to let the dust settle a little first, though. Griff is adjusting, but Fletcher keeps threatening to hitchhike back to Missoula. A dog might complicate things.**

Heaven forbid, Molly joked in reply. **Boone, LIFE is complicated.** She hesitated for a few moments then, and Boone withheld his response because he knew his sister wasn't finished. **Maybe some counseling would help,** she suggested, not for the first time. **This is a big change for all of you.**

Maybe, Boone answered. He'd had grief counseling after Corrie died. It hadn't helped. **I'll look into it.**

Bob's hurting a lot, Molly confided.

A wave of sadness swept over Boone as he absorbed those words. **I know, hon. I'm sorry—but stop worrying about us, because we're doing all right.**

The reply was a little smiley face and, **I'm doing my best not to sweat the small stuff, cowboy, but, hey, I'm a mom. Moms fixate and obsess. It goes with the territory.**

He smiled. **I love you, world's best sister.**

I love you, too, bro. Keep me up to speed on everything, okay?

Boone's throat burned a little, as though he'd gulped down a wad of rusty barbed wire. Griffin and Fletcher weren't the only ones who missed Molly. **Sure,** he thumbed. **And you do the same.**

The conversation was over, and

Boone's shoulders slumped slightly as he set aside the phone and went back to the refrigerator, this time for a jug of milk.

He poured a glassful for each of the kids and added silverware to their places at the table.

As for the counseling idea, Molly hadn't been the first person to broach the subject; a big believer in talk therapy, she'd taken the boys to see a child psychologist on a regular basis while they lived with her and that had been fine with Boone. After all, Griffin and Fletcher had lost their mother when they were practically babies and subsequently been uprooted from their home, and while he'd been sure they were better off with Molly and Bob, some kind of damage was inevitable in a situation like that.

He'd been a train wreck after Corrie's death himself, there was no getting around it. Without Slade and Hutch and a few other close friends, he might not have made it through the soul-fracturing cycles of grief and fury and every emotion in between.

Still, opening all that up again to some shrink, letting a "professional" poke and prod at all those sore spots, the most profoundly private regions of his psyche, had been beyond him. So he'd soldiered on, mostly alone, drinking too much alcohol when he was off duty, letting the patch of land—that he and Corrie had once had such grand plans for—fall to rack and ruin, getting through his days and nights, but not really living.

Eventually, Boone had tired of his own morose company and cleaned up his act a little, drinking beer only with his friends and always in moderation, and swearing off whiskey entirely. First as Slade Barlow's deputy and then as sheriff, Boone had dealt with too many mean drunks to delude himself. Trying to drown his sorrows in alcohol never worked and, besides, it was a dangerous road to travel.

The timer on the stove chimed suddenly, jarring him from his solemn musings. Opal's savory casserole was ready to come out of the oven.

"Supper!" he called to the boys, rifling through three drawers before he found a pot holder. The TV was still bullhorn loud.

Mercifully, one of them shut off the thing before he had to issue another order—the tube was never on unless Griffin and Fletcher were in residence, since Boone took in important football games on the big screen at the Boot Scoot Tavern in town and got the news that mattered off the internet or over the radio in his squad car—but these days, he had to choose his battles. Setting limits on how much television the kids watched was way down there on his priority list.

Both his sons marched into the bathroom and washed up without protest, and took their seats at the kitchen table when they came back.

Boone sat down to join them, scooped up some of Opal's fine-smelling concoction for Fletcher and set it in front of him, taking note out of the corner of his eye as Griffin reached for the serving spoon, making it known that he was big enough to help himself.

"Aunt Molly always says grace before we eat," Griffin remarked, moments later, when Boone picked up his own fork, ready to tie in. He was so used to his own sorry cooking, or takeout from the Butter Biscuit Café in town, usually cold before he got a chance to eat it, that the prospect of dining on something Opal had prepared made him double-hungry.

He stopped, mildly embarrassed. "Okay," he said, and waited.

The boys waited, too. Expectantly.

"If you want to pray, pray," Boone said.

"You're supposed to do it," Griffin informed him. "Because you're the grown-up."

Boone hesitated, cleared his throat, closed his eyes and improvised. "Thanks, God, for this fine food and for good friends and for letting us be here together." A pause, followed by a gruff afterthought of an "amen."

"Amen," the kids repeated in unison.

Boone suppressed a sigh. Back when Corrie was alive, she'd insisted on offering up a simple prayer before every meal, prevailing on Boone to do the honors once in a while, at Thanksgiving or Christmas, say, but most of the time, she'd been the one to say grace. They'd gone to church most Sundays, and she'd had both their children baptized by the time they were six weeks old.

Since the day Corrie had died, though, Boone doubted he'd said a single word to God, civil or otherwise. He neither believed nor disbelieved—some folks obviously took comfort from their faith, like Opal, for instance, and that was their own business—but now he sensed that he was being painted into yet another corner. This time, it was a spiritual one.

"I suppose your aunt and uncle took you guys to Sunday school pretty regular," Boone ventured, remembering the previous night when the little guys had said their prayers before bed.

Griffin and Fletcher nodded simultaneously, their eyes big with concern, and picked at their food.

"We went almost every week," Griffin said. His chin wobbled slightly. "The whole family."

Fletcher brightened a little. "And Uncle Bob always made pancakes when we got home," he added. "Waffles, too, sometimes."

Boone felt a sinking sensation in the pit of his stomach. While he was more than grateful to Bob and Molly for all the things they'd done for his boys, it seemed to him that they'd set the bar pretty high.

Pancakes and waffles. Sunday school. Grace before meals and prayers before bed. It was a lot to live up to.

Molly must have told him about all of it—she'd always kept him in the loop where the boys were concerned and sent pictures almost every day from her smartphone—but the embarrassing truth was, though he'd practically memorized those snapshots, he hadn't always *listened* all that closely. It wasn't that he hadn't cared—every mosquito bite, bad dream, skinned knee and wobbly tooth had mattered to him—but sometimes caring hurt so badly that he had to dial down his emotions a few notches just to stay in one piece.

If churchgoing and pancake breakfasts were part of his sons' routine, though, Boone decided, he'd honor the tradition as best he could. Before he got a chance to say so aloud, though, his cell phone rang.

He tipped back his chair on two legs and stretched to grab the device from the counter, where it had been charging.

"Sorry," he said to his sons, frowning at the caller-ID number. Deputy Treat McQuillan was on the line.

Not his favorite person, but he was the duty officer for the night, so Boone had to take the call.

"Boone Taylor," he said into the receiver, as he always did when he knew the call had to do with his job.

"Evening, Boone," Treat said, his tone slow and a little on the oily side. "Sorry to interrupt whatever you're doing at the moment, but we've got ourselves a situation."

"What kind of situation?" Boone asked, frowning. He had that instinctual prickling sensation at his nape, and he didn't try to hide his impatience to know what was up. In addition to his other faults, McQuillan had a flair for drama, liked to savor bad news almost as much as he liked to pass it on.

"Zeb Winchell's daughter called the office twenty minutes ago—she's up in Great Falls—and said she couldn't reach the old man on the telephone all day. She asked me to stop by his place and make sure he was okay," McQuillan continued in his own good time. "So I did."

"McQuillan," Boone prompted, making a warning of the name.

"When I got here, I found Zeb lying in the middle of his kitchen floor," McQuillan said lightly. He might as well have been recounting the details of a routine traffic stop, he sounded so casual. "Been dead a while. Probably a heart attack."

Boone closed his eyes, swore silently. Zeb Winchell had been a crotchety old coot, a prime candidate for one of those reality shows about hoarders, but damn it, he'd been a human being, a *person* with a life and a history. He'd loved his dog and his remarkably tidy vegetable garden and never bothered anybody, so far as Boone knew.

"Did you call the coroner?" he asked. Doc Halpern, a retired general practitioner, served as the county medical examiner.

"Yeah, but he's way over in Three Trees at some kind of a family shindig and he can't get here for at least an hour," McQuillan replied. "You'd better hurry on into town, Sheriff." He put a slight emphasis on that last word, probably still smarting because he'd lost the election last November.

"I'll be there as soon as possible," Boone replied, looking across the table at his sons, his mind clicking through the few options open to him. He couldn't take a couple kids on a death call, and he wasn't going to ask Opal to pinch-hit, either, since she'd put in a long and tiring day as it was. Hutch's bride, Kendra, would have helped out, but she was pregnant, due any minute, and Slade's wife, Joslyn, had a little one to look after, too.

Which left his next-door neighbor, Tara Kendall.

He finished the call with McQuillan, instructing the deputy to make sure

Zeb's neighbors didn't wander into the house, and quietly explained to Griffin and Fletcher that he had to go into Parable for a while.

He consulted the tattered list of near neighbors he'd taped to the inside of a cupboard door in case of sudden emergencies like fires and floods. He'd never programmed Tara's information into his cell phone, since he hadn't had any reason to call her, but he had scrawled her number at the bottom of the page once, after she'd given him a ring to ask when he planned to clean up his property.

Now, after choking down a chunk of his pride, he keyed in the digits.

"Hello?" she said on the third ring.

"There's a problem," Boone said bluntly, following up with a quick explanation and the necessary request that she look after Griffin and Fletcher until he'd finished up in town.

"Of course," Tara told him briskly. While she obviously had less than no use at all for him, she liked the boys, and she was willing to do the neighborly thing.

Thank God.

Fifteen minutes later, after wrestling both car seats into the back of the cruiser and loading up his sons and bumping over dirt roads, Boone pulled into Tara's driveway. At least the chickens had turned in for the night, so there was no squawking committee to greet him.

Tara came outside, still wearing the sundress she'd had on earlier, the half-grown golden retriever trotting at her side. With efficient goodwill, she rounded up the boys and sent them toward the open front door, where the twins hovered, clad in flannel pajama bottoms and T-shirts.

In a hurry, Boone thanked Tara for helping out on short notice and moved to slide behind the wheel again.

But Tara stood too close to the car, so he couldn't back up without running over her feet. "What's wrong?" she asked.

Boone saw no reason to sugarcoat his answer. "A man is dead," he told her.

She put a hand to the hollow of her

throat, and her eyes widened. "Oh, no," she said. "What—?"

"I'm not sure what happened," Boone said, ready to be gone, "but I'm betting on natural causes."

At that, Tara stepped back, lowered her hand from her throat, nodded in farewell.

Boone nodded back, shifted the cruiser into gear and drove off.

He didn't use the siren—there was no point in that, since poor old Zeb was already gone—but he flipped on the blue lights when he reached the main road and pushed the speed limit all the way into Parable.

Every bare bulb in Zeb's tar-paper-shingled house was blazing when Boone pulled up behind Deputy McQuillan's rig, and neighbors lined the chicken-wire fence.

Boone acknowledged them with a wave of one hand as he passed, sprinting up the front walk and then the porch steps, entering through the open door.

The distinctive smell of death hit him the moment he crossed the threshold, then wended his way along a trail between towering stacks of old magazines, empty boxes and God-knew-what-else to reach the back of the house.

McQuillan leaned idly against a counter stacked with junk mail, dirty paper plates, tin cans and other detritus, scrolling through various windows on his cell phone.

Zeb's spindly little frame lay sprawled on the filthy floor, facedown, hands extended over his head, as though he'd reached out at the last moment, trying to break his fall—or maybe just surrender.

Boone ached, saddened by the loneliness and the squalor and the body of the helpless old man on the floor.

He'd seen plenty of dead bodies in his time—there wasn't any violent crime in Parable County to speak of, but folks died of old age right along, like Zeb probably had, and there was the occasional farm accident or car crash, of course—but he never got used to the experience.

This one was all the more poignant, to his mind anyway, because of the small, shivering dog sitting patiently at Zeb's side, ears perked at a hopeful slant, keeping a vigil.

Boone crouched, checked Zeb's neck for a pulse even though he knew there wouldn't be one. "Get this dog some water," he told McQuillan brusquely.

"Like there's anything to put it in," McQuillan replied, barely looking up from his cell phone.

What was he doing? Checking his playlist? Updating his status on some social media site?

Disgust curled in the back of Boone's throat and soured there. Zeb, a good man, was *dead,* but McQuillan didn't seem to give a damn. "*Find* something," he said in a raspy undertone.

McQuillan finally put away the phone, shrugged his narrow shoulders, and, looking put-upon, started scouting around for something that would hold water.

Boone, still crouched, reached across the mortal remains of Zeb Winchell to pat the dog's head. It was some kind of terrier, he supposed, small and brindled and remarkably clean, considering the surroundings. The critter wore a spiffy red collar that looked fairly new, and there were the usual tags suspended from the little metal ring, license, proof of vaccination, etc. The one shaped like a bone was etched with a name and Zeb's phone number.

"Hello, Scamp," Boone said gently.

CHAPTER SIX

Griffin and Fletcher looked small and scruffy and a little bereft, standing there in Tara's entryway in their shorts and sneakers and striped T-shirts. They both sported a faint milk mustache, and their chins were speckled with remnants of their supper—something with tomato sauce.

Her heart went out to them, and she thought how ironic it was, this tendency of hers to mother nearly every child she met, when she'd never given birth herself. Did the loving count, the fierce, ferocious loving? Or was she a potential case study for a team of dedicated psychologists exploring obsession?

Earlier when Boone's call came in, Erin and Elle had been getting ready for bed, finally willing to admit they were tuckered out from a long travel day. Now they stood nearby, sleepy but curious.

"Are we spending the night?" Griffin asked point-blank, looking up at Tara with wide-eyed concern. He groped for his brother's hand and grasped it tightly, though whether he was trying to reassure himself or Fletcher was anybody's guess.

Most likely, it was both.

"That's a possibility, I suppose," Tara answered quietly, resisting the urge to gather both children into her arms and hold them close for a moment, promise to keep them safe, swear an oath that everything would be all right, they'd see.

They'd visited earlier, with Opal, so the place and the people weren't entirely strange to them, but there was a world of difference between playing in a sunlit backyard and drinking lemonade on the porch and being dropped off at night, with little or no preparation. "Would that be a problem?"

Griffin looked down at his brother, then back at Tara. "It might be," he said, with an air of grave confidentiality.

"We don't have pajamas," Fletcher put in staunchly.

Griffin blushed. "We *have* pajamas," he clarified, raising his chin slightly. No doubt he was remembering the exchange with Elle that afternoon, concerning the double-wide trailer that was suddenly home. "It's just that we didn't bring them with us and—" The little boy paused, glanced at Fletcher again. Swallowed whatever else he'd meant to say.

"I'm sure we can come up with something you can borrow, if the need arises," Tara said, eager to put the children at ease. There was no way to know how late Boone would get back.

Griffin slanted a wary glance toward the twins. "We don't want anything a girl would wear," he specified firmly. He was clearly more amenable than his younger sibling, but the statement was a line in the sand, nonetheless. These boys had pride, like their father, and it was inborn, probably woven into their very DNA, like an extra helix.

Tara hid a grin. "I have some old T-shirts that might do," she said, ready to dismiss the subject of sleepwear. "I don't suppose you're hungry?"

They shook their heads.

"We had dinner," Griffin said.

"It's all over your face," Elle confirmed, though not unkindly.

Tara tossed the girl a look.

"Oops," Elle said.

"We could sit on the back porch for a while," Erin hastened to suggest, playing her usual role: the peacemaker. "It's warm out, and the stars are amazing. In New York we hardly ever see them because of light pollution."

Fletcher, somewhat to Tara's surprise, agreed to the plan with a circumspect little nod. "Okay," he said, and followed Erin and Elle through the house, toward the kitchen and the back door.

Tara felt another pang of love for her lively stepdaughters, wished for the millionth time that they were her own flesh and blood, so James would at least have to share them with her. Because of that moment's woolgathering, she didn't immediately notice that Griffin had stayed behind when the other kids went out, standing with his spine very straight.

She rested a hand on his shoulder, but lightly, much as she would have gathered up a stray chick, frightened and fragile. "Was there something more you wanted to say, Griffin?" she asked, knowing there was.

Griffin nodded earnestly and dropped his voice to a whisper. "Sometimes," he confided, "Fletcher wets the bed. It's because he's little, I guess. He did it last night, and Dad had to wash the sheets and sleep on the couch."

"Oh," Tara said thoughtfully, steering the child gently toward the kitchen, touched by his concern for his younger brother. "Well, you're perfectly right, of course. It's only happening because Fletcher's so young." *Because he's scared and disoriented, after being wrenched from one home and summarily plunked right down in another.* "It's not his fault."

Griffin looked vastly relieved. "Do you have a washing machine?" he wanted to know, hedging his bets. "And a dryer, too?"

Again, Tara suppressed a smile, though this time, it was a sad one. They'd reached the kitchen by then, and sweet Lucy, who had been standing at the back door, inadvertently left behind when the others went outside, turned to wander over and give Griffin's cheek a welcoming lap of her tongue.

"I certainly do," Tara replied, indicating the doorway leading into the nearby laundry room. "Right in there." Then, because she couldn't help herself, she bent over and placed a light kiss on the bristly top of the boy's head. His dark hair was buzz-cut, like his brother's, but it was so thick she couldn't see his scalp. "Don't worry about anything, okay? Whatever happens, we'll deal."

Griffin blinked, offered up a tentative smile in response to her words. "That's what Dad says," he told her. "That we can deal with stuff, I mean. Kind of figure things out as we go along."

Tara's oft-bruised heart softened even

further. She had her reservations about Boone Taylor, to put it mildly, but for good or ill, she was falling in love with his boys, just as she had fallen permanently, irrevocably in love with Erin and Elle.

It was her destiny, she guessed. To pinch-hit for missing mothers.

Be careful, she warned herself, too late like always.

"That's very wise," she said aloud.

Griffin nodded again. Now that he'd gotten the bed-wetting issue out of the way, he seemed to relax.

"Don't you want to go outside and look at the stars?" Tara asked presently, in order to break the small silence that followed.

"I'd rather stay here with you, if that's all right," Griffin answered. "You kind of remind me of my aunt Molly, and I miss her a whole bunch. So does Fletcher."

Tara's eyes burned, and she swallowed the lump that rose in her throat. "It's definitely all right if you stay with me," she managed to say.

Then she settled the boy in a chair at the kitchen table, washed her hands at the sink, took a plate from one of the glass-fronted cupboards and filled it with freshly baked snickerdoodles from her vintage ceramic cookie jar.

Using a moistened paper towel, she wiped off Griffin's supper-smudged face, a matter-of-fact gesture, very casual.

"Your house is really nice," Griffin commented after Tara stepped away and tossed the damp paper towel into the trash. He eyed the plate of cookies, resting at the center of the table, and shyly reached for one. "Everything is pretty."

"Thank you," Tara said, thinking of the decrepit double-wide trailer across the narrow outlet of the river and wondering what it was like on the inside. Opal had spent most of the day there, taking care of the boys, so the place must be reasonably clean, but that didn't mean it was comfortable, let alone cozy. It probably looked like what it was—bachelor's quarters, a man cave, a place to crash between long shifts of keeping Parable County safe for truth, justice and the American way.

An odd combination of irritation and pity rose up in Tara as she pictured Boone inside that run-down trailer, doing whatever he did when he was at home. Most likely, he lounged in a beat-up recliner patched with duct tape, consumed copious amounts of off-brand beer and watched marathons of *Pimp My Ride* and *Pawn Stars* on a TV the size of a picture window.

While all these thoughts were unfolding in Tara's mind—and she wasn't particularly proud to be thinking them, since they were undeniably bitchy—Lucy lingered in the kitchen instead of attempting to join the trio of chattering stargazers outside, standing next to Griffin's chair and resting her furry muzzle on his lap, her glowing brown eyes rolled up toward him, beatific as a saint's, as he petted her silken head.

"Dad said we could maybe get a dog," Griffin told Tara, his tone as wistful as his expression. "Sometime. When the dust settles."

"When the dust settles?" Tara echoed, confused.

Griffin flashed her a grin, dazzlingly

reminiscent of his mostly dour but sometimes-cocky father. In a few years, when Griffin Taylor was approaching manhood, that grin would become a lethal weapon. There should be some kind of advance-warning system in place, for the sake of unsuspecting girls everywhere.

"I guess he means when Fletch and me get used to living with him instead of with Aunt Molly and Uncle Bob," the future heartbreaker explained manfully. He seemed so grown-up that it was easy to forget he was only seven. "I don't mind it so much, because I know Dad's doing the best he can, but my little brother just wants everything to be like it was before." A look of sadness passed over Griffin's face then, bringing the lump back to Tara's throat and the sting back to her eyes. "Maybe Fletch thinks if he just pees the bed enough times, and acts like a brat, Dad will get fed up with raising kids and send us back to Missoula for good."

Once again, Tara yearned to take this brave child into her arms and comfort him somehow, but the connection between them seemed as delicate as a single strand of a spider's web, and she couldn't risk breaking it. So she sat very still in her chair, with her hands clasped together in her lap, where they were out of Griffin's sight because of the tabletop.

"Is that what you want, too?" she asked carefully, quietly. "For your dad to send you back to your aunt and uncle, I mean?"

Griffin pondered the question. "I miss Aunt Molly and Uncle Bob and our cousins," he finally replied, having weighed the matter in his sharp little mind. "But Dad—well, he's our *dad*—and I think we ought to be with him."

Tara didn't know how to answer, so it was a good thing the twins and little Fletcher chose that instant to come clattering back inside. Spotting the plate of cookies on the table, all three of them dive-bombed it.

"There are *bajillions* of stars out," Fletcher said excitedly, pointing his cookie-free hand toward the ceiling. Maybe he was a budding astronomer—

like his brother, he was smart for his age.

"At least that many," Tara agreed.

"I'd like to *sleep* outside sometime," the little boy continued, with his mouth partially full of snickerdoodle and crumbs on his chin. "That way, I could count stars *all night long.*"

Tara smiled at the image. "That sounds lovely."

"Except for the mosquitoes," Elle said, with a little shudder, scratching at a bite on her left forearm.

"And the bears," Erin added, eyes big with delicious dread.

"And you only know how to count to ten anyhow," Griffin reminded his brother.

The wall phone rang then, a sudden, shrill jangle that startled Tara. Elle, being closest, reached for the receiver and said hello.

"It's for you," she said, after listening for a few seconds, seeming mildly disappointed as she held out the phone to Tara, stretching the cord as far as it would reach. "The sheriff."

She must have hoped James would

call, which, of course, he hadn't, jerk that he was.

Tara took the receiver. "This is Tara," she said.

"Boone Taylor," was the gruff reply. "We're wrapping things up here—it's all pretty cut-and-dried—so I'll be stopping by your place to get the boys within an hour or so, if that's not too long."

"They'll be ready when you get here," she replied. There was so much more she wanted to say, wanted to ask, but she'd be prying if she did and she didn't have that right and she didn't have the words ready anyhow. "Are you—is everything—all right?"

"As 'all right' as things can be, under the circumstances," Boone answered flatly, but without sarcasm. Then, after a brief goodbye, he ended the call.

Elle took back the receiver and studied it quizzically before returning it to its hook on the wall unit. "Is this an actual antique?" she asked. "Or is it just vintage?"

Tara chuckled. Shook her head. "Not quite either one," she answered. In Dr. Lennox's New York penthouse, the phones were all wireless, of course, sans cords and completely portable. She turned back to the Taylor boys. "Your dad will be here to pick you up in a little while," she told them.

Fletcher didn't react to the announcement in any overt way, but Griffin was clearly glad they'd be going home instead of spending the night. No sleeping in borrowed T-shirts, no danger that his little brother would embarrass himself by wetting the bed.

"Come on," Erin said, producing her state-of-the-art cell phone from the pocket of her pajama bottoms and joggling it from side to side a couple times. "I'll show you how to play 'Angry Birds' while we wait."

"I *know* how to play 'Angry Birds,'" Griffin told her, still touchy, but Fletcher was already across the room, stretching out a hand for Erin's phone.

"Show *me,*" he cried eagerly.

Elle allowed Fletcher to take the phone, but her gaze was fixed on Griffin. "Are you still bent out of shape because I called your house a trailer this afternoon?" she asked, in good-natured challenge. "I didn't mean to hurt your feelings or anything like that."

Griffin glowered at her, but a reluctant twinkle sparked in his eyes.

Breezily, Elle pulled back a chair at the table, dropped down onto the seat, and started showing an already-enthralled Fletcher the rudiments of the popular video game.

"Dad's going to build a *real* house," Griffin told Erin, since both of them were on the sidelines, his tone marginally friendlier than his expression but still taut. "I saw the plans. He keeps them in a drawer in the cabinet under the TV."

"Awesome," Erin said sincerely, producing her own cell phone from the pocket of her pajama bottoms. "Think you can beat me at Mario?"

Griffin beamed, sun-parting-the-clouds style. "Yeah," he said.

"Bring it," Erin replied, as they joined Elle and Fletcher at the table.

Tara, feeling a little restless, brewed herself a cup of herbal tea and stood leaning against the kitchen counter while she watched the kids manipulate those smartphones with the skill of stealth pilots at the controls of a fighter jet.

Boone would be there soon, and her feelings about that were mixed. On the one hand, her nerves buzzed with low-grade anxiety.

On the other, she couldn't wait.

The little dog whimpered pitifully when the EMTs finally loaded the shell of Zeb Winchell onto a gurney, inside a body bag and zipped him in, ready to roll him outside to the ambulance for the short trip to the Sunrise-Sunset Funeral Home, which doubled as the county morgue when necessary.

"Want me to drop the mutt off at Martie Wren's place?" McQuillan asked, with an annoyed glance at Scamp. Martie ran Paws for Reflection, the local animal shelter, and she had a heart as big as the Montana sky. By now, she was probably in bed, deep in the sleep of the kind and the just.

Irritated anew, Boone shook his head, stooped to pick up the dog when it tried to scrabble after the departing gurney. The little critter felt light against his chest, trembling and squirming and making a mournful sound, low in its throat.

"No," he said. "I'll see that he's taken care of."

McQuillan remained unfazed, both by the dog's obvious sorrow and Zeb Winchell's lonely demise. He lifted one skinny shoulder in a shrug and then straightened, finally dropping the cell phone he was always fiddling with into the pocket of his uniform shirt.

Silently, Boone wished being an asshole was grounds for dismissal—he'd have fired the deputy on day one if it had been.

"Be sure the report is on my desk when I get to work tomorrow morning," he said, heading for the door with Scamp still wiggling under his arm.

McQuillan responded with an insolent salute and a smirk and followed Boone outside, where the neighbors were waiting, watching the ambulance pull slowly away, taillights red in the humid darkness of a summer night.

Boone paused to address the gathering, while McQuillan sauntered on through the gate, climbed into his squad car and drove off.

"Zeb's passed on," Boone told the neighbors, quite unnecessarily. "Probably a heart attack. We'll know more tomorrow."

People in bathrobes shook their heads in collective sadness, murmuring to each other—*it's a shame . . . you just never know . . . poor little dog, left all alone*—

Gradually, they dispersed, went back to their nearby houses, sorry for what had happened to Zeb and yet, in that perverse way common to all humans, guiltily glad that death had knocked at someone else's door instead of their own.

Reaching his cruiser, with its large gold sheriff's insignia painted on both doors, Boone stepped around to the passenger side and carefully set Scamp on the seat.

"Stay," he said very quietly, without a hope in hell that the dog would obey. Scamp was still jittery and fretful, but he was showing signs of exhaustion, too.

How long had the poor little critter sat there, beside Zeb's dead body, willing him to wake up? When had he eaten, or had water to drink?

The images saddened Boone so deeply that, if he hadn't been going back to Tara's place for his boys, and if Scamp hadn't been in the car, he might have suspended his personal moratorium on hard liquor and stopped by the Boot Scoot Tavern for a stiff drink.

As he drove away from the curb, Scamp stood up in the seat, paws scratching at the window glass, and whimpered desperately.

"There, now," Boone said. "Everything's going to be all right."

Was it? he wondered grimly.

Bob, his brother-in-law, his good friend, his sister's beloved husband, the father of three kids and as good as one to Boone's own two sons, was recovering from serious surgery, and in a lot of pain.

Griffin and Fletcher were like the proverbial fish out of water, far from the only home they really knew, living with a virtual stranger—him—in what amounted to a giant metal box, rusting at the corners, nearly swallowed up by overgrown grass.

And as for Boone himself? Well, he was in way over his head. Love those boys though he did, he knew jack-shit about raising children, especially when they were trying to cope with an upheaval in their lives. It would be a wonder if he didn't scar them for life, just by being his ordinary old lunkhead of a self.

Scamp stopped whimpering as they passed the city limits and settled down on the seat, muzzle on paws, with a desolate little sigh and one more shiver.

"Sometimes things just suck, and that's all there is to it," Boone told the dog.

Scamp sighed again, more deeply this time, as if in agreement.

A few minutes later, they pulled into Tara Kendall's driveway. The chickens were asleep in their rickety coop by then, so there was no wing-flapping uproar to announce their arrival.

Tara stepped out of the house as Boone was exiting the cruiser, putting on his hat, adjusting the brim out of nervousness, rather than vanity. Still in her sundress, she was hugging herself with both arms, though the night was warm.

She looked so pretty, even in a frazzled and tired state, that Boone felt something shift inside him. He stopped where he was, in the middle of her front walk, and took off his hat.

"I appreciate your looking after my boys the way you did," he said.

"No problem," she replied. Bathed in porch light, she bit her lower lip. "I was wondering if we could—" she went on tentatively, before stopping again "—if we could talk sometime."

Boone watched her, curious and a little unsettled. Whatever she wanted to talk about, it wasn't going to be good. Probably, she meant to rag on him about the sorry condition of his property or offer him some salient suggestions on the art of child-rearing. "Whenever you say," he told her, already dreading the conversation. It wasn't as if he didn't realize he lived in a junkyard, after all. He knew what needed to be done over at his place, especially now that his sons were living with him, but where was he supposed to get the time? He'd lost a couple deputies to budget cuts, and he often worked twelve-hour days.

Griffin and Fletcher slipped through the open doorway behind Tara just then, stood one on either side of her, like they were fixing to grab at her skirt and beg to stay right there on the chicken farm. *Don't make us go home with* him, Boone imagined they were thinking.

But Fletcher was peering past him, toward the cruiser. "What's that?" he said.

Boone glanced back over one shoulder and saw Scamp with his front feet up on the dashboard, looking through the window.

"It's a *dog!*" Griffin shouted, before his dad could say a word. He and Fletcher both bounded down the porch steps and blew past Boone like he was standing still. Which, of course, he was.

Tara smiled a little, as though she thought there might be some hope for him as a parent, after all, however vague and flimsy.

Boone simply nodded his thanks and

his farewell and turned to follow his kids back to the car.

How was he supposed to tell them that he'd only brought Scamp home to keep from waking up the nice lady who ran the animal shelter in town? That even if they *had* been ready to take in a pet, there was still a pretty good chance that Zeb's daughter would come back to Parable and claim her dad's dog?

Griffin and Fletcher had the passenger-side door open, admiring Scamp and fairly exuding eager goodwill.

Scamp, for his part, eyed them warily, hunkered down on the seat.

"Hop in," Boone told the kids, anxious to get going. "It's late."

Remarkably, they obeyed without sharing an opinion, shutting the car door, scrambling into their safety seats in the back behind the folding grill.

Boone made sure they were both fastened in, glanced back toward Tara's house, and saw that she was still standing on the porch, watching them.

She gave a little wave goodbye as Boone settled behind the wheel, and he waved back.

"Where did you get the dog?" Griffin piped up from the back.

"What's his name?" Fletcher said at the same time.

"His name is Scamp," Boone said, turning around the cruiser in the dirt driveway. "He ran into some hard luck recently, and he needed a place to spend the night."

A brief but weighty silence followed.

"You mean we don't get to keep him?" Griffin asked, his voice quavering and small. "He's not our dog?"

Boone's heart staggered inside his chest. Ready or not, Scamp was in their lives and hell or high water, he decided suddenly, the dog was going to stay. If he had to buy the critter from Zeb's daughter, he would.

"He's your dog," Boone said.

"Really?" Griffin hardly dared hope it was true, that much was clear from his tone.

"Could we change his name to Ranger?" Fletcher inquired brightly.

Boone had to chuckle then, and damned if it didn't feel good. "I think he answers to Scamp," he explained, keeping his gaze on the road except for a brief glance at the rearview mirror. "Might be confusing to him if you start calling him something else at this late date. And besides—he's pretty sad just now."

"Because his person died?" Griffin proffered.

Boone's throat tightened. "Yeah," he said with a sidelong look at the dog. Scamp lay curled up on the cruiser seat and every few seconds, a little shudder went through him, like he might be crying on the inside. "I reckon Scamp's probably scared, too."

Like you guys are, Boone thought glumly.

The yard was dark when they pulled in—again, Boone wished he'd left a light on inside the double-wide earlier, but he'd been in too much of a hurry at the time, too stressed out.

His place wasn't a *complete* write-off, though, he thought. Night softened the edges of the trailer with shadows and hid the rust, pines and a few oaks and maples whispered in the breeze, as if they were sharing tree secrets, and moonlight shimmered on the sliver of water between his place and Tara's. Her windows glowed in the near distance like a warm smile.

"What are we going to feed Scamp?" Griffin asked. The instant they'd stopped, he got out of the car, opened the door opposite Boone, and gathered the dog gently in both arms.

"Dog food, I guess," Boone replied. "We'll pick some up tomorrow, in town."

Huddled against Griffin's narrow chest, the dog stopped trembling, at least for the moment, and ventured to lick the boy's cheek once.

Fletcher was out of his car seat before Boone could help him, running around the cruiser to stand at Griffin's elbow. "Do you think he's hungry *now,* Dad?" Fletcher fretted.

Dad. Where had *that* come from? Griffin called him that, but Fletcher didn't.

Boone had to clear his throat before he could get a reply out. "I don't guess he is, Fletch," he said, heading for the double-wide, the kids and the dog flanking him. "Old Scamp's kind of in shock, I think."

He mounted the porch steps, unlocked the door, reached inside to switch on the kitchen light so Griffin and Fletcher wouldn't have to stumble around in the dark.

Griffin carefully set down the dog on the worn linoleum and regarded him with concern. "How old do you think he is?" he asked Boone.

Boone got a bowl out of the cupboard, filled it at the faucet and placed it on the floor for Scamp. "I'd guess he's pretty young," he answered. "Zeb didn't have him all that long, as I recall."

He remembered seeing the old man around Parable over the years, always in the company of a dog. Zeb had gotten most of them as pups, one at a time, raised them and walked them and, when they grew gray-muzzled and teetery, he made allowances, slowing his own pace, cooking up special food for them. When the end came, he buried them in the lot behind his house and marked each one of their graves with a stone carried up from the riverbank, on which he had stenciled their names.

"Zeb?" Griffin asked. "That's the man who died? The one Scamp used to live with?"

Scamp looked at the water bowl, hesitant, then tottered over and drank, lapping slowly at first, then with growing thirst.

"Yes," Boone answered. Zeb's warm, animal-loving heart had been hidden from the rest of the world behind a cranky temperament and stacks of tattered magazines, years of newspapers and junk mail, and other assorted garbage.

"He's drinking a lot," Fletcher said, sounding worried as he watched the dog lap up water. "What if he wets the bed?"

"Dogs don't wet the bed," Griffin said with a sort of benign contempt.

"I don't want him to get in trouble, that's all," Fletcher persisted.

Boone crouched, so he was face-to-face with this child he and Corrie had made together out of their love. "Nobody's going to get in trouble," he said quietly. "Not the dog, and not you."

Fletcher studied him earnestly. Swallowed. Then, suddenly, he flung his small arms around Boone's neck, nearly toppling them both.

Boone held the boy, closed his eyes for a moment, overwhelmed by emotion. *Look at them, Corrie. Just* look *at them. Our boys.*

Soon enough, Fletcher pulled away, wary again, though not quite as on guard as he'd been before.

They made a bed for Scamp in the little room the boys shared, folding an old blanket in quarters and setting it on the floor. Scamp ignored the bed and headed back to the kitchen, stood with his nose pressed against the back door.

"He wants to go home," Griffin observed.

"There's a lot of that going around," Boone replied.

They took the dog outside, waited while he did his business, gave chase when he lit out down the road, probably headed for town, caught him and brought him back to the double-wide.

Clearly, Boone and the boys weren't the only ones with some adjusting to do.

CHAPTER SEVEN

Getting two kids and a dog ready for a new day was like trying to herd weasels, as far as Boone could see. He'd barely gotten them all out the door when Scamp took off at warp speed, zigzagging through the knee-high grass like a bullet ricocheting from one boulder to another. Griffin raced after him, and Fletcher took advantage of the chaos to make a mad dash of his own, darting in the opposite direction, then making a one-eighty, bolting toward the county road.

Boone, freshly shaved and showered,

wearing his best jeans and his last clean shirt, went after the boy, swearing under his breath as he sprinted along the driveway. Fletcher, most likely Missoula-bound, might break a leg if he didn't slow down for the cattle guard.

He managed to scoop up the little boy at the last second. "Whoa," he said, whirling Fletcher around with a low, gruff laugh born of relief, not amusement. "What's the hurry?"

Fletcher, furious at being thwarted, set his back teeth and refused to answer.

Boone, still holding his son, pointed to the cattle guard spanning the base of the driveway. It was essentially a deep hole in the ground with heavy planks of wood set in sideways, having four to six inch gaps in between. "You want to look out for these things," he said mildly. "In Montana, they're everywhere."

"I caught Scamp!" Griffin called from up in the yard, and Boone grinned when he looked back to see his eldest holding the squirming dog in both arms and beaming with pride.

"Good job," Boone replied, setting Fletcher back on his feet and taking a firm but gentle grip on the kid's shoulder, lest he make another run for it—this time he'd have skirted the cattle guard, quick study that he was, though he'd still have been caught.

Fletcher didn't try to pull away, and Boone didn't ask where he'd thought he was going because he already knew.

Missoula. Back to Molly and Bob, Ted and Jessica and Cate. His family.

Weary sadness washed over Boone, but he shook it off immediately, as usual. It was a new day and there was work to be done.

Once the boys were buckled into their booster seats in the back of the squad car and Scamp had resigned his small dog-self, for the moment, anyway, to riding shotgun, Boone all but collapsed behind the steering wheel. He hadn't done a lick of work yet, and he was already starting to sweat.

He made a mental note to stop off at the dry cleaners in town first chance he got and pick up the batch of shirts he'd left there to be laundered nearly a week before. That way, if necessary, he could put on a clean one when he got to the office.

"It's miles and miles to Missoula, you dummy," Griffin informed his brother, lowering his voice in the vain hope that it wouldn't carry to the front seat and Boone's ears.

"I was going to take a bus," Fletcher responded matter-of-factly, causing Boone to bite back a low chuckle.

"You can't just get on a bus and go somewhere," Griffin said. "You'd have to buy a ticket first, and you don't have any money."

"I have thirty-five cents," Fletcher answered. "From my allowance."

Allowances, Boone reflected. Yet another thing to figure out. Should he just hand them a few bucks once a week, or give them chores to do in return for the money?

Griffin gave a small, disdainful hoot in answer to Fletcher's statement. "That isn't enough to do *anything,* butt-face," he told his brother.

"Cool it with the name-calling," Boone put in, without much hope that the order would stick. As a little kid, he'd called Molly by a dozen different names, the more annoying the better, and she'd returned the favor. Maybe it was just the way siblings interacted, a natural thing.

Still, it smacked of bullying, and that was something Boone wouldn't, *couldn't* tolerate, as a father, as a man *or* as sheriff. In fact, he worked closely with the local school board to nip that kind of orneriness in the bud whenever and wherever it happened to sprout.

He was still deliberating over the allowance thing as the squad car bumped and jolted over the cattle guard, and Boone signaled a left turn onto the county road, even though he knew there were no cars behind him. It was force of habit.

"Doesn't Scamp want to live with us?" Griffin inquired presently, just when Boone was getting used to the silence. "Is that why he tried to run away?"

Boone glanced over at the dog, now standing on his hind legs, with his front paws resting on the edge of the window and his snout pressed to the glass, making a smudge. He figured there was no point in trying to pretty things up; the truth was always best, even when it stung a little.

"Yep," Boone answered. "Scamp's lonesome and confused, and he doesn't understand why he can't stay at the old place, with Zeb."

"Same as Fletcher," Griffin observed.

"Shut up, Griff," Fletcher said.

"Same as Fletcher," Boone agreed, but kindly, as one corner of his mouth twitched upward in a reflexive grin. By then, they were passing Tara Kendall's driveway, which was a rutted, twisting dirt road, no fancier than the one leading to his place, for all her lofty opinions on the upkeep of private property.

There was even a cattle guard, a twin to his, right next to the mailbox. A valuable deterrent to stampeding chickens, he thought wryly. Except that they could fly, of course. But, then, you couldn't expect a city slicker to remember everything.

Boone had always enjoyed making fun of Tara's chosen vocation, if only in his own head, but today there wasn't much juice in it. Damned if he hadn't begun to *like* the woman—a little.

The boys exercised their right to remain silent the rest of the way into town, and even Scamp dropped his paws from the window's edge to curl up on the passenger seat, a disconsolate little lump of dog.

The Parable peace accord came undone when they pulled in at the community center, however. Fletcher dug in like a mule knee-deep in the thick mud Montanans call gumbo, folding his skinny arms tightly across his chest, ducking his head and repeating the word *no* over and over again, in a stubborn monotone.

Boone unbuckled the kid's seat belt and unloaded the board-stiff little dickens as gently as he could. In the unguarded meantime, Scamp jumped into the back and then shot through the open door, disappearing into the bushes with Griffin in hot pursuit.

"Let him go," Boone called to Griffin, trying not to sound exasperated. "I'll pick him up after we're done here."

Slowly, sorrowfully, Griffin ambled

back to the parking lot. The stooped set of the boy's shoulders just about bent Boone double.

That was when Shea, Slade's stepdaughter, appeared, striding out of the community center's main doorway and smiling warmly at Fletcher. Shea was a pretty eighteen-year-old, college-bound in the fall, and she definitely had a way with kids.

"Hey," she said to Fletcher, her dark hair gleaming in the sun, her nearly violet eyes twinkling with welcome and the promise of mischief. "Remember me?"

Fletcher, still about as flexible as a crowbar, stood beside Boone, nodding glumly. She'd been the boys' babysitter, on occasion, during their visits to Parable, and part of most social gatherings. "You're Shea," he murmured, not looking at her.

"And you're Fletcher," Shea said, casting a don't-worry-I'll-handle-it glance Boone's way. She put out a hand to the little boy. "I'm volunteering at the community center this summer," she explained when Fletcher reluctantly allowed her fingers to close around his.

"Thing is, if somebody runs away, that'll make me look bad, and I might even be out of a job."

Fletcher blinked up at her, concerned at the looming specter of teenage unemployment.

Silently, Boone blessed the girl.

Griffin joined the circle. "What about Scamp?" he fretted, looking toward the bushes that had swallowed the dog.

"He'll be fine," Boone said. "I promise."

Shea greeted Griffin with a dignity kids her age normally reserve for their friends. "How do you feel about swimming lessons?" she asked. "They start tomorrow."

Griffin lit up at the announcement, and even Fletcher looked a tad less likely to bolt, whether it made Shea look bad or not.

"Can we sign up, Dad?" Griffin asked.

"Sure," Boone said.

"Let's go inside," Shea told the boys with another glance at Boone. "There's some cool stuff planned for today, and we don't want to miss anything, do we?"

With that, she led away Griffin and

Fletcher, one on either side of her slender, blue-jeaned frame.

Neither of the boys looked back.

Even though he was already fifteen minutes late for work, Boone made good on his pledge to find the dog right away. Not surprisingly, he found Scamp sitting on Zeb Winchell's back porch, waiting patiently to be admitted to the only home he knew. Since there was a strange car parked in the driveway, Boone knocked, watching the dog out of the corner of one eye.

No sudden moves, he thought.

A slender woman appeared on the other side of the screen door, wearing work clothes and rubber gloves, with her hair tied back under a bandanna.

Boone recognized Zeb's daughter, Nancy, even though she'd been about five years ahead of him in school and left town to get married around the time she got her diploma.

She smiled, though a long acquaintance with grief showed in her eyes. Rumor had it that she'd hitched herself to a series of losers before giving up on love. "Hello, Boone," she said. She noticed the dog then, and looked surprised. "Dad's?" she asked, making no move to unlatch the door.

Boone nodded. "Name's Scamp," he said.

"Poor little thing," Nancy replied. "I suppose I'd better take him over to Paws and ask Martie to find him a good home."

"My boys and I would like to keep him," Boone ventured. That was surely the understatement of the week. "If you wouldn't mind?"

"The last thing I need is a dog," Nancy answered, though there was no meanness in her tone or her expression. She was simply stating a fact. "You're welcome to him."

"Thanks," Boone said.

"I'd ask you in," Nancy went on, "but the place is a wreck. I'm trying to get this dump cleaned up so I can sell it. The money would come in real handy."

"That's all right," Boone replied, scooping up the dog in one arm, much as he'd done with Fletcher when he was making straight for the cattle guard at home.

"The funeral service is Saturday," Nancy said, looking as though she expected him to make polite excuses. "Over at Sunrise-Sunset. Two o'clock."

"I'll be there," Boone said, only then remembering to take off his hat. His manners, he reflected grimly, seemed to be in the same sorry state as his yard.

The dog had gone still in the curve of his arm, evidently resigned to capture.

Nancy tried to smile, and failed. "Thanks," she said.

"Your dad was a good man," Boone told her quietly, with a slight nod of his head.

Something lightened in Nancy's time-weary face. She looked older than she was, and tired; life had ground her down and taken the shine off the few bright hopes she'd probably had in the first place. "He was—different," she allowed, with another wobbly attempt at a smile.

Boone nodded again. "No law against being different," he said in parting. Then he turned around, Scamp drooling on the front of his shirt, and returned to the squad car.

He heard the hinges squeak on Zeb's screen door, and turned his head to see Nancy standing on the porch. Her expression was tentative, fretful.

"Did he suffer?" she asked, in a shaky voice. "Dad, I mean?"

Boone shook his head. "I don't think so. According to Doc Halpern, it probably happened fast."

Nancy's narrow shoulders sagged with bleak relief. "Good," she said, opening the door to go back inside and resume cleaning up her father's house.

Boone was pulling away from the curb, Scamp riding shotgun again, when he saw Opal drive up in front of the Winchell house in the big station wagon, at the head of a caravan of other cars. There must have been a dozen church ladies in those vans and subcompacts and pickup trucks, and it was immediately apparent that they were ready for action, dressed in old clothes, armed with cleaning buckets and scrub brushes, brooms and buckets and mops and all kinds of other supplies, including a couple of picnic baskets and three jugs of sun-tea.

Onward, Christian soldiers, Boone thought.

He smiled, raising a hand in greeting as he passed. Classic Parable, he thought. When there was a need, large or small, people pushed up their sleeves and waded in to help out.

It was a welcome indication that the world might not be going to hell in a handbasket, after all.

"We need overalls if we're going to be dealing with chickens," Elle announced at breakfast without preamble.

Tara and Erin paused between bites of scrambled eggs to absorb the implications of the statement. Tara, who hadn't slept well because she kept thinking about the way Boone Taylor looked in a pair of jeans, wasn't quite with the program yet. She'd done her chores in a sort of stupor.

"You're *afraid* of the chickens," Erin challenged her sister at some length, adjusting her glasses with a practiced jab of one index finger. "You told me so, Elle Lennox, just last night, before we went to sleep."

Tara hid a smile, and suddenly she was time-traveling. When she'd first taken possession of the farm—it had been sadly run-down back then and she'd looked at it numerous times before finally making an offer—she'd bravely ordered chickens from the feed store in town, and they'd arrived in stacks of cardboard boxes with airholes in the sides, chirping masses of yellow fluff. Faced with the reality of it all, she'd been terrified of hurting the little birds somehow, maybe stepping on them. Making a mistake.

It was, she supposed, even possible that the tiny birds might turn on her, harmless and cute as they seemed, and peck her to death like the hapless victim in some horror movie. Starting at ankle-level.

Fortunately, one of the local women, an earth-mother type named Darlene Jennings, had taken note of Tara's fear-paled face while a couple teenage boys carried the boxes into the feed store parking lot, stacking them beside her tiny sports car and exchanging doubtful, amused glances.

Darlene, who, as Tara later learned, raised gloriously colorful flowers—peonies and zinnias, daisies and roses, and clouds of tulips and daffodils in the early spring—to sell at a roadside stand, took pity on the newcomer.

"You boys load those chicks in the back of my truck," she'd commanded good-naturedly, through her rolled-down window, before shoving open the door and stepping out onto the gravel.

Tara had looked at her gratefully, walked over to introduce herself.

Darlene, dead just six months later of a pulmonary embolism, had not only delivered the chicks to Tara's place, she'd stayed to help her unload them in the ramshackle coop. They'd set out shallow pans of water—"You've got to keep an eye on these little fellas, or they'll drown themselves sure as taxes are due in April," Darlene had warned—and then she'd shown Tara how much feed to give them, and when. "Keep them inside the coop till they're bigger," the older woman had added. "Otherwise, they'll be bait for hawks and coyotes, among other things."

Tara had taken in every word, nodding constantly.

After Darlene's departure for home, Tara had sat down on the top porch step, cupped her chin in her hands and cried, completely overwhelmed by the enormity of what she'd gotten herself into.

Leaving Manhattan, where she'd lived since college, had seemed like such a good idea, in theory, after a shattering divorce. She'd been emotionally bloodied and battered and in desperate need of a change after the breakup—the more drastic, the better. By then, her parents, to whom she'd never been particularly close in the first place, were divorced from each other, remarried and living on separate continents.

Being an only child, Tara found herself with no one to turn to—most of her friends had drifted away since she'd tied the knot with James. She was always too busy with her husband, the demanding doctor, or with Elle and Erin, or her job, to make time for bistro lunches, heartfelt conversations and girls' nights out.

Sitting there on the porch step, though, with the dust whirling behind Darlene's departing truck just beginning to settle, she'd wondered what on earth had possessed her to buy a farm outside a Podunk town like Parable.

What did she, a city girl through and through, know about *chickens,* for pity's sake? Never mind cows and horses. She knew all about makeup and wine, museums and books, and the posh parties James loved to attend. She knew that primary colors looked good on her and grasped the major political issues of the day.

But she hadn't a *clue* about country living in general, or chickens in particular, and now she had a coop full of tiny golden lint balls, all depending on her for protection and food and a hundred other needs she hadn't thought of yet.

Blessedly, Darlene had returned less than an hour after she'd left, bringing special warming lamps to set up in the coop, along with extension cords and lots of advice about fire prevention. Though some of the chicks didn't make it through the next few weeks—this, according to Darlene and the man at the feed store and somebody she chatted with at the post office, was inevitable—the majority of the birds thrived, turning into honest-to-God chickens. The yellow down had given way to gleaming feathers, mostly russet in color and iridescent in the daylight, and Darlene, who stopped by often in those early days, had eventually hauled away all but one of the roosters, crated and crowing in protest, in the back of her truck.

Tara had never asked what became of those roosters, though of course she'd had her suspicions, especially when she came down with a summer cold that August and Darlene showed up with a pot of chicken soup topped by dumplings.

"Hello?" Elle chimed, waving a hand in front of Tara's face and bringing her back from those not-so-thrilling days of yesteryear with a mild jolt.

"Overalls," Tara said, to show she'd followed the ongoing conversation, which, of course, she hadn't.

"Overalls are stupid," Erin remarked,

frowning across the table at Elle. "Why can't we just wear jeans, like regular people?"

Elle looked world-weary for a moment—a cute trick, for a twelve-year-old. "This is the *country,*" she said, frowning back. "We'll look weird in our jeans—they have rhinestones and embroidery on them, remember?"

"You think we wouldn't look weird in *overalls?*" Erin countered.

"We'll go shopping," Tara interjected, glad the twins were even interested in helping out with the chickens. Glad they were *there,* in her kitchen, on a sunny summer morning, eating scrambled eggs and toast. "Plain jeans, overalls, whatever strikes your fancy."

"I wouldn't be caught dead in overalls," Erin decreed, her mind made up.

Tara wore them all the time, but reminding her stepdaughter of that would serve no purpose.

"Fine," Elle snapped back. *"Whatever."*

Lucy, waiting patiently nearby, looked from one woman-child to the other, hopeful and trusting that the formerly placid discussion would not give way to mayhem.

Tara finished her orange juice, then toasted Elle and Erin with her empty glass. “I’m taking Lucy for a short walk after I clear the table,” she said. “Be ready to go into town by the time we get back, please.”

With that, Elle and Erin left the table, bickering and giggling as they raced, elbowing each other up the back stairs to get dressed for the day.

Humming contentedly, Tara rinsed off the breakfast dishes, stacked them in the machine and fetched Lucy’s leash from its hook just inside the laundry room door.

Swishy-tailed with delight, Lucy was on her feet, eager for her walk.

Their normal route took Tara and Lucy down the long driveway, amid roaming, clucking chickens, across the cattle guard, which the dog had learned to navigate safely long before. For the hundredth time, Tara thought of filling in the pit, using dirt and river rocks, but the prospect was daunting, especially in the summer heat, so she again tabled the idea.

It was approximately a quarter mile from her mailbox to Boone's, and as she strolled, Lucy trotting happily at her side, she told herself she wouldn't so much as glance toward the overgrown yard and the gloomy-looking double-wide. If she looked, she knew, she'd just get her back up again, and what good would that do?

She concentrated on the gloriously blue sprawling sky overhead, the glistening green and Christmassy scent of the pine trees along either side of the winding road. She listened to the song of the river off in the near distance, and smiled in contented gratitude because Elle and Erin were staying with her, because she had her health and so did the twins, because she had good friends and wide-open spaces.

She passed Boone's place without so much as turning her head in that direction, walked, with Lucy, as far as the old covered bridge, with its weathered boards and long drop to another shallow, rocky tributary of Big Sky River, paused for a few moments to enjoy the sparkle of sunlight on clean, flowing water.

For all the challenges, for all the early misgivings, Tara knew she'd made the right decision, moving to Montana and starting a new life. At some point, there had been an almost imperceptible shift in the place where her mind and spirit met, and Parable had become her home.

CHAPTER EIGHT

Boone had picked up his clean shirts over at the cleaner's, and when he and Scamp got to the office, he ducked into the men's restroom to change into one of them. He'd barely begun scrolling through his email—the day deputies were already out patrolling the county and the receptionist/dispatcher was supposedly sick at home—when a skinny girl no older than twelve or thirteen burst in, breathless and pale.

Before Boone could place her, she blurted out, "Come quick! My brother just now fell off the water tower and his eyes are closed and he's not moving!"

Boone's blood ran cold as the image crystalized in his mind. He bolted toward the now-trembling child, speaking rapidly into the microphone of the small radio attached to his shoulder, summoning an ambulance and any available deputy, on or off duty, steering the girl out into the corridor by the nape of her neck.

"Stay here," he ordered gruffly, when Scamp tried to follow.

The dog obeyed, dropping to his belly and resting his muzzle on outstretched forelegs; evidently, this was a command he knew.

Once Boone and the girl were both inside the squad car, he flipped on the lights and siren and laid plenty of rubber pulling away from the curb.

Folks gawked from the sidewalks and other cars pulled to the side of the road as the cruiser streaked past.

"What's your name?" Boone snapped, instantly regretting the sharpness of his tone. The ambulance fell in behind him, siren shrieking, and various private vehicles trailed after, ordinary men who wanted to do whatever they could to help.

Parable was that kind of town.

The little girl, clad in a faded sundress and barefoot, shivered inside the passenger-side seat belt, her stick-thin arms wrapped around her upper body. She was sniffling now, and her freckles stood out against the waxen pallor of her cheeks. “Angie McCullough,” she said. “Maybe I should have gone to get Mama, but she’s way down at the Bide-A-Night Motel, cleaning rooms.” She paused, swallowed visibly. “My brother—Dawson—is he going to get in trouble?”

Boone shook his head. “You did the right thing, coming to me,” he said evenly, taking care to keep his voice gentle as he made a hard left onto the road leading to the water tower. He didn’t slow down for the ruts, deepened by decades of hard rains and wicked winters, and wondered briefly if the shocks on his squad car would hold up to the strain. “Nobody’s getting in trouble,” he reiterated. At the moment, this was all the reassurance he could offer.

The water tower loomed up ahead in the middle of a large, meadowlike clearing, a part of the town and yet separate from it, too, hidden among towering pine trees that had probably been mere seedlings when it was built.

A group of kids clustered in a circle, looking down. One of them, a gawky boy, all knees and elbows, turned to vomit into the tall grass.

“Stay in the car,” Boone told Angie McCullough, who nodded, her ears poking between strands of long, stringy brown hair. He shut off the siren, put the cruiser in Park and leaped out, leaving the rig running as he sprinted toward the kids.

They backed away as he approached, revealing a still form sprawled on the ground, arms and legs akimbo, eyes closed. The boy didn’t stir, either when Boone spoke his name or when he crouched beside him, feeling at the hollow of his throat for a pulse. He found one, but it was faint and dangerously irregular.

The EMTs broke through the small crowd just then, carrying their gear, kneeling on either side of Dawson McCullough's unmoving body. Boone moved out of their way, herded the horrified teenagers back a few steps. His gaze sliced from one face to another.

He knew every kid in town, by sight if not by name, and he'd had to chase this crew away from the water tower more than once in the past.

"Exactly what happened here?" he prompted, when nobody spoke.

"He fell," offered one of the girls, in a tremulous voice. Boone focused on her.

"It's not like he jumped or anything," added the boy who'd lost his breakfast a few moments before.

Boone drew in a deep, slow breath, to steady himself, and rested his hands on his hips. A glance toward the cruiser showed Angie's face floating behind the windshield, an oval moon, white as milk.

"Is Dawson—is he—dead?" someone else asked.

"No," Boone said, aware that the EMTs were working fast, one talking to the unconscious boy as he rigged him up to an IV line, the other racing back to the ambulance for more equipment.

"Not yet, anyway," he added glumly, sweeping off his hat to run the splayed fingers of his right hand through his hair in frustration. "What part of *stay away from this place* did you people not understand?" he asked, addressing the first girl, because she seemed the most composed.

The kids, cocky during previous encounters, exchanged meek glances.

The girl answered. "Dawson was being stupid, that's all," she said, a sly note creeping into her voice. "Nobody dared him to climb up there or anything like that."

Boone knew a lie when he heard one, but he didn't call her on it.

This wasn't the time or the place, he told himself. But for a moment, he didn't dare speak or move, because he was red-zone pissed. A human being, one of their friends, was badly hurt, maybe already dying, and the whole sorry situation could have been avoided if they'd only listened.

Did you *listen?* challenged a voice in the back of his mind. *You and Hutch and Slade?*

He became aware of the pickups and cars that had followed him and the ambulance to the scene. Men got out of them, stood at a distance, with their arms folded and their hats low over their eyes, watching, waiting.

That was when Deputy McQuillan roared up in his county car, stopped with a lurch and bounded out. A few more pieces fell into place in Boone's mind when Patsy McCullough, mother of Angie and the still-unresponsive Dawson, leaped from the passenger seat and shot past the deputy.

She was a thin, bedraggled woman, no older than Boone himself—he'd gone to high school with her—and, like Nancy Winchell, she looked hard-done-by and heart-bruised as she ran toward them. Her clothes, her face, her hair—all were colorless, as though she'd been slowly fading into invisibility from the day she was born.

The EMTs put a neck brace on the boy, and one of them called to the onlookers to bring the board and a gurney.

Boone stepped in front of Patsy, just

when she would have flung herself on her son, screaming his name over and over, and took her firmly by the shoulders.

"Let the paramedics do their job, Patsy," Boone told her quietly.

"I told him to stay away from this place," Patsy sobbed, every word hitching in her throat, raw and hoarse, painful to hear. "I told him—" Then she paused, watching in bleak disbelief as the EMTs carefully eased Dawson onto the board that would, they hoped, keep his spine stable, and strapped him in place.

With help from several of the other men, they hoisted the board onto the gurney, secured it. McQuillan, meanwhile, gathered the kids into a scared, sullen bunch and started grilling them.

Boone was pretty sure no crime had been committed, but he didn't interrupt the process. He was still holding Patsy upright, though he let her go when she turned, every nerve gravitating toward her injured son as he was carried past. By then Angie had bolted from the squad car and, once Dawson was loaded into the back of the ambulance, she and Patsy both scrambled in behind him.

"Charlie told me to tell you that they're calling for a helicopter," a familiar voice said, from just behind Boone's left elbow. "They're going to airlift the kid to Missoula, or maybe Helena—whichever they can get to faster."

Boone turned his head, saw Hutch Carmody standing there, and felt a twinge of relief at the sight of his closest friend. He hadn't noticed him before.

"It's bad then," Boone muttered rhetorically. He hadn't had a chance to ask about the boy's condition, but part of him, he knew now, had been hoping for a miracle.

Hutch's gaze moved from the departing ambulance to the water tower. "It's bad," he confirmed, frowning at the structure standing tall against an innocent blue sky. "That thing should have been torn down years ago," he finished. Some of the other men, standing nearby now that they'd done what they could to help the EMTs, nodded in solemn agreement.

"Yeah," Boone said, the word riding a raspy sigh. "Tell it to the town council and the mayor. Every time the subject comes up, some die-hard history buff backs them down."

"Maybe they'll listen now," said Art Farrington, a middle-aged rancher with a face as weather-beaten as the water tower itself. He adjusted his hat, a move that conveyed his agitation.

"There's been enough talk," Hutch replied grimly. "It's time to *do* something."

Art and the others did some more nodding.

The ambulance screeched away, headed toward the town's single airstrip, which was used mostly by the Hollywood types who came and went in private jets.

Hutch was rolling up his shirtsleeves as he strode toward his rig, parked with the others at the edge of the clearing. "I've got a winch on my truck," he called over one shoulder without bothering to look back. "Who's with me?"

To a man, the other locals trooped after him, rolling up their own sleeves as they went.

A protest rose in Boone's throat—he knew what they meant to do, of course—but he gulped it back. The water tower was town property and, since there was no municipal police force in Parable, it was his job to step in.

Never, not once, had he looked the other way when somebody took the law into their own hands, not when he was a deputy and certainly not since he'd been elected sheriff, but the inevitable had finally happened. A kid had been critically injured, taking a fall from the damned thing. Dawson McCullough might be breathing his last at that very moment, and for what?

"Get these kids out of here," Boone told Treat McQuillan. "Take them home and tell their parents what happened, and that I'll be stopping in for a word later on."

For once, McQuillan didn't argue or drag his feet. "You heard the sheriff," he said, addressing the teenagers, who looked even more badly shaken than before. “Let’s go.”

The kids straggled over to the deputy’s car and squeezed themselves in, heads down and evidently at a loss for the back talk that normally came so easily to them.

Hutch backed his rig to within fifty yards of the tower and, at the flip of a switch on his dashboard, steel cable rolled off the cog beneath the bed of his truck. Moving purposefully, without one glance at Boone and no visible hesitation, he got out of the rig again, picked up the cable and strung it to the base of the tower. There he fastened it around one of the four unsteady poles that supported the structure and fastened a hook to lock it in place.

Two other men did the same with cables unspooled from their own trucks. Normally, the winches would have been used to pull a rig out of a ditch or haul a cow from a mud hole. Today, they were being used for a very different purpose.

Once again, Boone considered putting a stop to the proceedings, but he couldn't make himself do it. He'd climbed that tower many times as a youth, and so had Hutch and Slade and practically everybody they knew—girls included. In a few years, his own boys would probably think it was smart to shinny up that rickety ladder, just as he had back in the day, on a dare or to impress some girl.

He closed his eyes for a moment, but the image of young Dawson McCullough might as well have been branded on the insides of his lids, it was so vivid. In his mind, the deathly still face became Griffin's, and then Fletcher's.

Bile scalded the back of Boone's throat.

"You might want to move to safer ground, Sheriff," Hutch suggested mildly, as he walked past Boone on the way back to his truck.

Boone hesitated for another moment, then shook his head and walked to his squad car, slipping behind the wheel but keeping one foot on the ground as he watched, as though he might spring out again, at the last moment, and put a stop to it all.

But he didn't.

There were three separate winch lines attached to the legs of the tower now, and a loud, grinding sound filled the muggy air as the cables grew taut. The tower swayed, timbers creaking, swayed again. The winches roared as their operators ratcheted up the power. The tower swung wildly from side to side, the word *Parable* painted in fading letters across the face of the massive, rust-trimmed tank, and then it toppled, the whole works, striking the ground hard enough to cause a noticeable tremor.

At last, the monstrosity lay on its side in the grass, splintered poles and boards scattered around it like giant toothpicks. Dust roiled for long moments after the collapse, and Hutch shut off his truck, burrowed through the wreckage to unfasten the hook so his winch-line could be wound back into place. As before, the others followed his lead.

Finally, Hutch approached the squad car, dust covered and grinning wanly at Boone, though his whole countenance was sad as he gazed briefly in the direction of the airstrip outside of town, where a helicopter would be landing soon—if they were lucky. Both Missoula and Helena were miles away, and it wasn't as if there were a lot of choppers waiting to lift off. Furthermore, nobody knew if the boy was going to make it or not and, even if he managed to survive, there was no way things would ever be the same for young Dawson, or any of the McCulloughs.

"I'll send a crew over to clear away the debris," Hutch said presently, meeting Boone's eyes again and holding his gaze. "If the mayor wants somebody's head for this, offer him mine."

With that, Hutch turned to walk away.

"Wait a damn minute," Boone nearly barked, getting out of his car and walking fast to catch up with Hutch, who barely slowed his stride. "You and Kendra have a baby on the way, damn it. You can't take the blame for this, Hutch—not all of it, anyhow—I won't let you."

Hutch sighed. He waved to the last of his partners-in-crime as they drove away, then rested that same hand on

Boone's shoulder. "Whatever happens," he answered, "we know one thing for sure. The McCullough kid was the first kid to fall from that water tower, and by God, he'll be the *last* one, too."

Boone surveyed the remains of a town landmark, nodded glumly. It looked like something out of a disaster movie, that pile of boards and metal and grime, and some folks around Parable weren't going to be happy about what had happened, but what was done was done.

And he was glad.

"I guess I'd better go break the news to the appropriate authorities," Boone said finally, dreading the prospect. Because he was an elected county official, he didn't have to answer to the town, but that didn't mean he wouldn't catch three kinds of hell from old Hannibal Hale, Parable's crusty mayor.

Hale's great-great-grandfather had been one of the first settlers in that part of Montana, and he and some other businessmen had overseen the construction of the water tower, a ploy to bring the railroad through Parable, thus putting the place on the map. The bold move had worked, too, though the tracks, lost in grass and the rubble of time, hadn't borne the weight of a train in fifty years.

Hutch nodded again, as though he'd read Boone's thoughts, lifted his hand from his shoulder, and continued toward his waiting truck. His cell phone played a few bars of a country love song as he moved, and Boone saw him stop dead in his tracks as he listened to whatever the caller was saying.

"I'll be right there," Boone heard Hutch say. "Hold on."

"The baby?" Boone asked.

"On its way," Hutch replied, looking both panicked and pleased. An instant later, he was in his truck, starting the engine, backing up to turn around the rig, and speeding away.

Boone silently wished Hutch and Kendra the best possible luck, climbed into his squad car and headed for the mayor's house on River Bend Road. Hannibal was a caustic old SOB, but he wasn't heartless. He'd be as sorry about Dawson McCullough's accident as anybody else, though of course the town's potential liability would come quickly to mind.

Once he'd spoken with the mayor, Boone meant to return to the office and dig in for the duration. Folks would be calling and showing up in person, most of them asking about Patsy's boy, but there were bound to be a few bent on reading him the riot act over the destruction of the water tower.

He glanced in his rearview mirror, taking in what remained of the monument one more time before turning his full attention to the road, and the tasks, ahead.

"Good riddance," he said in parting.

A sleek silver jet raced along the short runway just outside of Parable and lifted off, flashing against the blue sky. Knowing the plane belonged to Casey Elder, and having spotted the ambulance parked near the one and only hangar, Tara had pulled over her SUV to the side of the highway and stopped.

Elle was in the front seat this time, having won the coin toss before they left the mall over in Three Trees, while Erin rode in the back.

"That looks just like Dad's jet," Erin remarked.

Tara frowned, but, alarmed as she was by the sight of the ambulance driving slowly toward the highway, she didn't pursue the matter.

"He's only part owner," Elle said matter-of-factly. She glanced over at Tara, already wearing the lavender overalls she'd chosen when they'd gone shopping for chicken-tending clothes. "Why are we stopped?"

"Something's wrong," Tara said distractedly. Private planes came and went, but Casey, a famous singer and the new owner of the mansion Kendra had once owned, was a friend, and Tara knew she'd just wrapped up a long stretch on the road. Upon her return, she'd invited Tara, Kendra and Joslyn to lunch at her place, remarking wearily that it would take a bomb to blast her away from Parable in general and her children in particular.

The ambulance reached the road and

Charlie, sitting on the passenger side, waved at Tara as they passed.

Still parked, she grabbed her purse, rummaged for her cell phone, and speed-dialed Casey's landline.

It was a relief when Casey answered with a low-energy "Hello, Tara." If one of Casey's children had been injured or ill, in need of emergency medical care, she'd have been onboard that jet with them.

"I just saw your jet taking off," Tara began, feeling awkward now. "The ambulance was there—"

"A teenage boy fell from the water tower today," Casey explained. "They were going to send for a helicopter, but my jet was right there on the runway, and the situation was urgent, so I called my pilot and asked him to make the flight."

Tara's stomach did a slow backward roll, then lurched forward again. "Oh, God," she whispered. "Who— How badly was the boy hurt?"

"He's critical," Casey said. "I didn't catch his name."

Tara thanked her friend and hung up.

She was shaking as she put the SUV back in gear and pulled carefully onto the highway.

"What's going on?" Elle asked, her voice small, her eyes big.

"There's been an accident," Tara answered, her tone wooden.

"Did something happen to Dad?" Erin whispered, from the backseat.

"No, honey," Tara replied quickly, trying to smile but not quite succeeding. "I'm sure your dad is fine. Once we're home, I'll find out the details and let you know, okay?"

"Okay," the twins chorused, still worried.

At home, the chickens greeted Tara and the girls with hungry squawks and flapping wings. The distraction was welcome, at least from Tara's viewpoint. For a few brief, shining moments, she didn't think about the terrible accident Casey had mentioned on the phone.

Elle, already clad in overalls, wanted to get right down to business and start feeding chickens, gathering eggs and mucking out the chicken coop with a pitchfork. Erin, shopping bags in hand, hurried inside the house to change into the very ordinary, no-name jeans she'd chosen on the shopping expedition.

Lucy, shut up in the house while they were away from home, bounded down the steps and rushed Tara, barking for joy. The way that dog acted, a person would have thought they'd been apart for days instead of mere hours.

As always, Lucy's enthusiastic presence and unquestioning adoration lifted Tara's spirits. She smiled and bent to ruffle those golden silky ears in greeting. "Hello, girl," she said fondly. "It's good to see you again, too."

Tara spent the next half hour showing Elle and Erin how to gather eggs—even though she'd done that first thing that same morning, there were more now, some speckled and some brown, and a few that were *almost* white.

"They don't look like the ones our housekeeper buys," Erin remarked seriously.

Elle, meanwhile, looked around at the floor of the temporarily vacant coop, nose twitching. Clearly, her interest in shoveling manure was already waning.

"What are we supposed to *do* with all this poop?" she asked Tara. She looked a sight, standing there in her pastel overalls, face solemn with second thoughts.

Tara grinned at her stepdaughter. "I load it into a wheelbarrow and haul it around back—*way* back—behind the tractor shed. This fall, and again in the spring, I'll till it under to season. The flower beds and the vegetable garden love the stuff." She paused for dramatic effect, enjoying Elle's obvious consternation. "All of which, as it happens, are in constant need of weeding and watering and lots of loving encouragement."

The flower beds, burgeoning with colorful zinnias, gerbera daisies, fat roses dopey on sunshine and numerous other horticultural delights, would have been impossible to miss, even in the excitement of arrival and the process of settling in. It was obvious, though, that Elle hadn't spotted the vegetable garden, a fenced area behind the rickety old barn Tara had been meaning to tear down since she'd moved onto the farm. She probably spent more of her time there than anywhere else on her property, happy to kneel in good Montana dirt and tend the rows of lettuce and beans, corn and various herbs.

"Where did you think those lovely sliced tomatoes we had at supper last night, drizzled with olive oil and buffalo cheese, came from?"

"The supermarket?" Elle asked tentatively.

Erin laughed and shook her head and went in search of the wheelbarrow, Lucy swinging her plumed tail as she followed.

"Gardening is hard work, isn't it?" Elle asked Tara. She hadn't moved an inch, and she was still holding the none-too-clean egg she'd taken from one of the rows of straw-filled nests lining the walls of the coop.

"Yes," Tara replied frankly, "but it's also good for the soul. You'll see."

With that, she patted her stepdaughter's shoulder reassuringly, smiled again and went off to change into work clothes of her own—jeans, a T-shirt and the pair of ugly, hopelessly filthy boots she kept on the back porch.

Joslyn called just as she was heading back outside.

Tara grabbed her cell phone from the kitchen counter, where she'd left it on the way in, and greeted her friend with a subdued "Hello," remembering that there had been an accident earlier that day—no doubt Joslyn was calling to tell her about that.

"Did you hear?" Joslyn asked immediately.

"About what happened at the water tower, you mean?" Tara said, as she descended the back steps and started around the side of the large farmhouse to rejoin the twins at the chicken coop.

"That, too," Joslyn said.

"'Too'?" Tara echoed. Good heavens, what *else* could have happened in or around Parable so quickly?

"Let's talk about the happy news first," Joslyn responded.

Tara's heart lifted a little, and she smiled to see Elle up ahead, diligently shoveling chicken manure into the waiting wheelbarrow while Erin scattered feed on the ground for the hens and rooster to peck at. "Happy news?" she repeated, confused. "What—?"

"Kendra's in labor," Joslyn said. "She's at Parable General Hospital even as we speak—Slade went over to lend Hutch some moral support, and he just called to say everything's going well. Hutch was suiting up to go into the delivery room with her as of five minutes ago."

Tara's eyes misted over; she knew how excited Hutch and Kendra were over the coming of this child. They both adored their adopted daughter, Madison, regarding her as their own, but they'd traveled a long and broken road to find each other again, after bitter years apart. The new baby, conceived in the passion of renewed love, would be born—and raised—within the vast reaches of their joined hearts.

"That's *wonderful,*" she whispered, feeling, and acknowledging, the tiniest twinge of jealousy. What could be better, she wondered sadly, than to love and be loved by a good man, as Kendra loved and was loved by Hutch, and to produce a child by that union?

Once, she'd fully expected to live out

her life as a wife and a mother and possibly even a grandmother someday. Instead, she had married Mr. Wrong and, in the end, lost everything. She slowed her pace and instinctively gazed at her stepdaughters.

Straighten up, she told herself sternly. *This isn't about you.*

"So," Joslyn went on, "once the baby actually gets here, Slade will call me with the news and I'll pass it on to you."

"I'll be waiting to hear," Tara said softly. She'd go shopping again, as soon as she knew whether the new arrival was a boy or a girl, and buy tons of baby presents.

Joslyn sighed. "The other thing," she began, before her voice fell away.

Between her husband Slade's tenure as former sheriff and the fact that Opal Dennison kept house for them, Joslyn usually knew about everything that went on in Parable County.

"Casey said a teenage boy fell from the water tower?" Tara prompted, after gulping hard and stopping before she reached the twins. "She didn't know who he was, though."

"Dawson McCullough," Joslyn replied sadly. "It's touch and go, from what I've heard. Opal is already talking about raising money to help out with the costs—Patsy, Dawson's mom, is a single mother, barely making ends meet."

"No father in the picture?" Tara asked.

The twins, probably reading her expression, had stopped doing their chores to stand staring at her, their faces worried and earnest and so incredibly young.

"He's doing time, out of state," Joslyn said without judgment. Her own stepfather, Elliott Rossiter, had died in prison, and she knew how hard incarceration was on families.

"Let me know if I can do anything, anything at all," Tara said, feeling ineffectual. Sure, she could write a check, say a few prayers, gather vegetables from her garden to take to the McCulloughs, but that didn't seem like much in the face of such a tragedy.

"Of course," Joslyn told her gently. "I'd better get off the phone—Shea and Opal just pulled in, and Boone's boys are with them—probably means Boone's going to be working all night, poor guy."

Tara felt another twinge, this time of guilt, rather than envy. Boone might be obnoxious, but he *was* her neighbor. Just the night before, he'd brought his children to her for safekeeping, after old Zeb Winchell was found dead. Rather than ask for her help again, he must have turned to Opal this time.

For some reason that hurt.

"Talk to you soon," she told Joslyn, ending the call and tucking the cell into the pocket of her jeans.

"You said you'd tell us what happened," Erin reminded her, standing a little closer to Elle. "In town, I mean."

Tara nodded. Then, as best she could, she explained about the water tower, and how teenagers and even younger kids were forever climbing the thing, and now a boy had fallen. His name was Dawson, she told them, and she didn't know how badly he was hurt.

"Badly enough to need a jet to get him to a hospital," Elle said. As doctor's daughters, both girls knew how serious the situation was.

Erin nodded, her hands gripping the handles of the brimming wheelbarrow, then frowned. “Isn’t there a hospital in Parable?” she asked. “I thought we passed one today, on our way out of town.”

“There’s a hospital,” Tara confirmed, remembering that Kendra and Hutch’s baby was being born there, right then. “But it’s not equipped for the kind of care Dawson will need.”

“Oh,” said Elle.

After that, all three of them went back to work, thinking their own thoughts.

CHAPTER NINE

Things are never so bad, Boone thought ruefully, as he drove away from Mayor Hale's stately home a little over an hour after the disaster at the water tower, *that they can't get worse.*

Hale, a portly man in his mid-sixties, with a head of white hair that reminded Boone of Mark Twain, had been waiting on his veranda—with all that fretwork and gingerbread, the thing was too elaborate to be called a mere porch—looking as though he might bite his unlit cigar in half. Obviously, word of the incident had already reached him.

"This is what we get for depending on your department to keep Parable safe for decent people!" he'd raged, before Boone had even managed to open the front gate, let alone step through it. "Setting up a municipal police force would strain the town's budget, but it sure as *hell* would have been cheaper than the multimillion-dollar lawsuit we're probably facing now!"

The town's lack of its own law enforcement agency, however modest, had been a sore spot with Hannibal Hale since his election, way back in the early eighties. He'd never liked being dependent on the sheriff's department, and thus the county, but the council members had repeatedly voted to table the matter.

Too bad the mayor hadn't been as concerned about that damnable water tower, and the threat it presented to generations of kids.

"Has there been any word about the boy's condition?" Boone had asked evenly, fighting back the impulse to jump straight down the mayor's throat and set him straight on a few things. He knew the old man would have made calls by then, and not just to the town's attorneys, a citified bunch with offices over in Three Trees, but to the administrators of the most likely hospitals in Missoula and Helena, as well.

Some of the bluster had gone out of Hale at the reference to Dawson McCullough, and Boone had seen his hand tremble as he removed the cigar from between his piano-key dentures and lowered it to his side. "Spinal injuries," he'd replied gruffly, the first signs of chagrin gathering in his wide, bulb-nosed face. He'd extracted his pocket watch and snapped open the case to check the time. "He'll be heading into surgery right about now."

"Prognosis?" Boone had asked, bracing himself for the answer.

Hale, clad in his customary summer garb, a white suit that made him look like a character in some fifties movie set in the Deep South, had shrugged his beefy shoulders, but they'd slumped noticeably when he lowered them again. He'd shaken his head, sighed. "If that young man comes through," he'd replied, raspy-voiced, "he'll be in a wheelchair for the rest of his life. No question about that, I'm afraid."

It struck Boone then that a person could be shocked by something without being surprised. He'd known this was coming, and yet he felt sucker punched.

After a moment or two of private recovery, Boone had asked for the name of the hospital Dawson had been taken to, so he could check on the kid personally. After making a mental note, he'd bitten the proverbial bullet and said, "About the water tower—"

Hale had interrupted brusquely. "Heard about that, too," he'd growled. "*Damn* it, Boone, why didn't you step in? Accident or no accident, that water tower was the oldest structure in the county. It was a historical *landmark,* for God's sake. The Parable Preservation Committee is going to peel off a strip of my hide when they find out it's been torn down—and yours, too, unless I miss my guess."

"The thing was a menace," Boone had replied flatly. "I wasn't sorry to see it fall, and I think most people around here would agree."

Most. But definitely not all.

"You'll change your tune when the complaints start rolling in," Hale had retorted, gesturing with the cigar to drive home his point. "I'll expect you to charge Hutch Carmody and the others with destruction of public property before this day is over, *Sheriff.* And you might want to think about turning in your resignation, too."

Boone's spine had stiffened. "Don't hold your breath, sir," he'd answered, stepping back through the mayor's front gate onto the uneven sidewalk. "On either score." With that, he'd turned to leave.

He'd felt the mayor's furious gaze boring into his back as he returned to the cruiser.

Recalling the exchange as he pulled into the courthouse parking lot a few minutes later, Boone spotted the waiting media vans—how had the reporters gotten to Parable so fast?

With an inward sigh, he parked the cruiser in the usual slot, near the door to his office and the county jail adjoining it, and took his cell phone from its holder, affixed to his belt. He wouldn't be getting off work in time to pick up the boys at the community center that afternoon, that much was a certainty. There would be reports to write, interviews to give, calls to make, concerned citizens to deal with.

He speed-dialed a familiar number.

After two rings, Joslyn Barlow answered the phone at Windfall Ranch, where she and Slade lived, and Boone reluctantly asked to speak to Opal. When she came on the line, he asked her to get Fletcher and Griffin from school when three o'clock came around and keep them with her until he could pick them up.

Bless her, Opal agreed right away, as he'd known she would. "And Boone?" she ventured, when he was about to say thank you and goodbye.

"What?" he asked wearily.

"It isn't your fault, what happened today," Opal said. "You couldn't have kept that child from falling. Fact is, it's a miracle nobody's gotten hurt long before this."

Boone let her words sink in. "Thanks for that," he told her. "But I don't think Mayor Hale and the Parable Preservation Committee see things quite the same way as you do."

"Hannibal Hale," Opal sputtered dismissively. "*That* old buzzard should have retired *years* ago!" For her, one of the kindest people Boone had ever known, this was a virtual outburst of anger. "Don't you pay any mind to what he says. The *sensible* people in this town will understand, you can count on that. In fact, they'll be *grateful.*"

Boone sighed again. He wondered if Patsy McCullough would be grateful—or hopping mad because that tower had been left to stand for decades after it should have been dismantled. "I hope you're right," he said, gazing through his dusty windshield at the crowd of newspeople and assorted locals bearing down on him.

They ended the call.

Boone got out of the car, shoved the door shut behind him and shouldered his way through the growing throng. The back entrance to the courthouse, and beyond that, his office, seemed to recede farther into the distance with every step he took; he might have been wading through knee-deep mud, so sluggish did his progress feel.

Several microphones were shoved into his face.

"Sheriff, is it true that you stood by and allowed the destruction of an historical monument?" asked a woman he recognized from the five o'clock news out of Missoula.

"Yes," he said, still walking. "It's true. But right now, I'm a lot more concerned about the seventeen-year-old boy who took a fifty-foot dive off the thing. Dawson's undergoing emergency surgery right now, after all, and his condition is critical."

The newscaster didn't flinch, or even blink. "Shouldn't the county have taken safety precautions?" she pressed. "Prevented this tragedy somehow?"

Hindsight, Boone reflected glumly, *is always twenty-twenty.*

"The water tower is—*was*—within the

town limits of Parable," Boone said, lengthening his stride, doing his best to move forward without shoving anybody out of his way. "Strictly speaking, it isn't in the county's jurisdiction."

"Will charges be filed against the men who tore the tower down?" another reporter asked, shouting to be heard over the others, all of them clamoring for a scapegoat, somebody to take the blame.

What *was* it with these people? Boone wondered fractiously. Were they really more worried about some negligible "historical site" than the well-being of the community's kids?

"Not if I have anything to say about it," he bit out. Hutch and the other two men *had* broken the law, but Boone wasn't about to arrest any of them. As far as he was concerned, they'd simply done what nobody else had had the guts to do.

Finally, he pushed open the side door and stepped into the corridor leading to his office, trailed by the crowd, only to be greeted by all six members of the historical preservation group, every one of them irate—and not all that well preserved themselves, in point of fact.

At least the dog, Scamp, was glad to see him, wriggling happily and licking at the toes of his boots. Boone bent, scooped up the animal, and figuratively dug in his heels.

"It's a girl," Joslyn announced, bypassing "hello" completely, when she called Tara that evening. She and the girls were having supper on the front porch, watching Lucy chase end-of-the-day butterflies in the yard and enjoying the peace and quiet of a country evening. The resident noisemakers, the chickens, had retired into their coop for the night.

Tara felt such a rush of joy at the news—*weary* joy, since she and the twins had been working hard all afternoon—that her throat tightened and her eyes stung for a moment. "She's healthy? The baby, I mean? And Kendra's all right?" she managed to ask.

Overhearing, and immediately connecting the dots, Elle and Erin smiled.

"Baby and Mama are doing great,"

Joslyn replied, with a soft laugh. "Hutch, on the other hand, seems to be in some kind of daze. So says my handsome husband, anyway. Slade just got home from the hospital a few minutes ago, and he filled me in on the details before he went out to the barn to feed the horses."

"Does Baby Girl Carmody have a name yet?" Tara asked. A car went by on the road, slowed to turn in at Boone's place, jostled over the cattle guard. She recognized the station wagon Opal drove.

"If she does, Hutch and Kendra aren't telling," Joslyn replied, a smile warming her voice. "We might not find out until the christening."

Watching the goings on over at Boone's as she listened, Tara saw Opal and the little Taylor boys as they got out of the station wagon, walking through the gathering twilight toward the double-wide. For reasons she couldn't have put a name to, the sight caused a tiny pinch in her heart.

"What a day this has been," Tara said, thinking how strange life could be, brimming with happiness *and* sorrow, all of a piece. "Is there any word about—about the boy who was hurt over at the water tower?"

"Dawson came through surgery alive," Joslyn replied, solemn now. "But things are still touch and go. Poor Patsy must be beside herself with worry."

"Yes," Tara agreed as the lights blinked on in the trailer across the narrow branch of the river. She sucked in a deep breath, squared her shoulders. "Thanks for letting me know about Kendra and Hutch's baby, Joss. I'd love to see her, as soon as visitors are allowed."

"Me, too," Joslyn answered. "I'll call when I find out—we can go together."

After that, the two women said their goodbyes, and Tara turned to the girls to relay what they'd already gathered from her end of the conversation.

Elle and Erin listened closely, finished with their supper and casting glances in the direction of the double-wide.

"That's awesome," said Elle.

"Are we old enough to babysit?" Erin wanted to know.

"It *is* awesome," Tara agreed. "As for

the babysitting part—well, actually, no, I don't think you're quite old enough."

There was a brief silence.

"Could we walk over and say hi to Opal and the rug rats?" Elle asked, first to change gears. "And take Lucy with us?"

Tara considered the request—all the while resisting a crazy urge to keep the twins close, like a hen sheltering chicks beneath its wings—and finally nodded her consent. Elle and Erin might not be grown-up enough to look after newborn babies, but they were twelve years old, capable of navigating one of the largest cities in the world, not only on foot, but via the buses and subway system, too. Besides, there was less than a quarter mile between her house and Boone's, and most of it was clearly visible from her yard. "I guess," she agreed aloud, gathering up plates and glasses and silverware to take back to the kitchen. "Just be careful, okay? And don't stay longer than half an hour."

After fetching a leash for Lucy and grabbing a flashlight "just in case," Tara's stepdaughters set out, taking the path that wound along the water's edge instead of the road. There was a narrow place where someone had laid out boards as a makeshift bridge, and Tara watched as the girls went straight for it. Their voices floated back to her on a warm breeze scented with country smells—mud and grass, mostly, along with pine trees and sun-dried laundry and the faintest whiff of chicken manure.

Tara lingered on the porch, her hands full of supper dishes, watching with a love-swelled heart as the girls, on the fast track to womanhood, and the dog paused on the other side of the sliver of water to examine an old rowboat, half-sunken and mired in gluey mud.

She wondered fretfully if she should have gone along with them. Until today, she'd considered Parable an almost mystically safe place, but she'd been proven wrong, hadn't she? Even here, terrible things happened, people got hurt—

She shook off the mental image of the water tower, and the long drop to the ground from its height.

Think about Hutch and Kendra's baby, Tara told herself. *Think about Elle and Erin, and what a blessing it is to have them here with you.*

Soon, she went inside, carried the dishes to the kitchen sink and looked up Boone's home number. Then she picked up the receiver on the wall phone and punched in the digits.

Opal answered with a cheery, "Sheriff Taylor's residence. This is Opal Dennison speaking."

Tara smiled, amused. "Hello, Opal Dennison," she replied. "This is Tara Kendall. I'm just calling to alert you that Elle and Erin are on their way over even as we speak. They wanted to say hello to you and the boys."

"That's fine," Opal said heartily. "Have they had supper?"

"Yes," Tara answered. "We just finished eating."

"That's too bad," Opal responded. "Griffin and Fletcher and I picked up a pizza in town, and I think our eyes were bigger than our stomachs. Rented a couple of movies, too. Would it be all right if the girls stayed for a while? The boys will enjoy the company and I'd be glad to drop them off at home later on when I leave." She paused. "Of course, that won't be until Boone turns up, and there's no telling what time that'll be."

Tara was torn between a certain possessiveness—her time with Elle and Erin was limited, and she treasured every moment of it—and the need for a little solitude, so she could sort through some things.

"Tell you what," she said, after some thought, "if Boone isn't back by the time the second movie ends, call me, and I'll come over and get Elle and Erin myself. Lucy's with them, by the way—that's all right, isn't it?"

"Sure it's all right," Opal said, her voice as warm and motherly as a hug. To Tara and many other people, the woman represented everything that was good about Parable, Montana, and all the towns like it, and just talking to her made Tara feel more hopeful. "Here they are now, peeking in at me through the screen door." Her voice changed as she turned from the receiver to call out a welcome. "You girls come on in, and bring that dog with you."

Smiling, Tara thanked Opal, and they both said goodbye and hung up.

Alone for the first time since the twins had gotten off the airplane in Missoula, without even Lucy to keep her company, Tara stood very still, there in her empty kitchen, listening to the relative silence.

Her first response was a rush of loneliness, the achy kind that a homesick child feels at sunset. Clearly, solitude wasn't all it was cracked up to be.

Shaking off the feeling, she loaded the dishwasher, tidied up the kitchen, brewed herself a cup of herbal tea and returned to the porch, planning to sit on the steps for a while, watching the first stars pop out and enjoying the twilight songs of bugs, a few birds settling into their nests and the soft breeze.

Unfortunately, the mosquitoes were out in full force by then, and Tara was forced to retreat to her home office. There, she switched on her computer, waited for it to boot up and finally went online. So much for counting stars and generally communing with nature on the porch steps on a summer night. She was as much an internet junkie as anybody else.

There were emails awaiting her, including a cell-phone photo of Baby Girl Carmody bundled in her proud mother's arms, a hospital-room shot, no doubt taken by an *equally* proud father. The message itself had been sent by Kendra, however, which must have meant she was recovering nicely. **We'll be home tomorrow. Come and see us,** she'd written.

Tomorrow. Tara smiled and dashed off a quick Reply. **She's absolutely beautiful. What's her name?**

Not expecting an answer right away, she went on to her other emails, all of which had come in since that morning, and noticed there was one from James. Given that the subject line—I NEED A BIG FAVOR!—was written all in caps, the cyber equivalent of shouting, she knew she couldn't have missed it when she scanned the list the first time. No, James's email must have come in while she was admiring the photo of Kendra and the baby, which might mean he was still online.

Any contact with James Lennox unnerved Tara, especially when she wasn't expecting it. He was effectively a stranger. But, then, that was nothing new. She'd never *really* known him at all, she reflected, even when they were married.

Bracing herself, she drew a deep breath—*don't say you want me to send the girls back to New York right away,* she pleaded silently—and opened the message.

Getting married, James's missive began, typically blunt. No caps, no punctuation. Evidently, he'd used up his supply of those writing the subject line. **We're thinking of a honeymoon cruise—around the world. It'll take six weeks—any chance the twins could stay with you until school starts again, right after Labor Day?**

Tara just sat there for a moment, staring at the screen. Sure, she was relieved that James wasn't cutting Elle and Erin's visit short—*more* than relieved—but as far as she knew, the man hadn't said anything to his daughters about getting married again. Was he expecting her to break such important news to them, so he wouldn't have to?

The thought of her ex avoiding a huge responsibility like that one made Tara seethe—how could James *be* so callous, so selfish, so inconsiderate of his own children?

Be reasonable, Tara. You're jumping to conclusions. Okay, so maybe James *had* told Elle and Erin what his plans were. But surely, if that was the case, the girls would have *mentioned* it to her, wouldn't they? It wasn't as if they were eager to acquire another stepmother, after all.

Slowly, Tara let out her breath. She hit Reply, waited a few beats and typed, **Elle and Erin are welcome to stay here as long as they need to, of course. But do they know you're getting married again?**

She paused, afraid James would think she was jealous or hurt that he planned on remarrying—and nothing could have been further from the truth.

He responded almost immediately,

confirming her suspicion that he'd been lurking, waiting for her answer. **That's great,** he wrote. **You're great. By the way, I sent you a check today—you know, in case the kids need anything.**

Do they know? Tara fired back.

It won't come as a surprise, James hedged, after waiting so long that Tara was beginning to think he'd left his computer. She could picture him hunkered over the keyboard of the laptop he kept in his den.

You need to tell them, James.

Another long pause followed, then, **I think they might take the whole thing better if they heard about it from you.**

Tara rested her elbows on the edge of her desk, splayed her fingers wide, and shoved them into her hair as she lowered her head and indulged in a silent scream. Then, feeling slightly more composed, she answered, **That isn't fair to Elle and Erin, James. You're their father. You're getting married. You need to level with them—now.**

I've got to go, James replied briskly, this time with no hesitation.

And Tara knew it would be useless to argue.

Still, she grabbed up her cell phone and dialed James's home number.

She got his voice mail, of course. "You've reached Dr. Lennox. Leave your information and I'll get back to you as soon as possible."

Yeah, right.

Tara steamed. "You can't do this," she protested, after the beep. "It's wrong!"

Nothing. If James was at the penthouse, rather than his clinic or the hospital, and she knew he must have been because he never sent personal emails from anyplace but home, he was ducking her call.

The bastard.

She pushed back her desk chair and got to her feet, wildly annoyed.

What did James plan to do? Send his daughters a postcard from wherever the cruise ship stopped? *Guess what, kids! You have a new stepmother—isn't that wonderful?*

Tara paced, trying to vent some of her frustration, but pacing didn't help.

She still wanted to pick up something and throw it.

So she marched outside, mosquitoes be damned, and headed for the vegetable garden, a shadowy, moonlit space, and ruthlessly weeded three rows of carrots. At least she *hoped* she'd been pulling up weeds.

After a little while, the adrenaline began to subside, and she stood up. Left the garden. Of course the knees of her jeans were wet and stained, where she'd knelt in the dirt, as she came around the side of the barn, just in time to see headlights bumping over the cattle guard and swaying up the driveway.

Recognizing Boone's squad car, she waited in puzzled consternation, fitfully slapping at mosquitoes as they landed on her shoulders and bare arms.

He parked the cruiser, shut off the lights and got out. His dog bounded out after him, a four-legged deputy trotting at his side.

Without a word, Boone approached, took Tara gently by one elbow and squired her up the porch steps and through the front door.

"What—?" she asked, still confused, balking once they were over the threshold.

A single lamp burned in the entryway, and Boone looked wan in the thin light, even a little gaunt. The dog sat down at his feet, small and watchful, looking up at both of them, ready for anything.

Boone gave a ragged sigh, took off his hat, shoved a hand through his already-rumpled hair. "Don't ask me what I'm doing here," he said, "because I don't have the first damn idea what the answer is supposed to be."

Tara touched his arm, feeling strangely stricken. There it was again, joy and sorrow, all rolled into one. "Come in," she said quietly. "I'll make coffee."

He nodded once, but said nothing.

As she led the way to the kitchen, Tara was aware of Boone Taylor in every fiber of her being, aware of his heat and his strength and his uncompromising masculinity.

"You've done a lot with this place," he commented when they'd reached the kitchen.

Tara recalled that Boone had grown

up in the house, looked back at him as she approached the single-cup coffeemaker on the counter. “Have a seat,” she said, indicating the table and chairs in the center of the big room.

Boone dragged back a chair, sighed again and sat.

Suddenly, it was ridiculously easy for Tara to imagine that he *belonged* in this kitchen, that they lived here together as man and wife.

Maybe in a parallel universe, she thought sadly. In this one, they weren’t even friends—just neighbors who each wished the other one would move away.

Tara crossed to take his hat from his hand, hung it from one of the pegs near the back door, returned again to the caffeine-machine.

“I talked to Patsy McCullough a little while ago,” Boone said presently. It came again, that strange sense that it was *normal* for him to sit at this table, and tell her about his day. “Dawson’s mother.”

Tara set a mug under the spigot of the coffeemaker and pushed the brew button. She nodded. He’d had news, obviously, about the boy who'd fallen from the water tower in town that day. Instead of speaking, Tara simply waited, letting Boone take his time.

Finally, and with an effort that probably meant he'd dredged up the words from somewhere deep in the unfathomable silence within him, his dark eyes haunted, he continued, "The good news is, Dawson came through the surgery all right, and he's doing as well as can be expected. The bad news is—" Here, he paused again, cleared his throat, shoved a hand through his hair once more. Tara suppressed a need to walk right over and smooth her fingers through it, offering him comfort. "The bad news is, there was some serious damage to the boy's lower spine, and he isn't going to walk again."

Tara's throat scalded, so she swallowed hard. "I'm sorry," she said very softly. She was sorry for Dawson McCullough, sorry for his mother—and sorry for Boone, strong as he was.

The emotion felt dangerously intimate.

She moved stiffly as she brought him

the coffee, then went back to the machine to brew a cup for herself. Now it was a certainty—she wouldn't sleep well that night, if she slept at all. Something about the set of Boone's shoulders, the look in his eyes, a combination of vulnerability and stubborn courage, made her nerves pulse with a kind of sweet urgency that reminded her of desire. She was stunned to realize that, more than anything, she wanted this man to hold her, even make love to her.

And damn the consequences, forget the morning after.

She took an automatic step back, nearly spilling the cup of coffee in her hand.

Boone's gaze held steady—no way he could know what she was thinking, what she was feeling—the man wasn't psychic. At least, she hoped he wasn't.

Fingers stinging from the mild burn, Tara took herself resolutely to the table and sat down opposite Boone, wishing he would leave, wishing he would stay.

The inner conflict was so intense, so tangled, that heat surged into her face, and she set her cup on the tabletop, hoping Boone would think the blush was a reaction to hot coffee.

"I shouldn't have come here," he said gruffly, scraping back his chair, abandoning the coffee she'd made for him only minutes before. He started to rise.

"Stay," Tara heard herself say. "Please."

Boone slowly lowered himself back into his chair. The dog, having shot to its feet, lay itself down again with a resigned little sigh.

Boone smiled at the critter.

Tara smiled at Boone.

Watch it, warned her better judgment.

"I'm sorry," Boone told her, "for busting in on you like this. I ought to be at home, putting the boys to bed."

"They're watching movies with Opal and the twins," Tara said. She propped her elbow on the tabletop, cupped her chin in her palm and regarded Boone as objectively as she could, given the crazy gyrations of her nerves. "And there's no reason to apologize for dropping in. We're neighbors, aren't we?"

His grin was a mere tilt of one corner

of his mouth, but his eyes danced behind that sheen of weariness. "If you say so," he allowed lightly, taking a sip of his coffee and savoring it for a long moment before going on. "But we got off on the wrong foot, you and I. There's no denying that."

"No, I guess not," Tara said, wondering what had changed between the two of them, and when. She'd never hated Boone Taylor, but she hadn't liked him, either. He was too sure of himself, too good-looking, too hardheaded, too *everything.*

He drew a deep breath, let it out slowly and met her eyes. "Today was a hell of a day," he said, as though coming to a quiet realization.

"You probably get a lot of those in your line of work," Tara offered. "Maybe you just needed to tell somebody about it, in a familiar kitchen, over a cup of coffee."

Boone regarded her solemnly, but a touch of amusement lingered in his eyes. "Maybe," he admitted. Then he looked around. "Not that this kitchen is all that familiar. When we lived here—

Mom and Dad and Molly and me, I mean—it had ugly gold appliances, scuffed linoleum and bad wallpaper. *Really* bad wallpaper."

Tara laughed then, surprising herself.

Had she ever laughed in Boone's presence before? No. She'd hardly even *smiled.*

The title of an old Bob Dylan song ran through her mind.

The times were definitely changing.

CHAPTER TEN

Nothing had happened between him and Tara, Boone silently insisted as he and Scamp left her place later that evening, but something had *changed,* something profound, and it was a burr under his hide trying to figure out exactly what the shift meant.

Hell, he still wasn't sure why he'd wanted to see Tara so badly in the first place, and never mind her tentative suggestion that, after a hard day, he'd probably just "needed to talk to somebody." The fact was, there were plenty of people he could have spent time with—

close friends, any of his deputies (except McQuillan), the bartender over at the Boot Scoot Tavern. The waitresses at the bowling alley snack bar, for God's sake.

Instead, he'd chosen Tara Kendall, of all people. The pseudo chicken rancher. The big-city sophisticate who looked down on his battered double-wide, his sorry-looking yard and, most likely, she disapproved of the fact that he'd left the boys with Molly and Bob for so long.

To her, he was probably still just the redneck sheriff of a nowhere county, irresponsible to boot. Secretly, she probably marveled that he had all his teeth and no broken-down appliances rusting on his sagging porch.

Okay, yes, Tara had been genuinely concerned about Dawson McCullough, the McCullough family and the accident that, even in the best-case scenario, would turn Patsy and her children's lives upside down. Anybody with half a heart, with a *shred* of compassion for their fellow human beings, would care about a tragedy like that, and care deeply.

What nettled Boone was that he

hadn't just *wanted* to be with Tara, hadn't simply chosen to be with her. It was that he'd *needed* to, the way he needed his next breath, his next heartbeat. Bottom line: he hadn't had a choice.

And Boone didn't like not having choices. Before tonight, he would have sworn he didn't have an impulsive bone in his body. Despite all that, he'd left the office with the dog, hours after his usual quitting time, and driven straight to the chicken farm, like he was on autopilot or something, a moth winging its bumbling way into the bright core of a flame.

Finally home, but still sitting in his cruiser, with the headlights washing over his weedy yard and Scamp watching him expectantly from the passenger seat, pointy ears perked and fuzzy head tilted to one side, Boone tightened his grip on the steering wheel, remembering Corrie and how much he'd come to love her after the first dazzling passion began to let up a little.

They'd been nothing but kids when they got together, he and Corrie, awash in hormones and the kind of reckless optimism only the very young can sustain for long, but all too soon the realities of grocery bills and rent and car payments, along with an unexpected pregnancy, had matured them considerably. For all the challenges, totally against the odds, they'd made their marriage work.

"If we don't give up," Corrie had said to him once, after a yelling match and a bout of Olympic-quality makeup sex, "we'll be okay, Boone. All we have to do is keep trying to get this right, and, one day, we will."

Boone's heart clenched as he recalled those wise words and felt again the softness of Corrie's cheek resting on his bare shoulder, the warmth of her skin, her blind confidence that they had a future together, a good long one.

They were both naive and idealistic. Neither of them had much of an adult support system, with Molly gone off to live the life she'd put on hold for his sake. His folks were dead by then and hers were far away, divorced from each other and disapproving their one common link: their daughter. Back then,

Boone was making next-to-no money as a brand-new sheriff's deputy, a job he'd immediately loved. He'd pulled overtime whenever he could get it, just to make ends meet, and taken extension courses through the community college over in Three Trees as well as online.

His goals had been clear: he'd wanted to be a good provider, a good husband and father. The rest, he'd figured, would take care of itself.

The plan, simple as it was, had made sense to him and to Corrie, too. They'd had the piece of land Boone had gotten after his and Molly's parents had died, and a ramshackle trailer bought for less than a thousand dollars, the entirety of their combined savings. They'd had a baby coming and they'd had each other, and for the time being, anyway, all of that was enough.

In a few years, with discipline and more hard work, they'd reasoned, they'd be on track financially. They'd have more children and later on, Corrie would go back to school, get a degree of her own.

Trouble was, it turned out that “a few years” were all they were ever going to get.

By the time Boone earned his degree in criminal justice, he and Corrie had two fine, healthy sons, and they’d paid off their secondhand car, too. Nights and weekends they spent hours sketching out preliminary designs for the house they meant to build, doing much of the work themselves. The place would be modest, definitely not a mansion but big enough to accommodate a growing family. There would be a fenced yard, and Boone planned on building a play area for the boys. They’d even had a construction loan in place, one that could be converted to a mortgage later on, when the earth flipped on its axis.

One ordinary morning, while showering, Corrie found a hard, pea-sized lump in her left breast. She’d called Boone in from the kitchen, where he was overseeing Griffin’s cold-cereal breakfast and spoon-feeding Fletcher in his high chair, a hand-me-down from Molly’s kids, and there was a slight quaver in her voice.

Back then, as a deputy, he'd worn starched uniforms, and he carried Fletcher with him, tucked in the curve of one arm and held at a little distance, in hopes that the toddler wouldn't drool or spit up on his shirt.

He'd found Corrie shivering in the tiny bathroom, a towel clutched around her otherwise naked body, her eyes huge.

Without a word, she'd guided his hand beneath the towel to the soft underside of her breast. He'd felt a distinct swelling beneath her silky, still-damp flesh.

They'd just looked at each other for a long moment, both of them struck silent by cold, elemental fear.

Just an hour later, the babies were in a neighbor woman's keeping and Boone and Corrie were on their way to the local clinic. Blood tests, exams, a mammogram and lots of frightening questions followed. A biopsy was scheduled for the next morning.

Of course the news was bad, and the fear grew into something that made Boone's breath catch in his lungs and the backs of his eyes scald like fire.

Ever the devoted sister, Molly came right away, leaving her own kids in Bob's care, and Corrie had undergone the dreaded double mastectomy. Since radiation would be required, reconstructive surgery had to be put off until later.

Boone still choked up when he recalled the first words she'd said to him, his beautiful, funny, tenderhearted wife, when she woke up and saw him standing beside her hospital bed.

"You'll still love me, won't you, Boone? Now that I'm flat-chested and scarred?"

He'd nearly lost it then, replied hoarsely that he'd *always* love her, no matter what.

"But you're a breast man," she'd said with a small, sad flicker of a smile.

"I'm *your* man," he'd managed to get out in a raspy whisper. "Nothing's going to change that, Corrie. *Nothing.*"

At first, they'd been hopeful. After all, Corrie was young, and otherwise healthy, and cancer wasn't an automatic death sentence the way it used to be; what with all the new drugs and streamlined treatments and experimental programs, people recovered from the disease all the time. Went right on to enjoy happy, productive lives.

Things didn't happen that way for Corrie and Boone, though. An infection swept through her already-weakened system and, despite massive doses of antibiotics, she couldn't fight back.

Slowly, bravely and sometimes painfully, when she'd refused her meds because they made her "dopey," Corrie had wasted away, become a ghost weeks before she'd actually breathed her last in Boone's arms.

Forcing himself back into the present moment, if only because he couldn't stand the past, Boone squeezed his eyes shut for a moment, tried to shake off the images. Scamp let out a little whimper and scrabbled at the inside of the car door, tired of being confined.

Methodically, as though he'd been programmed like a machine, Boone shut off the headlights and the engine, leaned across to open the passenger-side door so Scamp could jump to the ground. He hoped he wouldn't have to chase the critter back to Zeb Winchell's again, because he was just plain tuckered out by then, physically *and* emotionally.

He pulled that door shut, opened his and got out of the cruiser.

To his relief, Scamp lifted a leg against the side of an old tire, took care of business and then trotted off toward the porch, just as the door swung open. A rectangle of yellow light splashed into the yard, and Opal Dennison's tall, sturdy frame filled the gap.

"Their movie is almost over," she said, evidently referring to the kids, stepping out onto the rickety porch to greet Boone. "It's an ice-age cartoon—" Opal paused, chuckled appreciatively, having the gift of finding joy in little things, shook her head as though there were no end to the marvels of ordinary life. "One of the characters is a wooly mammoth with an Elvis haircut, believe it or not. And here are all those folks claiming *the King* is dead."

Boone chuckled wearily, mounted the steps, walking into the double-wide behind Opal. He locked away his service revolver first thing, like always, then put his cell phone on the charger. While he washed up at the kitchen sink, leaving his badge on the windowsill beside a potted plant he didn't recognize, Opal scooped two huge slices of pizza from a box on the counter onto a plate, long strands of cheese trailing, and zapped the works in the microwave.

Boone didn't have the heart to tell this good woman he wasn't hungry and probably wouldn't get that way, at least in the immediate future. His brain was wrung out, his emotions were as snarled and spiky as a coil of rusted barbed wire and his stomach was as cold and heavy as if he'd swallowed a bowling ball.

All he really wanted to do was shower, fall into bed and sleep, grab a few hours of blessed oblivion before the sun rose and the whole show started up all over again, but the days when he could be that self-indulgent were over.

He moved to the living room doorway, looked in. Griffin and Fletcher were on the floor, too close to the TV, while Tara's preteen stepdaughters lounged, respectively, on the couch and in

Boone's battered recliner. The golden retriever pup at their feet looked up, too.

Griffin, meanwhile, turned back over one T-shirted shoulder and grinned a welcome at Boone. "Hey, Dad," he said offhandedly. "Be with you in a sec. This is the best part of the movie."

Boone smiled. *Be with you in a sec.* At least *one* of his kids wanted to spend time with him. "No rush," he said quietly, as Scamp darted across the floor and landed square in the middle of Fletcher's narrow back, frantically licking the boy's nape and one of his ears.

Fletcher burst out giggling, and rolled over to wrestle with the dog, careful to be gentle, since Scamp was small. The sight made Boone's throat pull in tight and ache a little.

The girl in the recliner—Erin? Elle? he couldn't begin to tell the sisters apart—looked at him with startled, worried eyes. Was he that scary, even without his service revolver and his badge?

"Shall I get out of your chair?" the girl asked, poised to bolt.

Boone shook his head, figured her dad must be one of those guys who tended to be territorial about their favorite lounger. “Stay put,” he said mildly. “I’m good.”

Then, bemused, he turned and went back to the kitchen. Thinking of the girls’ father led to thinking about Tara with a husband, and he didn’t want to go there.

Not now, anyway.

In the interim, Opal had set the plate of reheated pizza on the table, along with a paper napkin and some utensils, and though she hadn’t picked up her purse, reached for her well-worn summer cardigan or rattled her keys, she was clearly gearing up to leave.

“I promised Tara I’d drive Elle and Erin and Lucy home after the movie,” she said, studying Boone solemnly, seeing too much, as she generally did. Then she gestured toward the food. “That’s not the most nutritious supper in the world,” she added with some regret. “But you still need to eat.”

Boone sighed. Maybe he could fake it until she was out the door, pretend an interest in the pizza, but that seemed like a stretch, given that all four kids were still glued to the TV and Opal was nobody's fool. "I know," he said. "In a minute."

Opal walked over, drew back a chair at the table, sat down across from him. "Hutch and Kendra's baby came today," she said. "A fine and dandy girl, healthy as any one of her daddy's horses. Weighed nine full pounds."

Boone's flagging spirits climbed, then dipped a little; of course he was happy for his friends, but there was that usual small twinge of something uncomfortably similar to envy, too. He and Corrie had hoped to give the boys a baby sister or two, when the time was right, and now, like so many other things, that was never going to happen. "I knew Kendra had gone into labor," he said finally, his throat dry as dust. "I was there when Hutch got the call. What with all that was going on, though, I never got around to following up."

Opal nodded understandingly, apparently seeing no need to comment. "How is the McCullough boy?" she asked presently, taking off her glasses and polishing the lenses with a corner of her cotton apron. Opal Dennison always seemed to be wearing one, usually with big pockets and a few ruffles, always ready for a cooking or cleaning crisis.

"Dawson's holding on," Boone said. If he'd been asked that question once that day, he'd been asked it a dozen times, and he was tired to the center of his soul, but this was Opal, after all. Not some busybody, or big-city reporter.

"What's poor Patsy going to do?" Opal fretted, shaking her head. "She cleans motel rooms, for pity's sake, and I know she doesn't have health insurance."

Subtly, he hoped, Boone slid aside the pizza, rested his forearms on the tabletop. He recalled his conversation with Mayor Hale, and, later, the go-round with the good people who made up the Parable Preservation Committee. They'd been spitting mad over that stupid water tower, especially after Boone pointed out that they could have maintained the damn thing a little better if it meant so much to them, made it safer, if only to live up to their pompous-assed name.

Needless to say, they hadn't appreciated the reminder. They were clamoring for arrests, and for his resignation, neither of which, he'd pointed out, were forthcoming. Unless, of course, hell froze over.

"I don't know," Boone said honestly, in reply to Opal's question, thinking that money, though it would definitely be a problem, was probably the least of Patsy McCullough's worries right about then. "I ran into Walker Parrish a few hours ago when I went over to the Butter Biscuit to pick up a sandwich, and he told me that Casey's setting up some kind of trust for Dawson—plans to fund it with at least one benefit concert." He paused, cleared his throat. "People will step up as best they can, Opal—this is Parable, remember?"

She relaxed a little. Even smiled. "Yes," she agreed. "This is Parable. And it's generous of Casey to help out, given that she's pretty new in town."

Boone nodded. Casey had loaned the McCulloughs her private jet, too. For somebody so famous, she struck him as surprisingly down-to-earth.

"Speaking of Walker," Opal went on

thoughtfully, "whatever happened with that case Treat McQuillan was threatening to bring against him for that tussle they had over at the Boot Scoot Tavern that night?"

Boone permitted himself a smile, though it probably looked more like a grimace to Opal. Over a year ago, Treat and Walker had gotten into it after Treat made a move on Walker's kid sister, Brylee. Walker had decked the offender, pronto, and Deputy McQuillan had sworn he'd press charges.

"I guess they must have settled that privately," he said. "Walker and Treat, I mean."

Opal made a little *harrumph*like sound. "I wouldn't have given Treat McQuillan credit for that much good sense," she said.

"Me, either," Boone agreed. He supposed some money must have changed hands, but then, payoffs weren't Walker Parrish's style. He probably hadn't regretted throwing the punch that landed Treat in the sawdust and peanut shells covering the barroom floor for so much as a moment.

Closing-scene music swelled from the TV; the movie was over.

The tube went blessedly silent, and four kids and two dogs wandered into the kitchen.

"Did Scamp try to run away again after you went and found him?" Griffin asked, standing close to Boone's chair.

"Nope," Boone replied. "But tomorrow's another day. We'll have to keep an eye on him for a while, I think."

"Aunt Molly called tonight," his elder son continued, the sudden remembering plain in his earnest little face. "She said you were on the TV news. And that you're up to your backside in alligators."

Fletcher's eyes widened. "Alligators?" he repeated, after a hard swallow. "Like the one in *Peter Pan?*"

"That was a crocodile," one of the twins put in, matter-of-factly. The young retriever stood patiently while she hooked a leash to the animal's collar. The bigger dog showed a studied lack of interest in Scamp, who was trying to get some kind of canine game going.

Fletcher didn't look away from Boone's face. He wanted answers.

Boone's mouth twitched, and he risked rubbing the top of the boy's buzz-cut head with one hand, was gratified when the kid didn't pull away. "It was just a figure of speech, buddy," he assured the child. "Among its other charms, Montana is both an alligator- and crocodile-free zone."

Fletcher let out a long breath. "Good," he said, obviously relieved.

"We didn't see you on TV," Griffin added, looking disappointed. "Opal wouldn't let us turn the set on until after we had supper."

"Good for Opal," Boone said with a glance at her.

She was on her feet by then, distracted and efficient, saying good-night to the boys, herding Elle and Erin and the golden retriever outside to her car before Boone could so much as say thanks, let alone reach for his wallet and pay her.

"You didn't miss anything," he told his sons, after the door closed behind the others, recalling what a hard-ass he'd been in front of the news cameras that day. He was glad the boys hadn't been watching. "By not catching my TV debut, I mean."

They both just stood there watching him, the dog sitting between them. The boys seemed to expect something more from him—hell, maybe Scamp did, too—but what?

"Did your aunt say anything about how your uncle Bob is doing?" Boone asked, partly to break the silence and partly because he really wanted to know.

Griffin nodded, serious as the national debt. "She said he's super-duper grumpy, but he'll be as good as new in a couple of months."

"That's good," Boone said, making a mental note to call Molly the next day, or at least shoot a text or an email her way. "That he's getting better, I mean. Not that he's grumpy, even though that's understandable, given that he's just had knee surgery." He pushed back his chair to stand. He went whole days without saying as much as he had this evening, he thought, mildly amused. He was getting downright chatty in his old age. "Anybody want this pizza?" he asked, picking up the plate Opal had prepared for him earlier.

Both boys shook their heads no. “We had some before,” Griffin explained. “And then Opal made popcorn.”

Boone nodded, crossed the room and dumped the pizza into the trash.

After that, it was bath time—Griffin and Fletcher climbed into the tub together, since that was what they were used to—and there was some splashing and some laughing and, finally, the beginnings of a row.

Boone interceded quietly, bringing towels, checking ears and necks, knuckles and knees, to make sure they'd gotten clean.

Once they'd dried off, gotten into their pajamas and brushed their teeth at the sink, shouldering each other the whole time, they hopped into bed. Boone followed, figuring they'd want to say their prayers.

Instead, they settled against their pillows and regarded him with two pairs of dark eyes.

“Tell us about Mommy,” Griffin finally said.

The request struck Boone's heart like a pebble from a slingshot. He'd known this was coming, of course, but he hadn't expected it tonight.

He sat down on the edge of their small berthlike bed, sighed. "What do you want to know?" he asked, wishing he had clue-one how much Molly had told her nephews over the years.

"Was she pretty?" Fletcher asked, very softly.

Boone's breath caught, but he recovered quickly. "Not just pretty," he said. "She was beautiful."

"She got real sick and died," Griffin added.

"Yes," Boone rasped.

"But she loved us very much," Griffin recited, obviously repeating what his Aunt Molly had said, "and she wouldn't have left us for anything, if she could have helped it."

"That's right," Boone ground out. "You guys meant everything to her."

Griffin frowned. "How come there aren't any pictures of her? We had one on our bedroom wall back in Missoula."

The mention of Missoula tightened Fletcher's small face.

Scamp scooched past Boone to join the boys on the bed, settling between them.

"Yeah," Fletcher said. "How come there aren't any pictures?"

"We'll rustle some up tomorrow," Boone promised.

"For real?" Griffin pressed, looking doubtful. "I don't want to forget what Mommy looked like."

"Okay," Boone managed to say, going through the motions of tucking in little boys for the night.

Griffin frowned. "Sometimes, when I remember Mommy, I just see a lady, but she doesn't have a face."

Boone waited a beat, struggling with an onslaught of emotion. He had the same problem now and then, envisioning Corrie with her features blurred. When that happened, he panicked and got out the fat scrapbook she'd kept, studied her image until he could hold on to it in his mind.

"That's normal, buddy," he told the boy. "Nothing to worry about."

"Will you take us to put flowers on her grave?"

This time, Boone couldn't speak at all. He simply nodded and got to his feet.

His small sons closed their eyes then, and interlocked their fingers to say their bedtime prayers.

Molly had taught them well.

"Please help that boy who fell off the water tower to get better," Griffin said.

"And don't let Scamp run away anymore," Fletcher added.

"Amen," they said together.

Choked up, Boone left the room, shutting off the light as he went, whispering a gravelly "Good night," in the process.

Alone in his kitchen—programming the coffeepot for morning, making sure the back door was locked and finally flipping the light switch to off—he stood at the window over the sink, looking out at the scrap of river and the shadow of the house beyond it.

For all his missing Corrie, still a keen ache that pierced his middle like a spear, for all his mourning the life they'd shared and all the dreams and hopes and possibilities that had died with his sweet wife, it was Tara Kendall who filled his thoughts now.

He felt it again, that need to be near her, even if they didn't talk, or touch each other. He wanted to breathe in the scent of her, let her tentative smile and the soft light in her eyes soak into all his broken places like healing sunshine.

Moonlight stirred the little spit of river like a trailing index finger, and the stars blazed overhead like small, silver bonfires, full of desolate beauty.

It was happening, he thought grimly, the thing he'd sworn, to Corrie and to himself, that he'd never *allow* to happen.

He wanted a woman, a *particular* woman, and not just for sex, like the practically anonymous females he'd bedded now and then, when the loneliness got to be too much.

And that woman wasn't Corrie.

Tara waved goodbye to Opal, who remained behind the wheel of her station wagon, as Elle and Erin and Lucy erupted from the rear doors and raced toward her. They looked so happy, in the light of that sky-filling moon, the dog bounding alongside.

Opal tooted her car horn, backed up to turn around and drove away.

"We watched two baby-movies," Elle called out, as she came up the walk, "but they were pretty good, anyway."

Tara, still dealing with the combined effects of the email exchange with James and the unexpected visit from Sheriff Boone Taylor, smiled. "You had fun, then," she said. "I'm glad."

Erin, forever the responsible one, paused to close the front gate before following her twin and Lucy up the walk. "There are *no* crocodiles in Montana," Erin said. "Zero."

Elle laughed as the three of them came up the steps to join Tara on the porch.

"Oh, let that go," she told her sister, with a note of good-natured impatience in her voice. "You've made your point. We all get it, Professor Know-it-all."

Erin rolled her eyes but offered no argument.

Tara didn't ask what *that* conversation was all about. She had too much on her mind. James and—Bethany, wasn't it?—were about to change the dynamics of Elle and Erin's lives, throw everything into a tailspin.

True, James and his ladylove had every right to get married, and they certainly didn't need permission from the twins, but the way they were going about the whole thing bothered Tara. Not only did James expect *her* to tell them—*his children*—about the upcoming wedding, he apparently felt no compunction to include them in the big event at all. Shouldn't they *be there,* take part in the ceremony in some way?

"What's wrong?" Erin asked suddenly, frowning at Tara.

Tara moved to lock the front door for the night, wishing she had another kind of face, the sort that didn't show everything she was thinking and feeling.

"Tara?" Elle insisted, sounding worried.

Tara turned around to face them. She wasn't going to get out of this one, she realized. She'd been fooling herself, thinking she could hold off until tomorrow and suggest they give their dad a call.

"Let's go into the kitchen," she said.

Elle led the way, but she kept looking back at Tara with a worried expression.

The twins took chairs at the table without being asked, and Tara sat down, too, facing them, folding her hands in front of her on the table.

"No one's hurt or sick, it's nothing like that," she told them, holding their gazes even though she wanted to look away. "But I do have something to tell you."

Damn James, she thought with a sigh. He'd gotten his way—again.

"What?" both girls asked at the same time, nearly whispering.

"Your dad and Bethany are getting married," Tara said. "Soon."

Elle's mouth dropped open.

Erin reddened. "I knew it," she said, but, though angry, she was obviously as stunned by the news as her sister had been.

Elle found her voice then. "He couldn't tell us himself?" she asked as Lucy, eyes luminous with sympathy, came to stand between the girls' chairs.

"He asked me to do it," Tara replied gently.

"He's such a coward," Erin sputtered. Both she and Elle were stroking Lucy's coat, but their eyes were still fixed on Tara.

Tara ignored the comment, though, of course, she privately agreed. Still, it wouldn't be fair to criticize James in front of these hurt and bewildered children. They were, after all, his daughters.

Elle's little shoulders sagged. "He knew how we'd react," she said miserably.

"He's still a coward," Erin said.

"But it's sort of our fault," Elle told her twin, her eyes glistening with unshed tears. "Dad knows we don't like Bethany."

"*None* of this is your fault," Tara was quick to put in.

Erin turned to Tara, spoke in a soft, heartbreakingly fragile voice. "Couldn't we just stay with you?" she asked. "Please?"

Tara's heart broke into pieces. She tried to smile. "You'll be here until school starts," she assured them. "That's longer than expected and—"

"Bethany doesn't want us," Erin broke in, stiffening her spine. "She calls us brats. She and Dad will make us go to some boarding school—so why can't we stay here?"

Tara moved forward, wanting to take both girls into her arms and not quite daring to, because the act might unleash a lot of rash promises, ones she wouldn't be able to keep.

"I'd like nothing better," she admitted. "But it isn't my decision to make."

After that, the girls scraped back their chairs, stood up and left the kitchen without so much as a glance in Tara's direction or a muttered good-night.

Besides the arrival of Hutch and Kendra's baby girl, this day only had one thing going for it: it was over.

CHAPTER ELEVEN

Life in and around Parable settled into a peaceful lull over the next few days, or seemed to, anyhow, but Boone didn't trust the respite to last, and he remained vaguely uneasy, waking or sleeping.

The medical reports on Dawson McCullough came in on a regular basis, and they were cautiously hopeful. The ruins of the old water tower were quietly cleared away, the wood burned, the metal of the tank itself cut up for scrap and hauled off. The Parable Preservation Committee pulled in its figurative horns a little, and Mayor Hale didn't make any more noises about arrests and resignations.

Miss Shannon Carmody, Hutch and Kendra's new daughter, thrived, as did her happy parents.

Zeb Winchell's funeral was a somber affair, but well attended, and Boone brought Scamp to the services, on a leash, of course, and—this was the boys' idea—a bright blue bandanna around his neck, for his dress-up attire. The dog seemed to understand that this was goodbye, where he and his late master were concerned, and after that he never tried to run away again.

On the home front, Boone showed the boys Corrie's scrapbooks, and let them choose a picture of her to enlarge in the photo department of Walmart and subsequently hang on their bedroom wall. Talking about Corrie at all, let alone sharing stories about her, was painful for Boone, like standing too close to a blazing fire with a fresh case of frostbite, but it was getting easier. He took them to her grave, over at the Pioneer Cemetery, and they solemnly set a bouquet of yellow roses in a canning-jar vase in front of her headstone and ran small fingers over the engraved letters of her name, date of birth and date of death. Over the words *Beloved wife and mother.*

For all the sadness of it, and all the poignancy, something seemed to ease in both Griffin and Fletcher, though Boone doubted they really understood. Why had he never brought them here before during one of their visits from Missoula?

It was as if just having a special place to pay their respects to the woman who'd given them life was consolation enough, at least for the time being.

Though he didn't let on, Boone experienced a sort of closure himself, a sense that he was relinquishing things, almost against his will, things he'd sworn he'd hold on to forever. There was a degree of guilt, and a wrenching sense of the old, familiar sorrows being torn away.

In the silence of his mind, surrounded by graves and green rippling grass, by whispering pines and cottonwoods, with that amazing Montana sky arching over all of it, Boone came to terms with an uncomfortable but exciting truth: he was attracted to Tara Kendall. *More* than attracted, though it was way too early to go putting names to things.

Leaving the cemetery with his boys that quiet afternoon—he'd taken them to Sunday school that morning, though actually attending church was still beyond him—and stood in some awe of the continuous, ever-deepening shift going on in the most private regions of his mind, body and soul.

He felt like somebody waking up from a coma, even as though he was being *resurrected,* literally brought back from the dead. He could admit it then, at least to himself, as he herded the boys and Scamp toward the waiting cruiser: a big part of him *had* wanted to die with Corrie, rather than endure being parted from her.

The obvious flaw in that logic was this—he was *alive.* He had two boys to bring up. He had a job he loved, ninety percent of the time, anyway. He had a prime piece of land, however underdeveloped it might be, and for the first time since he and Corrie got together, he wanted something more from a woman than no-strings-attached sex.

All those were things to be grateful for, he thought, as he and the kids and the dog drove away, leaving the cemetery—and a lot more—behind. And none of it was a guarantee against the shit-storm he knew was gathering on the horizon.

"Can we get restaurant food?" Griffin piped up from his booster seat in back, behind the cruiser's sliding metal grill. He and Fletcher liked to pretend they were bad guys, being hauled off to the hoosegow—Boone hoped it was a phase.

"Scamp's with us," Boone reminded his son. "No dogs allowed inside the Butter Biscuit Café." A pause. "Guess we could leave him in the car while we went inside and chowed down, but it's pretty hot out, and if we leave a window open, he might head for the hills."

Scamp, riding shotgun as usual, looked at him askance, as though indignant at the suggestion that he might bolt. Since Zeb's funeral, he'd settled into his new family with an air of resigned relief.

"We could get burgers and fries at the drive-through," Fletcher put in. Though Boone suspected the kid still entertained ideas of hitching back to Missoula to live with Molly and Bob again, he seemed more accepting of the current situation. Probably, he was just biding his time, convinced that this visit would end at some point, like all the others before it.

"That way Scamp wouldn't have to wait for us all alone," Griffin added. "And he could have a cheeseburger."

Boone smiled. "Good plan," he said, his voice a little gruff, and headed for the local fast-food joint. In defiance of modern trends, Bernie's Best Burgers had held its own against the franchises over in Three Trees. The establishment boasted a covered outdoor dining area, with metal picnic tables painted army-green sometime in the late sixties. A neon sign shaped like a curvy girl—at night, the electric flapper winked and jutted one hip in and out—went back even further in time.

He was only slightly taken aback to pull into the lot and find Tara and her stepdaughters already there, along with Lucy, the golden retriever.

The girls smiled and waved from their picnic table when they spotted Griffin and Fletcher, and Scamp got all excited, too, probably thrilled to have another stab at making friends with Lucy.

Tara's gaze locked with Boone's as he got out of the car, soon followed by the boys and the dog. She didn't look away, and neither did he, but nobody smiled or spoke, either.

Boone nodded an acknowledgment and walked over to the window to place an order, with a lot of input from Griffin and Fletcher.

When he was through—the food would be delivered by one of half a dozen teenagers hired for the summer—Boone turned, half expecting Tara to be gathering up trash, suddenly eager to hit the road, put some space between the two of them.

Instead, she gestured for him to sit down at her table.

The kids and the dogs had wandered over to explore what passed for a play area, Bernie's only nod to the franchises. That was where the old man drew the line, though—there were no low-cal/low-fat/low-carb choices on *his* menu. Everything came with a high fat content and plenty of refined carbohydrates—one memorable offering was a burger called the Big Butt Special, and more than a few longtime Parable residents could attest to the accuracy of the name.

Boone sat down across from Tara, at a loss for words—not an unusual occurrence for him, though this was different. *This* encounter, like all the ones before it, was charged.

Tara, apparently, suffered from no such inhibition. She leveled those too-blue, gold-flecked eyes of hers at him and asked, straight out, "Is it just me, or is something happening between us, Boone Taylor?"

Boone was used to direct questions—hell, he was direct to the point of bluntness himself under normal circumstances—but Tara's words knocked him back on his figurative heels for a moment. Feeling like seven kinds of idiot because his ears and neck were suddenly burning—he might have been fourteen and all feet instead of a grown man—he cleared his throat. Cleared it again.

Tara simply waited and watched him. She did not look at all happy with the conclusion she'd drawn.

"I think maybe you're right," he finally said. Then, awkwardly, he hastened to add, "Not that it's love or anything."

She smiled first, and then she laughed, though not unkindly. Checked to make sure all four kids were still out of earshot and lowered her voice to a near whisper just in case. "Nobody said anything about love," she informed him. "We have to put a stop to this, whatever it is. *Now.*"

Boone was warming to the subject. He rested his forearms on the surface of the picnic table and leaned in a little. "Why?"

"Because it could never work," Tara said tautly.

"What if it's just a simple case of lust?" he suggested mildly.

To his satisfaction, she blushed a peachy pink. Was it an all-over kind of thing, or confined to her face?

"Of course it isn't *lust,*" she blustered out.

He chuckled. Let her simmer in the idea for a few moments.

It didn't seem possible, but Tara's color actually heightened. Her eyes widened and flashed. "It *isn't,*" she insisted. She was even more beautiful when she was royally pissed off. "Just because you're drop-dead gorgeous, *Sheriff* Taylor, and women probably throw themselves at you day and night, don't go thinking *I'm* like that, because I'm not!"

Boone arched an eyebrow, felt a strange, quickening sensation somewhere in his core. *Drop-dead gorgeous? Him?* He'd have said he was presentable enough in the looks department if somebody dragged the admission out of him with a team of wild horses, but he was just a guy.

And it wasn't as if women "threw" themselves at him, day *or* night. But the fact that *Tara* thought they did came as a pleasant surprise.

He merely shook his head, confounded.

"Passably handsome, perhaps," she clarified, embarrassed.

Boone's food came then, and that brought the kids and the dogs back from the so-called playground.

"We should probably be leaving," Tara announced, with a sort of fretful reluctance that only served to deepen Boone's intrigue.

Elle and Erin busily cleared the table, said goodbye to Griffin and Fletcher and, by extension, Boone, and went off to load the retriever into Tara's spiffy SUV.

Griffin and Fletcher were busy unwrapping hamburgers from greasy paper, dividing the spoils and making promises to a very attentive Scamp, so they barely managed a response to the twins' farewell. Tara and Boone were completely off the radar—which was fine with Boone.

He shifted awkwardly from one foot to the other.

"Casey's benefit concert is next weekend," he said, "out at the fairgrounds." Never mind that everybody in three counties knew that—the show had sold out so quickly that there was talk of a second performance over at Three Trees. "Want to go? With me, I mean?"

Smooth, Boone mocked himself silently.

Tara blinked. "What about the children?" she ventured, whispering again.

Boone had planned on taking the munchkin contingent along, but now, unbelievably, he was picking up some very different—and very interesting—signals from Tara. Was it even *remotely* possible that the lady had a whole other kind of evening in mind? Okay, maybe she wasn't thinking sex—Boone could barely think of anything *but* sex, now that they'd broken the proverbial ice—but some adult conversation might be a welcome prospect, maybe even a quiet dinner before the main concert and, what the hell, a little dancing afterward, since most everybody was bound to wind up over at the Boot Scoot Tavern once Casey took her final bow, too. They'd be too wound up by the fun and the music to head straight home.

Just imagining the scenario made Boone's nerves twitch under his hide. The last time he'd gone on a real date, he'd been taking Corrie to their high school prom. Pathetic.

"What about the children?" he countered at long last, wanting the ball to land in her court. She'd been the one to bring up the subject of kids, after all.

Tara bit her lower lip, and the move, though unconscious and completely ordinary, stirred Boone's blood, sent it buzzing through his veins. Damned if he didn't want to haul off and kiss the woman right there beside Bernie's Best Burgers, in broad daylight, where half the town would be sure to see.

"Casey's putting on a special early show at her place, for the kids, I mean. Afterward, there will be games and prizes and clowns and stuff, and then there's a campout in her backyard—with plenty of supervision, of course."

Tara paused, dragged in an audible breath, and Boone wondered, with some amusement, if she was wishing she hadn't brought up their attraction in the first place. "Elle and Erin have their hearts set on going—Casey has a son and daughter close to their age—and there will be a lot of little ones there, too, so . . ." Her words trailed off into a flummoxed silence.

God bless Casey Elder, Boone thought. Not only was she raising a serious chunk of money for the McCullough family, she was offering the local adults a chance to whoop it up for one night, babysitting provided.

"They'll want to be there, all right," Boone said with a glance at his boys, who continued to gobble up their food, oblivious to the grown-ups but sharing liberally with Scamp, while Boone's own meal grew cold in its leaky paper holder—not that he gave a damn.

He was going out with Tara Kendall, and Saturday night couldn't come soon enough to suit him.

"Then I guess it's decided," Tara said with great dignity, the breeze making a tendril of her dark brown hair dance against her cheek.

"I guess so," Boone replied, with a grin.

After favoring him with a pointed glare, Tara said a warm goodbye to the boys and Scamp, walked over to her SUV, where the twins were already waiting, and climbed behind the wheel. She looked back at Boone once, her face a study in annoyed bewilderment, and gave a halfhearted wave.

You started it, lady, Boone thought. He responded with a crooked grin and a motion of his right hand that was part casual salute and part "so long."

Tara drove away.

"Yes!" he said, under his breath, before turning back to the boys, the table, the burger awaiting him in a puddle of sauce and melted lard.

Griffin and Fletcher looked up at him, curious and munching away, but neither one of them spoke.

Boone sat down, picked up his burger and ate with rare appetite.

* * *

"Am I out of my mind?" Tara asked Joslyn over the phone an hour later, her tone plaintive. Before her friend could offer an opinion, one way or the other, she rushed right on. "What possessed me? *Boone Taylor,* for pity's sake—I have exactly *nothing* in common with the man!"

Joslyn chuckled. "Apparently you're both Casey Elder fans," she teased. "That's something."

Tara, alone on the back porch, looked down at her faded overalls, ragbag T-shirt and work boots, which, no matter how often she hosed them down, were speckled with chicken manure. "Who *isn't* a Casey Elder fan?" she all but snapped. "Joslyn, I'm *serious* here. I think I've taken leave of my senses—"

"Or you're just a red-blooded woman in need of a good time," Joslyn put in. Her voice took on a note of benign slyness—by "good time," she didn't mean a movie date, with shared popcorn and hand-holding. "Know what I think, my friend? *I* think Boone scares you half to death, that's what. He is, after all, one hot cowboy-sheriff. As long as the two of you were sparring over chickens and yard upkeep, you felt safe enough. But now that he's turning up the fire, you're terrified."

"Next," Tara whispered, "you're going to say that's how it was with you and Slade—that you could barely stand each other at first but boy-howdy, look at you now!"

Joslyn laughed again. "You know it's the truth," she said. "And remember how Hutch and Kendra butted heads every time they happened to cross paths? It's called *passion,* Tara."

"Passion!" Tara practically spat the word, glancing anxiously toward Elle and Erin. With some "help" from Lucy, they were busy feeding the chickens. "Sometimes, things are just exactly what they *seem,* you know. Boone and I took an instant and completely mutual dislike to one another on sight!"

"Then why didn't you just say no when the man asked you out?" Joslyn asked, pretending to be confused.

Tara felt her shoulders slump a little. "I don't know," she admitted.

"Well, I do," Joslyn replied with confidence. "You've been alone and lonely for too long, and so has Boone, and the sexual tension has reached critical mass." Another pause. "The tipping point, you might say."

"There will be absolutely *no* tipping!" Tara burst out.

That only made Joslyn giggle again. Then, recovered, she went on to say, "*You* called *me,* remember? What did you think I'd tell you, Tara? That, oh, horrors, you'd made a terrible mistake and ought to call off the whole thing?"

Tara was at a loss. "I don't know," she repeated miserably.

"I'm going to make a rash suggestion here," Joslyn warned, full of mischievous cheer. Five seconds after they eventually hung up, Tara suspected, Joslyn'd be on the phone to Kendra, the two of them tee-heeing like crazy.

"What?" Tara hardly dared to ask. She was clenching her cell so tightly that her fingers began to ache.

"Stop making such a big deal out of this," Joslyn counseled reasonably. "Go out with Boone, have some fun and see what develops. Just don't write a script in your head based on what you went through with James, because Boone is an entirely different kind of person and, anyway, you can't possibly *know* how things will shake out."

"I'm scared," Tara said, after a long and difficult silence.

Joslyn replied gently. "Don't be," she said. "This is a *date,* Tara—not a life sentence with no possibility of parole. Let go and *enjoy the evening.*"

"But—"

"You're still scared," Joslyn supplied with understanding. "That's okay, Tara—Boone probably is, too. He's no monk, but as far as I know, he hasn't asked a woman out on an actual date since before he and Corrie were married. This is big."

Tara did not want to deal with "big," or the concept of a dead wife, either. "Were you scared when you and Slade first got together?"

"No," Joslyn said. "I was *terrified,* and so was Slade, though he probably wouldn't have admitted as much."

Tara got a little of her sass back. "It isn't helping, you know," she said, flustered, "the way you keep drawing parallels between you and Slade and Boone and me. This isn't the same thing at all."

"If you say so," Joslyn answered, practically singing the words. When she went on, she was her usual reassuringly affable self. "Let's get together for lunch this week—you and Kendra and me, and Casey, too, if she can make it. Have ourselves some girl-time."

"Sounds good," Tara said, because it did. Of all the friends she'd made in her life, Joslyn and Kendra were two of the best, and Casey was fast becoming a part of the group. "Do you think Kendra's up for going out? It's pretty soon, after all."

"Are you kidding me?" Joslyn retorted happily. "She's one of those insufferable women who can give birth in the morning and go bungee jumping in the afternoon."

This time it was Tara who laughed, and the sudden release of so much tension left her a little dizzy. On this note, she and Joslyn ended the call.

The girls had finished feeding the chickens and were moving toward her, smiling tiredly, a pair of city kids rapidly going country, faces dirt-streaked, clothes in dire need of washing.

Neither of them had said a single word about James and Bethany's wedding, to which they were clearly not invited, nor about James himself. Their silence on the subject of this momentous change in their lives troubled Tara, hard as she tried not to worry so much. She would have felt better if they'd cried, or flown into a fit of temper and spouted fury. At least then she could have comforted them.

Her dizziness subsided, she stood, watching her girls.

As it was, she had to guess at what they were thinking and feeling, sensing as she did that asking them outright, for the moment at least, would be tantamount to poking at a fresh wound.

So she would wait and watch for an opening in their combined shells, and trust that things would work out okay in the long run, though she was afraid to engage too deeply or too often in certain hopes—that James would let the twins stay with her and attend classes in Parable this year, for instance, instead of insisting on boarding school.

But James was anything but predictable—he might be so wrapped up in his new marriage that he didn't want to be bothered with a pair of preteen girls at all. Leaving them with Tara would be an easy out—write a few checks, send a few superficial emails or texts, parent his children from a comfortable distance.

On the other hand, as image-conscious as he was, James might want to play the part of devoted husband and father, the professional man who had it all, fabulous career, loving family. Not that the charade would keep him from sending Elle and Erin away to some expensive and august learning establishment, because his personal convenience was even more important to James than outward appearances were, but he'd manage to come off looking like Dr. Wonderful just the same.

He was handsome, he was rich, he was confident. So what if he was an inch deep, all reflection and no substance?

Unlike Boone Taylor, a complicated man full of mysteries.

"You look sad," Erin commented when she and Elle reached the place where Tara stood, lost in thought.

She summoned up a determined smile. "I was just thinking hard," she said, and though the statement was deceptive, it wasn't exactly a lie. "That's all."

Just then, laughter floated from across the slice of river between her place and Boone's, and something leaped inside her. She turned to see Boone and his boys standing on the opposite bank, brandishing fishing poles.

"Do you think Mr. Taylor would let us try to catch a fish?" Erin asked, her tone as wistful as her gaze. They were on the outs with James, temporarily, Tara hoped, but in that moment both her stepdaughters showed distinct signs of daddy-envy.

Tara hesitated, watching Boone with his young sons, and smiled. She doubted that either twin would make it past baiting the hook, but maybe she was wrong.

"There's only one way to find out," she said. "Ask him."

With that, both Elle and Erin were off, running toward the gleaming strand of water, Lucy galloping tirelessly behind them.

Tara followed, at a much more sedate pace, nervous about another encounter with Boone after their conversation at Bernie's, but refusing to give in to cowardice by hanging back.

Boone looked up and saw her approaching, and he grinned a slow, sexy grin as he handed off his fishing pole to Elle, who was first on the scene. Showing all the symptoms of a little-boy crush, Griffin offered his fishing rod to Erin and began instructing her in the fine art of casting and reeling in.

Tara crossed the board bridge carefully, her arms folded against the slight chill of the evening, and Boone waited for her on the other side.

"I hope we're not intruding," she said.

Boone shook his head from side to side, just once, watching her with an unreadable expression in his eyes. His dog, Scamp, frolicked at his side, while

Lucy stayed with the children, as if afraid they'd fall in and drown if she wasn't vigilant.

When the girls finally went back to New York, Tara reflected, with a pang, poor Lucy would be lost.

Elle squealed suddenly, and both Boone and Tara turned to see her holding the fishing pole high, a shimmering catch at the end of the line. Boone walked over, deftly freed the fish and tossed it back in the river.

Elle and Erin both gazed at him in adoration. They were in the market for a hero, and it looked as though Boone Taylor was elected.

"We always throw them back," Griffin explained importantly.

Tara looked at Boone, mildly surprised. She wouldn't have pegged him for the sensitive type, at least where catching fish was concerned.

"Why catch them in the first place?" Erin asked, puzzled.

Good question, Tara thought.

"Because it's fun," Griffin told Erin, with exaggerated patience.

"Oh," Erin replied, and handed her

pole back to Fletcher. Evidently, her fascination with the sporting life was short-lived. Elle, on the other hand, wanted to try again.

Soon, Griffin, Fletcher and Elle, along with both dogs, formed a busy little huddle on the bank, while Erin sat nearby in the grass, her arms around her upraised knees, her head tilted back so the last dazzle of sunlight warmed her face.

Easily, Boone took Tara's hand, led her a little ways back from the water, and the two of them sat down on an old log, keeping an eye on the kids.

Tara didn't exactly pull her hand free of Boone's after they were seated, but she definitely withdrew it.

"Tell me about before," Boone said presently.

She knew he wasn't asking about her career, or what it was like growing up in a place like New York City. He was asking about her life with James. The remarkable thing was, she didn't mind answering.

She bunched her shoulders, then unbunched them again, with a sigh and a flicker of a smile, because the kids and the dogs were having such a good time, laughing and chattering and trying to catch fish. "It's not a very interesting story, really," she said, conscious of Boone close beside her, aware of his solid strength and the peaceful set of his broad shoulders. They weren't *quite* touching, but it was almost as good, for Tara, at least. "I was in love with a dashing young doctor, and the dashing young doctor was madly in love with himself, and there was no winning him over, though God knows, I tried." She sighed again, interlaced her fingers in her lap, deliberately relaxed them. "I knew it wasn't going to work, but I just couldn't seem to give up," she added after a few moments, her gaze resting on the twin reasons for staying with James as long as she had.

"They're great kids," Boone said.

Tara nodded. "I wish they were mine," she said.

"They seem to think of you as their mom. You're good with them, Tara." There was something faintly sad about Boone's remark.

"Thanks," Tara said, turning her head at last, taking in his profile.

Joslyn was right on all counts, she concluded. Boone Taylor was one hot cowboy-sheriff, and she was scared to death of him.

Why? Because if she wasn't very, very careful, she could care about him, care deeply and, yes, passionately. Ever since the divorce from James she'd managed to convince herself that her safe and peaceful life, with her fractured heart thickly swathed in pride and independence, was enough.

But it wasn't. The thing was, just the thought of loving again felt so risky that it almost took her breath away.

"What was Corrie like?" she asked gently, after a long but not uncomfortable silence had unfolded itself between them. "I mean, I know the surface details, that she was really pretty and everyone liked her and then she got terribly sick, but that isn't the same as knowing *her.*"

Boone didn't speak for so long that Tara thought he was going to get up and walk away from her without a word, rejoin the kids on the riverbank, pretend they hadn't had this conversation at all.

Then, gravely, he replied, "She was funny, full of life, always up for whatever came next. We had our share of dust-ups, there's no denying that—Corrie tended to throw things at me when she was mad and I could go three days without talking to her, knowing full well that it drove her crazy—but we were still, well, *partners.* We were both in for the long haul, right from day one. Giving up wasn't an option."

Tara smiled softly. She'd wanted, even *expected* to have that kind of forever-relationship with James, but, looking back, she could see that there'd never been any chance of that. James had loved himself, but she'd been no better, really, because she'd loved the *idea* of him, the potential he never quite reached, the husband and father he could have been but never was.

She'd loved Elle and Erin, a pair of cherubic, motherless toddlers, from the very beginning, though. Now, she realized how perilously easy it would be to take Griffin and Fletcher into her heart the same way, accepting their father as part of the deal. She was on dangerous ground, she decided.

Very dangerous ground.

CHAPTER TWELVE

When the mosquitoes came out and sunset was spilling purple shadows over the horizons on all sides, Boone rose from the rough-barked log near the water, where he'd been sitting beside Tara for much too long—and not nearly long enough—and held out his hand to her for the second time that evening.

She didn't need his help standing up, of course, but there was still such a thing as common courtesy, and Boone had been well schooled in that, first by his mother and then by his older sister, who had appointed herself Mama-Two, the sequel.

When Tara hesitated, then slowly placed her palm on his, he was quietly pleased—pleased and scared shitless, like somebody trapped on a carnival ride with a maniac at the controls.

"Time to call it a day," Boone told his kids, who were swatting at bug bites and starting to bicker, a sure sign that they were tired and probably hungry, to boot. They'd need supper, a bath and bedtime prayers, in that order.

Tara backed him up, over a chorus of protesting groans from all four of the children. "Thanks for letting Elle and Erin try their hand at fishing," she said. She'd softened toward him, Boone could tell that, but she seemed a little wary, too. Like she'd enjoyed their time together but still couldn't get away quickly enough.

Boone could relate to the dilemma. The urge to kiss her was overwhelming, and if the twins and his boys hadn't been there, he probably would have given in to the temptation. Inside, he was still reeling, out of control, roller-coaster-run-amok stuff.

"You're welcome," he finally found the presence of mind to reply. Then, in a gruff and hasty undertone, he added, with an abruptness that made the tops of his ears burn, "Remember, a deal's a deal."

Tara looked up at him, frowning slightly, making him want to touch the tip of an index finger to the little crease in her brow, smooth it away. "I beg your pardon?" she asked, with a note of caution in her voice.

Boone sighed, frustrated with himself. He'd never had a way with women, like his friends Hutch Carmody and Slade Barlow did, never learned how to flirt or make small talk because he and Corrie had both been so young when they had hooked up, and being together had always been enough. "I was just thinking you might back out—of going to the concert with me, I mean."

Amusement brightened her eyes and her highly kissable mouth crooked up at one side. "I'm a woman of my word, Boone Taylor," she said. Then she frowned again, as some wayward thought had just struck her like a tiny meteor. “Won’t you have to work the night of the concert, though? You *are* the sheriff, after all, and a chance to hear Casey sing is bound to attract people from all over Montana, if not Idaho and Washington, too. What about crowd control and all that?”

Boone realized he’d clamped his back teeth together and deliberately relaxed his jaws. The truth was, he’d forgotten all about his job, all about everything except the way this woman looked and smelled and how her hand felt in his.

He was up for a lot more touching.

“I’ll figure something out,” he said. *If it kills me.*

The kids had gathered the fishing poles into a tepee formation by then, and even the dogs looked worn-out, tongues lolling, heads and tails drooping.

Tara simply nodded, as though satisfied with Boone’s answer, and after that, the two families went their separate ways, Tara and the twins and the golden retriever walking back toward her place, and Boone, his sons and Scamp back to the double-wide.

Walking toward it in the twilight, Boone couldn't help noticing how much his home looked like a big metal box, left out in the weather for too long. It almost seemed to be hunkered down in the deep grass, settling into the earth, like it was trying to dissolve itself, atom by rusted-over atom.

He wanted to look back, watch Tara and her crew until they were safely across the spit of river and climbing the slope toward the farmhouse, but some instinct prevented him from doing so. If there was trouble, he reasoned, one if not all three of the females would probably let out a holler to alert him.

They didn't.

"Are you and Ms. Kendall going out on a date?" Griffin asked bluntly, a full hour after Boone had fed them a boxed mac-and-cheese supper with cut-up wieners added for protein, overseen their nightly bath and finally tucked them into bed.

Boone rubbed his chin, feeling the stubble of a late-day beard and wondering if he'd looked seedy to Tara, down there by the river. "Now why would you ask a question like that?" he stalled.

"You held her hand," Fletcher put in with alacrity.

"And both of you sat real close together on that log," Griffin elaborated.

"I like her," Boone finally admitted. He had to give them something, after all, or they'd just keep on pestering him till the cows came home. Which would be a long time, given that he didn't *own* any cattle.

Griffin smiled broadly, pleased. More surprisingly, so did Fletcher.

"She's nice," said the younger boy.

"And pretty," said Griffin.

"Is this conversation going anywhere in particular?" Boone asked with a tired grin. "Or are you two just trying to get out of saying your prayers and going to sleep?"

"We're just saying," Griffin told him airily. Boone wondered if they'd discussed the Dad-Tara situation between themselves, and if so, what they'd said.

Suddenly, as if on cue, both boys

clasped together their hands and tightly squeezed their eyes shut. Prayer time.

"Thank You, God, for the fun we had fishing with our dad," Fletcher said earnestly. "And for letting Scamp come to live with us."

Boone's throat tightened a little.

"And please give us a new mom," Griffin requested. "Our old one is up there with You, but I guess You know that already. Ms. Kendall would be perfect for the job, because she has a nice house and lots of chickens and she makes good cookies."

Boone squeezed the bridge of his nose between a thumb and forefinger and closed his eyes for a moment. Not only did the kids want a mom—he hadn't had a clue—but they'd already picked her out. And he hadn't missed the "nice house" reference, either.

He waited for the amens to ring out before he cleared his throat and said carefully, "You might be putting the cart before the horse when it comes to signing Tara—Ms. Kendall—on for mom-duty."

"Aunt Molly says God likes to hear

about stuff we want," Griffin said, unfazed.

"And we want a mommy," Fletcher chirped. A pause. "Aunt Molly's *like* a mom, but she's not *our* mom. We have to share her with our cousins and, anyway, she's in Missoula and that's far."

Kids, Boone thought, as winded as if the business end of a ramrod had just barreled into his solar plexus. *They can land a sucker punch without lifting a hand.* "You won't be going back to Missoula," Boone told his children kindly, but in a matter-of-fact tone of voice, "except for visits every now and again. And that won't be for a while, because your uncle needs some serious mending time."

"We're going to live here now," Griffin observed, and, though it was a statement, there was a question underlying his words.

"Yes," Boone said. He wasn't sure exactly when he'd made the decision—he'd waffled a lot, inside his head—but he knew it was final. "I'm your dad, and you're my sons, and we belong together."

The dog jumped up onto the bed just then and snuggled in beside Fletcher, who closed his eyes without another word. Just that quick, exhaustion caught up with the little guy and pulled him under.

Mildly surprised that his youngest hadn't raised hell about staying in Parable for good, Boone winked at Griffin, who was watching him with a broad grin and big, hopeful eyes.

"I love you, Dad," he said.

The announcement nearly brought Boone to his knees.

He bent over the bed, kissed his son's freckled forehead, and replied hoarsely, "I love you, too, buddy. Sleep tight."

After shutting out the light, Boone walked quietly down the corridor toward the kitchen, aching with emotions he'd managed to keep under wraps for a long, long time.

He felt restless, happy and terrified at the same time, and the double-wide seemed too small to contain him, so he stepped outside, under a giant yellow moon, and surveyed the familiar landscape with new eyes.

He ached, and yet he wanted to shout for joy, too.

He strode the several dozen yards to the site where he and Corrie had planned to build their house. The stakes, marking off corners and future rooms, were still there, though almost swallowed up by time and grass and shifting dirt.

Boone paced off the living room, the kitchen, the master bedroom, the dining area, the rooms where the boys would sleep, the spaces meant for other children, expected later.

He stood in the center of the invisible house, tilted his head back, and looked up at the star-spattered sky. His throat seized again, painfully, and he had to blink a couple times to keep his eyeballs dry.

"Corrie," he said in a gravelly whisper, when he finally managed to find his voice and put some breath behind it, "I loved you as much as any man ever loved a woman or ever will, but I'm still here and you're gone, and, well, the hard truth is, I'm lonesome as all get-out." He stopped again, choked up, then went doggedly on. "The boys are asking for a mother—maybe you heard them tonight, I don't know. I'm not sure who they'll wind up with, but I guess I ought to start looking for somebody, for their sake as well as my own. Just know this, sweetheart—we're not meaning to replace you. That would be downright impossible. I'll make sure our sons remember you, always, and you'll always be their mother, no matter what. It's just that—" He hesitated as his voice broke again, like an engine throwing a rod, and he finished what he wanted to say in his mind instead of aloud. *I'll always love you, Corrie. But I'm ready to love someone else—I* need *to love someone else—and I guess I'm asking you to understand.*

Boone was quiet for a long time after that, just standing there, not expecting an answer or anything, just imagining the house into existence, building it, board by board, wall by wall, in his head. He could almost smell the drywall and the sawdust, hear the buzz of electric saws and the rhythmic tattoo of hammers pounding nails into good Montana timber.

Yep, he was definitely alive, and it was wonderful, a jubilation that almost took his breath away.

But it hurt like hell, too.

"You like Sheriff Taylor," Erin said, when she and Elle and Lucy were all back inside the farmhouse.

Had there been a note of accusation in her voice?

Tara smiled, feeling strangely jangled *and* mellow. "Boone's nice enough," she said lightly. An understatement for sure, and quite a shift, considering that she'd disliked Boone intensely almost from the moment they had met, many moons ago, at the glamorous backyard party Kendra, as her real estate agent, had thrown in Tara's honor after she'd finally made a firm offer on the chicken ranch and signed on all the dotted lines.

A glance at Elle showed that she was, one, scratching mosquito bites garnered on the fishing expedition and, two, scowling with disapproval and hurt. Angry tears glinted in her eyes. "He's all wrong for you," she said. "If you marry him, you'll *never* come back to live in New York."

Tara was jarred, though she tried not to show it. Obviously, the child was upset enough. So she put both hands up, palms out, and said, "Whoa. Who said anything about marriage?"

Lucy gave a worried little whimper and plopped down on her haunches, an uneasy witness to the small drama.

"Adults *never* say anything about marriage," Erin retorted, nudging up her glasses with one finger. The lenses were smudged, and she had grass in her hair, Tara noted, with distracted affection. "They just go right ahead and have a wedding and everybody else just has to deal with it!"

This outburst was, of course, about James and Bethany, Tara realized, not so much herself and Boone. "Some adults do that," she conceded gently, silently willing James to develop male-pattern baldness and two left feet on the racquetball court. "But I'd definitely talk to you two before I said 'I do' to anybody. You have my word on that."

Erin sniffled.

Elle dashed at her grubby cheeks with the back of one hand.

There was a short silence during which Tara began to hope that the storm had blown over as quickly as it had arisen.

No such luck.

"You *like* the sheriff," Elle insisted, though with less bluster than before. "You were just *pretending* to think he was a jerk."

Tara had to grin at that, even though her heart felt bruised. "No," she said, moving to make herself a cup of much-needed herbal tea, "I wasn't pretending. I really, one hundred percent, believed Boone Taylor was a jerk."

Out of the corner of her eye, she saw Erin's knuckles whiten as she gripped the back of one of the chairs at the table. "But now?" the girl asked.

"Sometimes we make judgments about people before we really know them," Tara said, her tone mild, but with a distinct tremor. She certainly wasn't afraid of Elle and Erin—and how she lived her life wasn't their call, though she was willing to allow them some input. No, the small quaver in her voice had more to do with her growing attraction to Boone than anything else.

This development still came as a shock, and she hadn't *begun* to make sense of it. *Boone?* Good heavens, even his *name* was redneck.

"If you came back to New York," Erin said, more moderately now, "Dad might see what a mistake it would be to marry Bethany. He might figure out that it's really you he loves, and then we'd all be together again, like before."

Tara froze. Her movements were awkward, almost wooden, as she set her teacup on the counter to avoid spilling the contents, and turned to face her stepdaughters.

"Honey," she said gently, brokenly, addressing not just Erin, but Elle, too, "your dad and I aren't going to get back together, ever. It's really and truly over—he *doesn't* love me and I don't love him. I thought you understood that."

Both girls looked crestfallen.

Of *course* they hadn't understood, Tara thought with a stab of sorrow. They were *children,* carrying vestiges of magic and fairy tales in their hearts, and *hope,* which not only came naturally to them, like breathing, it died hard.

Tara crossed to them, gathered both girls to her, one in the curve of each arm, and held them. They buried wet faces in either side of her neck, and Erin's slender body trembled with silent sobs.

"Shhh," Tara whispered, kissing the crown of one blond head, then the other, fighting back tears of her own. After all, she was the grown-up here, and *somebody* had to hold it together. "I know it's hard right now, because everything is changing, but, trust me, you're both going to be all right. *Better* than all right. You're growing up into smart, beautiful women before my very eyes. You'll be happy, I promise, if you'll only trust that there's a plan."

Trust that there's a plan. Maybe, Tara thought, she ought to follow her own advice. Simply let life unfold, without any pushing and plotting on her part.

What a concept.

Tara managed a wobbly smile.

"The *plan,*" Erin all but wailed, "is for

Dad to marry Bethany and for Elle and me to rot away in some stupid, swanky *boarding school* until we're old enough for college! That way, he doesn't have to be bothered with us—"

"Hey," Tara protested, squeezing them both again. "Have a little faith, will you?"

More good advice. *Are you listening to yourself, Tara Kendall?*

Elle pushed back slightly, not quite pulling free of Tara's embrace, but stiffening as she looked up at her. Her cheeks, like Erin's, were awash with tears. "Faith?" she echoed, and there was a stubborn set to her chin while her eyes flashed. "We prayed every night for a year that you and Dad would get back together, that you'd come home and we could all be a family again and—and now look what's happening!"

Tara kissed the girl's forehead. No matter how many children she might be blessed with in the future, she knew she would never love any of them more than she did these two. Elle and Erin were a part of her, joined to her soul as well as her heart, the ties unbreakable.

"Things don't always turn out the way we want them to, obviously," she replied carefully, when she'd recovered a bit. "But that doesn't mean your prayers weren't answered." She smiled another wobbly smile. "You've heard that old Garth Brooks song, haven't you? The one about unanswered prayers?"

"Garth who?" Erin asked, plainly baffled.

Tara laughed, a ragged sound. "Never mind," she said. "The point is, we don't always know what's best for us, or for the people we love. We have to trust that Someone Else does."

The twins looked skeptical, each of their faces a near perfect reflection of the other's, but they were calming down a little. Even Lucy sensed the change in the atmosphere, leaping up to lick Erin's cheeks and then Elle's in a burst of dog-relief.

"Dad says there's no such thing as God," Erin announced, a few moments later. She scratched at a row of pink mosquito bites on her right arm. "He says people *invented* God because they were scared of being all alone in a big universe."

"He's entitled to his opinion," Tara said diplomatically. "Suffice it to say, there are lots of us who disagree. Like Opal, for instance."

"You believe in God?" Elle asked tentatively.

"You know I do," Tara assured her. "Remember how we went to Sunday school every week, at Marble Collegiate Church?"

"Sunday school is a social form, that's all," Erin said, obviously parroting James again. "People think it makes them look good."

"Maybe," Tara allowed, "and maybe not." She drew a deep breath, let it out slowly. "Now," she went on, "let me make you some sandwiches—you missed dinner, in case you've forgotten—and then you can take your showers, put some lotion on those mosquito bites—stop scratching, please—and turn in for the night. Tomorrow's another day."

Thank you, Scarlett O'Hara, commented a wry voice in the back of Tara's brain.

She'd expected some resistance, even open rebellion, but the twins simply nodded, went to the kitchen sink, washed their hands and splashed their faces, coming away with spiky lashes and pink cheeks.

They took their places at the table and Tara poured glasses of milk for them and whipped up a trio of grilled cheese sandwiches in a hurry.

The three of them ate in companionable silence—a relief to Tara, who was fresh out of inspiration—and afterward, while the girls cleared the table and loaded the dishwasher, Tara went outside with Lucy, waited on her, and then filled the dog's bowl with kibble when they were back inside.

Lucy ate heartily, like any self-respecting dog, and when the twins trooped upstairs, yawning and bantering about plans for the next day, the golden retriever brought up the rear.

Tara moved through the house, shutting off lights as she went, making sure doors were locked, pausing just briefly at one downstairs window to look toward Boone's place.

Without meaning to, she kissed the fingertips of her right hand and pressed them lightly against the glass before turning away.

"It's a hen party," Hutch Carmody explained bright and early the next morning, while he and Boone and Slade Barlow each tied into a breakfast special at the Butter Biscuit Café.

"Makes me nervous when women get together like that," Slade commented drily with a twinkle in his eyes. The planned gathering over at Casey Elder's place for lunch was evidently a "no men allowed" kind of thing. Kendra, Joslyn and Tara were all going, though Boone wouldn't have known that if his friends hadn't told him. It wasn't as if he was in the loop where Tara's social life was concerned.

"I need some deputies," Boone blurted out. "For the night of Casey's benefit concert, I mean."

Slade and Hutch exchanged amused glances.

Slade buttered another piece of toast, while Hutch took his sweet time savoring a sip of lukewarm coffee.

Boone felt himself reddening from the neck up, and his ears started to burn. "What?" he snapped, looking from Slade to Hutch and back again.

"It seems our friend here has a hot date for Saturday night," Slade finally commented, grinning across the table at Hutch.

"About time," Hutch drawled.

Boone loved living in Parable—it was home, pure and simple—but there were moments when he wished gossip didn't get around so fast.

Tara must have told Joslyn and/or Kendra that Boone had asked her out, and by now, everybody in the county was probably in the know.

"It's no big deal," Boone practically growled.

"Are you kidding me?" Hutch retorted, mischief dancing in his eyes. "This is *news.* Sheriff Boone Taylor climbs out of the coffin and rejoins the living. If this town still had a newspaper, that's what today's headline would read."

Boone felt steam building inside his ears, fit to shoot out and scald somebody.

Slade reached over and slapped him lightly on the back. “Take it easy, old buddy,” he said. “If Hutch and I josh you a little, it’s only because we’re happy for you.”

“Damn straight,” Hutch agreed. “You’ve been alone way too long.”

Boone, embarrassed but not angry, simmered down a bit. “You make it sound like Tara and I are planning to elope to Las Vegas or something,” he muttered, disgruntled. “I asked the lady to a concert, that’s all. But I’m still going to need somebody to cover for me that night.”

“I’d be glad to help out,” Slade said. A former sheriff himself, he had the know-how and the experience. “Maybe Three Trees will lend us a few officers—Casey’s planning a second concert in their fine community in a week or so, and you could return the favor by sending some of your people over.”

Hutch grinned. “I’d volunteer,” he said, “but I’m an outlaw now. That water tower incident has ruined my sterling reputation. I barely escaped arrest."

Boone almost choked on a sip of coffee. "Your 'sterling reputation'?" he countered, with a raspy chuckle. "In what universe do you have one of those?"

Hutch looked hurt, though it was all pretense, of course. He'd always been a rascal and a rounder, even prided himself on it, a born rebel, with or without a cause. Why, before Kendra came back into his life and loved off some of the rough edges, Hutch had been a wild man.

"And what's this 'now' crap?" Slade wanted to know, echoing Boone's silent observation on the matter. "You've been an outlaw for as long as any of us can remember."

Hutch shook his head slowly from side to side, as though disgusted. "When did *you two* turn into upstanding citizens?" he asked, holding back a grin. "You're not the only ones around here with a memory, you know. Slade, what about that time you let old man Darby's milk cows out, and we had to spend a whole day and a half rounding them up so Sheriff McQuillan wouldn't throw the whole bunch of us in the hoosegow?" He turned to Boone, his manner idle. "As for you, old pal, weren't you the one who used to pull up stop signs all over town, every Halloween night, without fail?"

"You should know," Boone said mildly, sitting back in his chair and folding his arms across his chest. "You were right there with me."

"Only because I'm a true friend," Hutch said, his expression downright angelic.

"Or because it was your idea in the first place," Slade put in. He and Hutch, half brothers though they were, hadn't been close in those days. Hutch's late father, John Carmody, had scandalized the whole county by siring Slade outside the bonds of holy matrimony, and they'd grown up brawling like Cain with a twin.

"Sheriff Wilkes McQuillan," Boone murmured, recalling the man they'd all both feared and admired. "Parable County's own John Wayne."

"Hard to believe Treat's any kin to him," Slade remarked. Deputy McQuillan hadn't been a favorite with him, either, back when he was wearing the sheriff's badge.

"I hear he's dating Nancy Winchell," interjected Susan, the waitress, suddenly appearing with a coffeepot and a speculative expression. "Treat McQuillan, I mean. She's been spiffing up her daddy's house all this time, and making all kind of noise about selling the place, but there's no For Sale sign in the front yard yet, I notice."

"Why, Susan," Hutch teased, mock-scolding the woman they'd all known forever, "not only are you a gossip, but an eavesdropper in the bargain."

"You shush," Susan told him, splashing a refill into his coffee cup. "Just because you've got a daughter now, that doesn't mean you can get all full of yourself."

"I have two daughters," Hutch pointed out, more serious than before. As far as Hutch was concerned, Madison was a full-fledged Carmody, and he wasn't shy about reminding people that he considered the little girl his child, period.

Susan paused to pat his shoulder fondly. "I know that, Hutch Carmody," she said, unruffled, "so just pull in your horns."

Hutch grinned. "Two daughters," he repeated good-naturedly. "Madison and Shannon."

"And more on the way, unless I miss my guess," Susan chattered. She filled Slade's cup and Boone's. She focused on him then. "Least Hutch and Slade are carrying on their family names. That's more than I can say for the sheriff, here."

Susan meant well, they knew that. She just lived to interfere, that was all. She mothered the whole damn town, and wasn't above nagging.

"Last time I checked," Boone retorted, "I had two sons. No doubt they'll both grow up and start making babies of their own, when the time is right."

Susan shook a finger at him. "You need a wife," she insisted. "And that's all I'm going to say on the subject!"

"Fat chance," Boone muttered, reaching for his coffee cup.

Susan sashayed away, giving other customers a good-natured ration of guff as she passed, headed back to the kitchen.

"She's right, of course," Hutch observed moderately.

"Yep," Slade agreed, favoring Boone with a lopsided grin as they all got out their wallets to divvy up the check and contribute to Susan's tip. "You definitely need a wife."

Even though Boone had already come to that conclusion himself, he didn't appreciate the reminder.

"You'll take over for me on concert night?" he asked, pushing back his chair and rising. "Joslyn won't mind?"

"She'll understand," Slade said. And what he *didn't* say registered just as clearly. Joslyn would probably have pinned on the sheriff's badge for concert night herself, if there was any chance of Tara and Boone getting together.

Boone nodded, not quite able to manage a thank-you, and left the restaurant, walking back to the courthouse, where he'd left his cruiser. Scamp had been holding down the office, along with Becky, the clerk/dispatcher who worked whenever her busy social schedule permitted.

Becky had worked for Slade and, before that, for Sheriff McQuillan. She took a lot of cruises, dyed her hair a different color every other week, and was almost as nosy as Susan over at the Butter Biscuit.

"The mayor's on his way over," she said the moment Boone stepped through the door and greeted his deputy-dog.

"Great," Boone replied grimly. "Did he say why?"

Becky shook her head. She was a redhead this time around, and her blue polyester pantsuit looked like it was struggling to contain her. "There's talk, though."

"Of course there's talk," Boone said. He walked to the coffeemaker, started to pour himself a mug of joe, and decided against it. He was nervous enough as it was. "Mind filling me in on some of the details?"

Becky never minded filling anybody in on anything. "My brother-in-law is on the town council," she said, in an oddly reverent tone, "and there was an emergency meeting last night, over at Mr. Hale's house. According to Dixie—that's my sister—"

"I know Dixie is your sister, Becky," Boone said, tight-jawed.

Becky prattled right on, as though he hadn't said anything, though she clearly disapproved of the interruption. *"According to Dixie,"* she repeated, "there are some big doings under way—"

Before she could finish, she was interrupted again, though this time it was the mayor's fault, not Boone's.

"It's time this town had its own police force," Hannibal Hale blustered, as he whooshed through the doorway. "And I've hired Treat McQuillan to head it up."

CHAPTER THIRTEEN

Since he knew the mayor's big news was meant to annoy him, Boone struggled hard not to grin, punch the air with one fist and yell, *YES!*

He'd been looking for an excuse to fire Treat McQuillan since the day he'd taken office, and now the matter had been taken out of his hands by the gods of municipal government. Of course, McQuillan might turn out to be a bigger pain in the ass as police chief than he'd ever been as a sheriff's deputy.

"Well," Boone drawled, finding it extra difficult to maintain his straight face and, for that reason, not daring to glance in Becky's direction, "I reckon that was bound to happen sooner or later. Is this going to be a one-man operation?"

Hale looked a mite let down at Boone's reaction, or lack thereof. The old man loved a good ruckus, which tended to make for some lively town council meetings. "We're starting out small," the mayor said, bending to pat Scamp on the head and thus proving that even cantankerous curmudgeons have some good in them.

"How small?" Boone asked mildly. McQuillan with no backup would be worse, in terms of law enforcement efficiency, than no Parable Police Department at all.

Hale forgot about the dog, nodded tersely to Becky, who was, after all, a voter, and replied, "I've given Treat leave to hire three men, all of them part-time, at least at the beginning." He paused to swell up a little, like a rooster smack in the middle of a flock of hens. "Unlike many communities—or even the U.S. government, I dare say—Parable's budget boasts a sizable surplus. Our first priority is to build a facility, and a committee will be duly appointed to oversee construction."

Boone hoped the mayor wasn't fixing to ask if the new police department could share his office and jail cells in the interim, for two reasons. First, it would suck, bumping shoulders with Treat McQuillan all day every day and, second, because this was the county courthouse, not the town hall. "You have a site picked out?" he asked, idly tapping a file folder against the palm of his left hand.

"We do," Hale replied, looking pride-swollen again. "Thanks to those damn vandals who tore down the water tower—and don't think I'm going to let that go, Boone, because I'm not—we're all set. Groundbreaking will be within a month."

"And in the meantime . . . ?" Boone ventured. Out of the corner of his eye, he saw Becky sitting up very straight in her office chair, ears practically perked forward, she was listening so carefully.

"Treat and the others can work out of my study until their own building is ready," Hale said. He paused and looked Boone straight in the eye, as if daring him to counter what he meant to say next. "In the event someone requires detainment, we've asked the county commissioner for permission to borrow one of your empty cells." Another pause. "They're empty most of the time, anyhow."

Boone's jaw tightened a little, for he knew what the old coot was implying: that there were all kinds of criminals running loose in Parable County, courtesy of the sheriff's department's—*his*—low arrest rate. He'd be a fool to take the bait, though, and since the mayor already had the county commissioner on his side, there was no real point in arguing.

It galled him, though, to know that McQuillan, that pompous ass, would soon be swaggering around town, flashing his badge and locking up everybody who jaywalked or spit on the sidewalk, and right here in his jail.

"Parable County has a *very* low crime rate," Becky put in snappishly, rising to Boone's defense. She was undependable and not all that efficient in her office skills, but at least she was loyal. "Thanks to Sheriff Boone Taylor and his deputies."

Boone made a mental note to send Becky flowers on Secretary's Day—whenever that was. His office assistant usually just skipped the middleman—Boone himself—and ordered her own bouquet at county expense.

"Of course I'll have to replace Deputy McQuillan," he said, all business. As if the local paperboy couldn't have done a better job than good ole Treat. "When can I post the employment notice on the county website?"

Boone hoped he hadn't sounded too eager; it would be just like Hannibal Hale to prolong McQuillan's hiring process just to spite his favorite adversary.

"I'm sure you'll want Deputy McQuillan to give at least two weeks' notice," Hale said. For the first time since he'd blown into Boone's office like a dust devil off the prairie, he didn't seem all that confident.

"I wouldn't want to hold up the process," Boone said generously, at last allowing himself to grin. “Your Honor, Treat McQuillan is all yours, with my compliments.”

And my sympathies.

“It’s hard to believe I used to live here, isn’t it?” Kendra said with a slight smile as she and Joslyn and Tara pulled up in front of Casey Elder’s mansion in Tara’s vehicle just before noon. Shea, having the day off from her job at the community center’s day care facility, had taken Elle and Erin over to Three Trees to have lunch and see a movie, while the Carmodys’ new nanny, Bella, looked after Madison and little Shannon out at Whisper Creek Ranch.

Joslyn smiled, a little wistfully, Tara thought. “Funny, I was just thinking the same thing about myself,” she said.

Tara shut off the SUV and gave both of them a look. Joslyn had grown up in the elegant monstrosity, still known as the Rossiter house back then, and Kendra and her first husband, Jeffrey, had eventually purchased the place and moved in. “Guess that makes me odd woman out,” Tara teased, pretending to envy the others. "I'm the only woman in our friendly foursome who's never lived in this house."

Joslyn made a comical face as she climbed out of the backseat and stood on the sidewalk, looking slender and cool in her summery yellow cotton dress and sleek sandals. Kendra, who was probably a walloping ten pounds overweight, post-baby, wore a pink-and-white-striped caftan that would be too big for her in another week or two.

"Poor Miss Penthouse Overlooking Central Park," Joslyn joked good-naturedly. "You've been so deprived. Stick with us, kiddo, and we'll show you how the fancy folks roll."

Tara laughed, though with anyone else, she probably would have retorted that the penthouse had never really been her home—it had always belonged to James. It was still a sore spot, she realized. Before she could think of a comeback, though, Casey appeared on the porch.

Tiny, with cascades of naturally red hair, now pinned up in a bulky ponytail, and impossibly green eyes, the famous singer looked almost ordinary in pressed jeans and a royal-blue silk shirt. Her feet were bare and her two cats, both coal-black and fluffy, curled around her ankles, purring wildly. Part of a litter born to Joslyn's near-human feline, Lucy-Maude, they bore no resemblance whatsoever to their mother, nor to the three other kittens from the batch, all of whom had gone to loving homes.

Joslyn, in charge of finding families for Lucy-Maude's thriving offspring, wouldn't have had it any other way.

"Howdy!" Casey called out, paying the cats no mind. "Come on in, ladies, the coffee's on and lunch is almost ready!"

With that soft Texas accent of hers, she could have been standing in front of a log cabin or a remote ranch house instead of the fanciest home in Parable County, Montana. Casey's down-to-earth ways, like her wholesome looks and her staggering talent for music in any form, were part of her charm—and charm was something she had aplenty. Men liked her, and so did women, children and all manner of critters.

Tara, Joslyn and Kendra all waved back, juggling purses and shutting doors, and then stepped through the gate and headed single file up the front walk.

Joslyn was carrying a big bouquet of roses, red and yellow and white, plucked from her garden out at Windfall Ranch. “Opal says hello,” she said, mounting the front steps and handing the flowers to Casey. “Coals to Newcastle,” she added, “since you’ve got one of the most amazing gardens I’ve ever seen.”

Casey waved off the compliment and readily accepted the roses, cradling them in her arms like a beauty queen. “I was hoping Opal could join us,” she said, after taking an appreciative sniff of the bouquet. “And, by the way, there’s no such thing as too many flowers.”

“Opal has a hot date with the Reverend Dr. Walter Beaumont,” Joslyn replied with a twinkle. “Though she claims it’s just business as usual, overseeing choir practice and helping to compile the new church directory.”

Just then, the cats bolted, zipping into the shrubbery near the front door in pursuit of unsuspecting prey, and Casey stepped back, gesturing for her three visitors to precede her inside.

The entryway was massive, with light spilling through magnificent skylights high overhead, but the house might have been a split-level rancher for all the heed Casey seemed to pay to its grandeur.

Three chocolate Labrador retrievers, all adopted, dashed up the spectacular stairway, right behind Casey's son, twelve-year-old Shane, and her daughter, Clare, who was thirteen. The dogs barked loudly and the kids laughed, egging them on.

"Try to pretend you're civilized," Casey called after the stampede with feigned exasperation. "We have *company,* in case you two haven't noticed!"

"Sorry, Mom," Clare shouted over the din, which subsided as the pack reached the second floor and headed for parts unknown.

Casey shook her head. "Those kids," she said, but she was smiling the whole time, and her eyes were soft with love. "They learned their manners from the roadies and the guys in the band, I guess. Maybe I shouldn't have taken them on the road with me so often, but, darn, I couldn't just leave them for weeks at a time."

"They're wonderful," Tara said, meaning it. Shane and Clare were bright, friendly and intelligent, as well as full of mischief, and despite Casey's remark about their manners, they addressed men as "sir" and women as "ma'am," among other unusual acts, like opening doors and carrying heavy things without being asked.

Which was not to say Casey's life, or the lives of her children, were the proverbial open books. Though she was officially a part of their group, Casey had still had her secrets—no small feat, given that the tabloids and stringers from numerous trash TV shows featured her often, showing no particular compunction to tell the truth, and were constantly on the prowl for the next scandal—and those secrets mainly centered around her children.

Though she had never been married, Casey's name had been romantically linked with various men in the music industry over the years. She'd gone into seclusion for both pregnancies, and she flat-out wasn't saying who the father or fathers were.

Given that Tara hadn't shared much of her past until recently, close as she'd been to Kendra and Joslyn, she wasn't inclined to judge—or pry. Casey would confide in them when and if she was ready, and that was good enough for everybody. Intimacy mattered in their four-way friendship, but so did privacy.

After crossing through the massive and sparkling clean kitchen, Tara saw that the table had been beautifully set on the screened-in sunporch at the back of the house, overlooking glorious gardens and a charming little guesthouse, where Joslyn had lived briefly before her marriage to Slade Barlow. The uniformed housekeeper, Doris, greeted them with a smile and a tray of rolled-up washcloths, steaming hot, cheery as a flight attendant in first class.

Everybody took one, wiped their hands, and set the cloth back on Doris's tray to be whisked away.

"Have a chair, you all," Casey commanded warmly. "Let's get the iced tea—and the girl-talk—flowing."

The chairs were fashioned of white wrought iron, and the cushions were as brightly colored as the gardens outside, as though someone had captured samples of zinnias and roses, daisies and ferns, and woven them right into the fabric.

They sat, and Tara took a moment to admire the china place settings, each piece rimmed in exquisitely painted morning glories, and the crystal glasses twinkled as if there were tiny fairy lights hidden in their stems.

She sighed with contentment and almost instantly relaxed.

"Everybody in Parable appreciates what you're doing for the McCullough family, Casey," Kendra said with quiet sincerity. A cool and classically beautiful blonde, she made an intriguing contrast to her husband's rough-and-tumble cowboy ways. "Lending them your jet—putting on benefit concerts—you are truly and totally amazing."

"Here, here," agreed Joslyn and Tara

in unison, lifting their ice-filled glasses in a toast, though the tea hadn't been poured yet.

Casey blushed slightly. "I'm not the only one helping out," she said modestly. "Opal's church is planning at least one event, and some folks from the community center are gearing up to build wheelchair ramps at Patsy's place, and widen some of the doorways, too."

"Still," Tara insisted. "You're making an incredible contribution, and you deserve some credit."

Casey's hand shook a little as she reached for the handle of a crystal pitcher, filled with brown tea and slices of lemon, and her smile wobbled slightly on her full lips. "I'm no stranger to trouble myself," she said, very quietly, not looking at any of the other women as she filled their glimmering glasses. "Besides, I've been so blessed in my life that giving back is the *least* I can do."

"You've been blessed," Kendra agreed gently, "but you've also worked very, very hard, and you have a great deal of talent."

Casey seemed to relax a little, putting down the pitcher and sweeping up her guests in a single friendly glance tinged with amusement. "You know what my old granddaddy used to say about talent?" she began. "It's not worth a heap of rusted bottle caps if you don't work like hell to develop it."

Doris reappeared just then, serving them each a luscious salad, sprinkled with fruit and walnuts and dried cranberries, before slipping away again.

Casey called a quiet "thanks" after the middle-aged woman, then picked up her fork and said, "There goes one of my biggest blessings. Doris runs this whole outfit—she's like a mama to me and a grandmama to the kids. She even fusses over the band and the road guys."

"Who would have thought there could be two Opals in the world?" Joslyn smiled.

"Amen to that," Kendra agreed. "If they ever joined forces, it would be the end of war, poverty and tabloid talk shows."

Everybody laughed, and the conversation turned to the "girl-talk" Casey and the rest of them had been anticipating all along.

There was no agenda—another refreshing thing, to Tara's mind—and nobody mentioned her "date" with Boone Taylor, which was fine with her.

She still couldn't believe she'd said yes, thereby opening a floodgate of disquieting possibilities—like sex with the cowboy sheriff. She'd never been much of a party girl—when it came to lovers, James and a grand total of two other men made up her entire dance card.

And she hadn't wanted a one of them the way she wanted Boone Taylor.

She colored up at the images and sensations that practically swamped her then, and she ducked her head a little, concentrating on the delicious salad—a concoction of greens, feta cheese, walnuts and dried berries of some sort—and on not choking, thereby requiring the Heimlich maneuver.

Kendra and Joslyn clearly noticed, but neither one offered a comment.

Just one of the many reasons she loved her friends—though there was no guarantee that they wouldn't grill her once they were all back in the SUV and driving away.

"Do you have another tour coming up soon?" Joslyn asked Casey after the second course, a cold pasta dish with pesto and pine nuts, had been served by the bustling Doris.

Casey shook her head. "I'm taking a year off," she said. "At least where going on the road is concerned. I've parked the tour bus and given all the road people a long vacation with pay, though the band and the techs are living here, so we can rehearse and do some recording."

It was common knowledge in Parable that Casey was in the process of converting the former wine cellar and recreation room downstairs into a state-of-the-art studio, complete with a small soundstage, specially designed computers and the latest digital equipment for making and transmitting videos. Folks weren't overimpressed with her celebrity, admired though she was—movie stars and captains of various industries came and went, in both Parable and the neighboring town of Three

Trees, buying or building spectacular hideaways and showing up only rarely to interact with the townspeople—but they *were* impressed by her down-home personality, small-town values and genuine interest in the community as a whole.

In addition, of course, that renovating meant a spate of regular paychecks, an important perk in an area mostly geared to raising cattle and the crops to feed them. Although all of the larger ranchers employed crews, the pickings were slim come winter, and there weren't enough service jobs to go around.

Casey Elder was putting food on the tables of ordinary, hardworking people, without acting like Lady Bountiful in the process, as some of the out-of-towners did, and they not only liked her, they were grateful to her.

Dessert, again brought in by the tireless Doris, was orange sorbet, formed into perfect balls and decorated with a sprig of mint. After dessert came coffee made from freshly ground beans, and after the coffee, the party began to wind down.

Kendra said she needed to nurse the baby soon, and Madison would be getting out of her summer program over at the community center in under two hours.

Joslyn had a toddler at home, and she started glancing at her watch and saying, "Look at the time."

Tara, with her stepdaughters at the movies with Shea, had no particular reason to hurry, unless you counted sweet, patient Lucy, who probably needed to go out, and the chickens, waiting for their sprinklings of poultry feed.

Everyone thanked Doris and, of course, Casey, as they took their leave. On the porch, Casey reminded them about the backstage party that would follow her benefit concert, saying they were all invited.

Maybe it was the reminder of the concert—Tara didn't know. But as soon as she was behind the wheel of her SUV again, with Kendra riding in the back this time and Joslyn taking the shotgun seat, they took their opportunity.

"What are you planning to wear? On

your date with Boone, I mean?" Joslyn inquired, sounding like a reporter at a presidential press conference rather than a close friend riding in the back of an SUV.

"Clothes," Tara quipped, but the joke didn't quite fly.

"Not for long, I'll bet," Kendra remarked, pleased as a cat just presented with a bowl of cream.

Tara reddened slightly as she pulled away from the curb in front of Casey's place, honked a farewell to her, since she was still standing on the porch, waving goodbye. As full as her life was, with her glamorous career, her beautiful children and her rollicking band of cats and dogs, she looked strangely lonely standing there, watching as her lunch guests drove away.

"Just because you and Hutch could never keep your hands off each other," Tara said sweetly, darting a brief glance in Kendra's direction, "it doesn't mean I'm planning on jumping Boone Taylor's bones the minute we're alone."

Joslyn giggled and leaned forward to land a reassuring pat on Tara's shoulder. "Chill out," she said. "We're on *your* side."

"There are sides?" Tara asked fretfully, biting her lower lip. She headed for Windfall Ranch first, since Whisper Creek, Kendra and Hutch's home, was nearer her farmhouse.

"Naive girl," Kendra teased, almost purring. "There's the male side, and the *female* side. And you can bet Team Boone—that would be Hutch and Slade—are coaching him to bring condoms and pour on the charm."

"And you two are Team Tara?" Tara's tone might have been a touch on the snarky side.

"Believe it," Joslyn confirmed.

"Given that you both seem as invested in getting Boone and me into bed together at the earliest possible moment, I can't really tell where one team ends and the other begins."

"Oh, for Pete's sake," said Kendra.

"What is *that* supposed to mean?" Tara shot back, navigating Parable's homey side streets as she wound her way toward the highway.

"You sound like a nun," Joslyn put in,

straining at her seat belt as she leaned forward, her head poking between the two front seats. "Pardon me for saying so, but you've been through a pretty long dry spell, unless you're keeping something from us. You must be *be-yond* ready for some sweaty, sheet-tangling, OMG sex."

"Is that how it is for you?" Tara asked, bemused. Had she missed something? With James, sex had been—well—*nice.* Soft orgasms, but never anything that twisted sweaty sheets into knots or made her cry out, *Oh, my God!*

"Better," said Joslyn.

"By a long shot," Kendra added.

"We haven't even *kissed,*" Tara said, and then blushed again.

"You're *kidding,*" Joslyn marveled.

"We didn't exactly strike sparks when we met, you know," Tara pointed out.

"Right," Kendra scoffed, in a tone that might have been sarcastic if it hadn't been so gentle.

"We were there, if you'll recall," Joslyn said. "He looked at you, you looked at him and fireworks lit the sky."

They had passed beyond the Parable

town limits by then, and Tara was relieved. Nothing but open road ahead of her. "Fireworks did *not* light the sky," she said. "Unless you and Slade sparked them, or Kendra and Hutch. *I* was an innocent bystander, and Boone couldn't have made it clearer what he thought of a New York city slicker in the chicken ranching business."

"Kiss him," Kendra suggested, without preamble.

Tara nearly drove off the road. *"What?"*

"Kiss Boone Taylor," Joslyn contributed, from the backseat. "Just *kiss* him, and you'll know."

"Know what?" Tara bit out, blushing again. Were her two best friends so complacent in their admittedly red-hot marriages that they believed love—not that whatever she had with Boone *was* love, of course—would reveal itself through one simple kiss?

"Just kiss him," Kendra urged.

"I dare you," Joslyn added.

"Have I mentioned that you two are no help at all?" Tara retorted, flustered. Suddenly, just imagining what it would be like to kiss Boone Taylor made her warm all over—*too* warm—and she turned on the SUV's powerful air-conditioning system with a poke of a button.

Kendra and Joslyn laughed.

"She's got it bad," Kendra said.

"Oh, yeah," Joslyn agreed.

For her part, Tara was glad when she pulled into Joslyn and Slade's driveway. Their house, recently renovated with a much bigger family in mind, rose majestically from a grassy rise. There was a new barn, and lots of horses wandering around in the pasture, which went on for acres and acres.

"Thanks for the lift home," Joslyn said as Tara stopped the SUV near the house.

Joslyn and Slade's dog, Jasper, rushed to meet her, as did Lucy-Maude, the cat, though she was more sedate in her exuberance.

Joslyn laughed, waved goodbye to Tara and Kendra, and bent to scoop up the big gray feline into her arms, nuzzling between its ears as she headed for the back door. Jasper jumped and yipped, overjoyed, at her side.

"Her life is perfect," Tara mused, and then wished she hadn't spoken aloud.

Kendra reached over to touch Tara's arm. She'd been in a teasing mood before, but now she looked solemn and gentle and very tender. "No," she said quietly. "But it's very, very good, and yours can be that way, too, Tara. Give things a chance—give *Boone* a chance."

Tara backed up the SUV, tooted her horn in farewell to Joslyn, even though she'd disappeared into the house by then, and made her way toward the main road at the base of the driveway. "Is there a reason why you and Joslyn are so convinced that Boone Taylor is the man for me?" she asked, her tone fretful and even a little impatient.

"Call it intuition," Kendra replied, smiling softly as she nodded.

Tara needed a while to digest that one.

Twenty minutes later, with Kendra safely deposited at Whisper Creek Ranch, Tara headed for home. She had a few extra hours on her hands, with the twins off in Three Trees, eating lunch and catching a movie.

Once she'd reached her own place, Tara let Lucy out of the house to run wildly around the yard for a while, drunk on the celebration of freedom, checked on the chickens, watered and weeded the garden, and found herself with way too much time on her hands, anyway.

When Boone drove up, less than half an hour after she'd finished her chores, she was sitting on the front porch, sipping iced tea and watching Lucy make good-natured attempts at herding the chickens from one part of the yard to another.

She wasn't having much success, silly dog, but she seemed to be enjoying the process, and the chickens must have known she was harmless, because they just went about their business.

Tara's first reaction to Boone's arrival was gut-clenching alarm. Had something happened to the twins, to Shea? An accident, maybe? Why *else* would the sheriff of Parable County be pulling into her yard at a little after two in the afternoon?

She stood up.

Boone, out of the cruiser by then,

must have read her body language, because he raised a reassuring hand. “Nothing’s wrong, Tara,” he said, and she gave him a few points for being unexpectedly perceptive. “I just stopped by to ask if you’d be willing to donate some chickens for the fundraising event at Opal’s church—the one to help with some of the McCullough’s hospital bills.”

Tara put a hand to the hollow of her throat, still playing catch-up. She’d heard about the project through Joslyn, but for some reason, she did some mental stumbling—in the privacy of her own head, she hoped—*Kiss him,* she heard Joslyn say, a friendly challenge in her voice.

Kiss Boone Taylor, and you’ll know, Kendra had told her, in so many words.

Boone was standing at the foot of the porch steps by then, greeting an exuberant Lucy with a chuckle and some serious ear-ruffling.

“Are *you* okay?” he asked, watching Tara. There was a mischievous light in his eyes, and it got to her, as surely as if he’d reached out and stroked her cheek, traced the line of her lips with the pad of a calloused thumb, or even caressed one of her breasts.

She swallowed hard. "What are you doing here?"

Kiss him, kiss him. Then you'll *know.*

That's stupid.

Tara Kendall, you're a coward.

The internal bantering—with herself, no less—rattled her even more.

"I just told you," Boone replied, his voice low. "I came to ask for chickens."

Tara blinked. "People would *eat* them?" she heard herself say, and in the next instant, she wanted to bite off her tongue. If Boone ever found out she'd never killed a single chicken, or even signed a figurative death warrant, he'd think she was a fraud—a tender-hearted, skittish female *posing* as a real farmer.

"That's the general idea," Boone said. Something flickered in his eyes—the beginnings of a grin, maybe? Was he on to her? "Is it a problem?"

Tara was a few moments catching her breath. Her heart skittered and she kept noticing that Boone's shoulders were wide, his eyes a piercing brown, his hair dark and silken, inviting her to plunge her fingers into it.

That was when, as she would claim ever-after, the devil made her do it.

She launched herself at Boone Taylor, right from the top step of the porch, wrapped both arms around his neck and kissed him. Hard.

He caught her in strong arms, rested his hands at either side of her waist, and kissed her right back, tentatively at first, but then with increasing boldness and a hunger that sent thrills rippling through every part of Tara. Soon, their tongues were involved and the sensations compounded themselves to the infinite power—each of them distinct and wildly delicious—and she uttered a little moan as Boone deepened the kiss.

OMG, Tara thought wildly, while the planet jolted off its axis. *Oh. My. God.*

This was so good.

This was so *bad.*

She was in *so* much trouble.

For all her native common sense, Tara knew there had been a mutiny—her body had wrested the controls from her mind, taken over.

She was vaguely conscious of Lucy, of Boone's little dog, apparently content to remain in the cruiser, of the chickens pecking at the ground around her feet.

It was time to get a grip, stop herself, put down the mutiny and batten down the hatches.

Except that Boone kissed her again, and she was utterly lost.

When he finally tore his mouth from hers, he looked deep into her eyes, chuckled once, then turned her gently around, steering her over the threshold, leaving the door open to the summer afternoon.

She half pulled him up the stairs, along the hallway to her room.

This is crazy, prattled that voice in her head, feverish now, and flimsy. *Stop, now!*

No way, Tara thought, in direct response. *This is it, and there's no going back.*

CHAPTER FOURTEEN

Tara's room, her personal sanctuary, was spacious and feminine, with lots of lace, both at the windows and on her antique brass bed; it was the same space, and yet it was different, too.

Despite the voices going back and forth in her mind, a quiet knowing came over her: she wasn't out of control. In fact, she'd never felt stronger or more self-possessed. She'd brought Boone Taylor to this room for one reason and one reason only—because she wanted him.

He smoothed her hair back off her

shoulders, a gesture so tender that it made her throat ache, and tilted his head to one side, regarding her with smoky eyes and a modicum of concern. "Are you sure you want this?" he asked, his voice gruff. A little grin cocked up one corner of his mouth. "This is me, you know. Boone Taylor. The redneck sheriff from next door, he of the beat-up double-wide and the weedy yard."

She smiled, relishing this strange and special freedom she was allowing herself, this bubble that held the two of them, somewhere outside of time, all the while knowing full well that she'd probably regret it later and still not giving a damn, and slid her arms around his neck. Her senses raced as Boone drew her close, her softness resting against the steely length of him. He smelled of soap and fresh air and something else she couldn't quite define, his own scent, she guessed, as unique to him as his fingerprints.

Boone arched one dark eyebrow, watching her, waiting for her reply. He was so solid, so substantial, and if there was any hesitancy, any uncertainty in him, Tara couldn't detect it.

"It was bound to happen," she said reasonably.

He gave just the slightest nod, then the corner of his mouth quirked up again. "I figured it would be on concert night, though," he observed.

"You'd rather wait?" she teased, looking up at him, longing to get lost in him.

"No, ma'am," he answered. "But some things have to be taken into consideration, just the same."

"I'm not using birth control," Tara confessed, and felt her soaring spirits sag a little.

Boone chuckled, pulled his wallet from the hip pocket of his jeans, opened it and brought out a small, battered packet. "'Be prepared,'" he quoted, his eyes twinkling with an irresistible combination of passion and mischief. "I've been carrying at least one of these around since high school."

Tara eyed the condom. "Not this particular one, I hope," she said, only half kidding.

He laughed, a low, masculine sound,

easy and real and unhurried. "No," he answered. "I've seen a little more action than that, as it happens."

"Kiss me again," Tara said. Some part of her longed to conceive a child, *this man's* child, but she knew it wouldn't be fair to Boone or to the baby. If things didn't work out—and there were so many reasons why they might not—Boone would want to be a part of the little one's life, wouldn't he?

And the baby would be born into turmoil and controversy. Tara wanted her children to be conceived in love, *raised* in a happy home, like Joslyn and Slade's little boy, and Hutch and Kendra's infant daughter.

"I like a woman who says what's on her mind," Boone answered, obliging.

If only you knew what's on my mind. You'd probably be out of here in two seconds flat.

Instead of clueing him in, Tara gave herself up to his kiss, to his mouth and the caresses of his hands, marveling that the floor seemed to pitch beneath her feet, dazed and dizzy and loving the wild physical and emotional responses Boone roused in her.

They kissed again and again, now hungrily, now in gentle exploration, and again the ordinary course of time seemed altered to Tara.

This is here, she reminded herself silently, joyously. *This is now.*

Still, things were shifting—constantly shifting—within her. How long had she and Boone been standing here, really? A few moments? An hour? A year?

A soft, country-scented breeze played over Tara's skin, and that was when she realized she was naked—somehow, without her noticing, her clothes had simply melted away.

And so, she soon discovered, had Boone's.

She found herself on her back, just midway across the width of her bed, with her legs dangling over the longer side. Boone murmured to her as he kissed and caressed her, sweet, senseless words that made her feel cherished, almost worshipped.

It was all so new to her, his governed strength, his slow hand, his warm mouth, tracing her neck, her breasts, her belly, that Tara felt virginal and, at the same time, powerful, very much in control of her own destiny.

Kneeling beside the bed, Boone kissed the insides of her knees, then her thighs.

She shivered with an anticipation so primitive, so undeniable, that she might have been a she-wolf, offering herself to her mate under a magical moon.

Boone parted her, found her most tender place and took her into his mouth, nibbled at her.

She gave a cry, part moan, part exulted gasp, and tangled her fingers in Boone's hair, holding him to her even as she began to whimper feverishly and toss her head back and forth in a frenzy of surrender.

He worked her skillfully, taking his time, bringing her to the very brink of release and then slowing down, easing up, making her knot her fingers in his hair and plead.

Again, the breeze flowed over them, pouring through an open window, perfumed by trees and wild flowers and the nearby river.

She begged.

He feasted on her in earnest then, brought her to a climax so fierce that her hips flew upward, seeking more of the incomprehensible pleasure and then still more. Her body buckled wildly, like a cable in a high wind, and still it went on, the rising from one pinnacle to another and then another.

When it finally ended, Tara sank, exhausted, settling deep into the mattress, *deep into herself and the sweet, soft glory of simply being a woman.* There couldn't be more, there just couldn't.

Except that there was.

Boone sent her soaring, again and again, untying all the hidden knots within her, opening floodgates of passion in her heart and even her soul.

After a long time, he turned her lengthwise on the bed, speaking soothingly to her as she slowly descended from impossible heights, airless places beyond the clouds, beyond the big sky itself.

She felt his body weight shift, knew

he was opening the packet, putting on the condom. Now, *she* would conquer *him,* pleasuring him until he gave himself up to her, spilled himself inside her, reveling in his satisfaction, already saturated by her own.

"One more chance to say no," Boone rumbled, resting on top of her, settling between her parted legs. His eyes searched hers.

In answer, Tara drew his head down, kissed him softly, tantalizing him with her tongue, then nipping lightly at his lower lip.

Boone groaned and then, in one long, powerful stroke, he was inside her, sheathed to the hilt.

Tara's eyes widened in surprise—she'd thought she was spent, that he'd already wrung every possible response from her—but a new and undeniable need swept over her, through her, instant and fiery and utterly ferocious.

She gasped his name.

Boone locked his gaze onto hers and seemed to be gazing into the very depths of her being, seeing a whole hidden landscape there, a place no other man had ever ventured into before, a place she herself had never charted.

And he began to move, his pace maddeningly slow.

She clawed at his bare back with her fingernails—until that moment she'd never known that really happened, even in the throes of passion—urging him to go faster, to increase the delicious friction until the world, indeed, *the universe,* exploded around them.

But Boone wouldn't be hurried, even though the set of his jaw and the corded muscles in his neck proved he was battling his own need to give in, to let go, to fall into her fire and allow it to consume him. All the while, though, he maintained eye contact, fierce as a warrior, but at the same time, so unbelievably gentle.

Tara wouldn't ask herself how such a contradiction could be until much later; at the moment, she was beyond rational thought. All she knew for sure was that she was a woman and Boone was a man and, together, they were being swept upward, into some kind of cataclysmic collision that would bond them in ways far more profound than the mere joining of their two straining bodies.

They climaxed at the same moment, Tara with a long, guttural, soblike cry, Boone with a raw, husky shout. They seemed to hang suspended in the aftermath, as though they'd been fused into one being, and finally they collapsed, exhausted, onto sweat-moistened, tangled sheets.

Tara had neither the strength nor the breath to speak, and Boone, too, remained silent, his heart pounding beneath her cheek, his arms tightly around her.

The old-fashioned clock on the bedroom mantel ticked, a disquieting reminder that time was passing.

The girls would be coming home soon. The chickens would need to be fed. And she would have to come to terms with what she'd just done.

Presently, Boone rolled away from her, scooped his clothes up from the floor, retreated into Tara's bathroom without a word. By the time he returned, he was fully dressed, though his hair was still mussed and his shirt looked rumpled.

"Do we have to talk about this?" Tara whispered, as the first waves of misery washed over her. She'd expected this reaction, but that didn't make it any easier to bear.

Boone bent, kissed her forehead, briefly. "Not right away," he replied.

And then he was gone. Tara lay very still, listened to his footsteps on the stairs, heard the distant creak of the front door opening, the snap of its shutting, the faint roar of Boone's car engine.

Lucy wandered into the room moments later, rested her muzzle on the bedding, and gazed soulfully at Tara, devoted and probably concerned.

Tara pulled up the covers to the bridge of her nose, reached out one arm to stroke Lucy's golden head. "You're such a sweetheart," she sniffled.

Why was she crying?

Tara couldn't have given a precise reason, not at that moment, anyway.

She'd never even imagined that lovemaking could be the way it had been between her and Boone—this was the stuff of storybooks, of romantic movies and very private fantasies.

But real life? Even now, it seemed impossible.

Tara's emotions rioted even as her body settled back into an ordinary rhythm, and they were epic in proportion, those feelings, as well as completely contradictory to each other.

She was scared. She was elated. She'd just made the mistake of a lifetime. She'd just been touched by something that was meant to be, written in the stars.

Only two things were certain, and they were both alarming. One, her life would never, ever be the same after this. And two, she was in love with Boone Taylor. It wasn't the polite, nearly platonic love she'd had with James, but the big, scary kind that seared an imprint into her soul.

The question was, did Boone feel the same way?

Or was he whistling under his breath, grinning a little, and thinking, *Slam-bam, thank you, ma'am?* That would be typical of a guy. Maybe he was even feeling a little cocky, thinking he'd scored one against the chicken farmer from the big city, gotten her back for all those snide remarks about his run-down double-wide and overgrown property.

The prospect was so awful that Tara wanted to hide in that bed until she got old and died, or at least until she could drum up some defiance, but neither one of those things was an option. She had the twins to think about, and sweet Lucy, and the chickens.

With a sigh, she threw back the covers, got out of bed, trailed into her bathroom and started the shower running. She stepped into the stall and let the hot water pummel her until it turned lukewarm, then got out, dried off and put on clean clothes, jeans and a worn T-shirt. Work clothes.

Downstairs, she took a store-bought lasagna from the freezer and turned on the oven. *One thing at a time,* she told herself. She fed Lucy her kibble, and then went outside to take care of the chickens, shutting them up in their cozy coop for the night.

By the time Shea brought Elle and Erin home from their expedition to Three Trees, the sun was going down and Tara figured she probably *looked* pretty normal, at least on the outside. On the *inside,* she knew she'd sowed the wind and reaped the whirlwind. She was a one-woman weather system, category-five.

She wasn't the type to get carried away, never had been, but this time she'd gone and opened her heart, not to mention her body, to a man she barely knew. She'd zipped right on past beginning to like Boone to *loving* him, but there was certainly no guarantee of happily-ever-after.

She and Boone had little in common, really. And he'd loved his late wife deeply—probably loved her still. After all, he and Corrie had gotten together as teenagers, planned a life, made two beautiful babies.

They'd shared big dreams and worked hard to make them come true, and Tara knew—everyone in Parable did—just how deeply Boone had grieved for his bride. According to Joslyn and Kendra, he'd shut down completely, just doing his job and *existing,* letting his sister and her husband raise his children.

The twins were bursting with excitement, their words tumbling over each other as they recounted the high points of the movie. They'd had Mexican food for lunch, but that was *hours* ago, and they were both starved. And Shea was awesome.

Looking at Tara, though, their prattle trickled off into silence. She hadn't fooled them, then—they knew something was wrong.

"What's going on?" Elle asked, straight out.

"Have you been crying?" Erin wanted to know.

"I'm *fine,*" Tara said. "Maybe just a little tired, that's all."

Tired, yes. But she didn't expect to get much sleep, with her insides churning the way they were. One moment, she felt ecstatic, the next, she was terrified that she was another notch in Boone's bedpost.

Both girls looked skeptical. And fretful.

Tara went to them, gave them each a one-armed hug. “Look,” she said quietly, “I’m going through some stuff, but it’ll pass, and there’s absolutely no reason for either of you to worry, okay?”

“You’d tell us if you were sick or something, wouldn’t you?” Elle asked, still troubled. “I mean if you had some terrible disease and—”

Tara chuckled, hugged the child close again. “Babe,” she said softly, “this isn’t a movie. I’m definitely not sick.”

“Did Dad do something?” Erin pressed, idly stroking Lucy’s gleaming golden back. “Say something mean, maybe?”

“No,” Tara said. “Let’s make a nice salad while the lasagna is heating up.”

“I get to tear the lettuce,” Elle said, making a dive for the refrigerator. She and Erin were used to racing each other for the best chair or the front passenger seat and any number of other desirables, and getting out the salad makings was no exception.

Tara interceded, reminding them to wash their hands first, and soon they were busy at the center island, chopping and slicing and tearing.

Supper was blessedly quiet, but just as they were clearing the table, the landline rang, unusually jarring and shrill, it seemed to Tara. Even before she picked up the receiver and said hello, she knew something had happened.

"Thank God I got you instead of one of the girls," James blurted. He sounded wound up, tight as an old-fashioned watch-spring. "Can you talk?"

Obviously the point of the call was for *James* to do the talking, not Tara. She drew a deep breath, let it out slowly, gestured to the twins to take Lucy outside.

"I can listen," Tara answered when the back door closed behind one eager dog and two reluctant young girls.

"I'm coming out there to get the twins," James announced briskly.

The words struck Tara like a punch in the stomach. Or the heart. "But I thought—what about the wedding—the honeymoon?"

"There isn't going to *be* any wedding," James informed her tersely.

Tara stretched the phone cord as far as it would go, sank into a chair at the table. "Okay," she said, at a loss for words. She was stunned, disoriented—first, Boone and about nine million second thoughts, and now this.

James launched into a long tirade about how he and what's-her-name had had a serious row. He felt duped, taken, *used.*

Tara didn't point out that she'd felt that way, too, when they had split up.

What it all boiled down to was, Bethany wanted children—lots of them. She'd thought James wanted the same things she did. Surprise. James was *over* raising kids. For Bethany, that was a deal-breaker, and the wedding was off.

When James finally lapsed into a charged silence, maybe catching his breath, Tara stepped out onto the proverbial limb.

"Why not let the girls stay here a little longer? After all, you're pretty upset. Maybe you need some time."

"I've found a good school for them—it's in Connecticut," James said. "Some of the kids spend the summers there, in addition to the regular term. They'll love it."

Tara closed her eyes. "James," she said, "they love it here."

"They're not your responsibility," James informed her. What he *meant* was, *Stay out of this. You're not their mother.*

"Couldn't we wait a few days?" Tara ventured carefully. "So you can calm down a little?"

James's tone hardened. "What's the use in that?" he countered. "My assistant will make plane reservations, and get back to you with the times and flight numbers."

Tara's eyes filled with tears. She blinked them back, swallowed.

The door opened, and Elle and Erin came through it with Lucy.

This time, she wasn't going to cover for James. "It's your dad," she said, holding out the receiver.

Elle got there first, but she turned the phone slightly so Erin could listen, too.

Tara sat still, too wobbly kneed to stand up, let alone flee the room, and watched the looks on the twins' faces as they absorbed what their father was saying.

"No!" Elle yelled suddenly. "I don't *want* to go away to some stupid school, and neither does Erin!"

Erin nodded rapidly in agreement, her cheeks flushed.

Had James told his daughters that he and Bethany had called off the wedding? Tara had expected that news to please them, if nothing else.

"We'll run away," Elle threatened, picking up steam. "We won't even get on the plane!"

"And you'll never see us again!" Erin elaborated.

Tara forced herself to her feet. "Girls," she scolded, very gently, shaking her head. "Give me the phone."

By this time, Lucy was beside herself with worry, poor thing. She and Tara normally lived quiet, uneventful lives, *sans* emotional drama.

Elle fairly shoved the receiver at her, crying hard now, her chin trembling. "We won't go back," she reiterated, "we *won't!*"

"You're scaring Lucy," Tara pointed out. "Take her upstairs—I'll join you in a few minutes, and we'll talk."

The girls obeyed, Lucy wagging her tail hopefully as she followed them out of the kitchen.

James was furious again, frustrated to the max; Tara knew that by the way he was breathing, even before he spoke to her.

"That was a dirty trick," he bit out. "You really put me on the spot, Tara, and I don't appreciate it."

The nerve of the man. *She'd* put *him* on the spot?

No more Ms. Nicey-Nice. The gloves were off. "Would you like to know what *I* don't appreciate, James?" she snapped out, not giving him a chance to answer before she rushed on, whispering in case the girls were eavesdropping at the top of the stairs. "I don't appreciate your arrogant disregard for other people's feelings. Elle and Erin are your *children,* not puppets you can jerk around on strings, and all you can think about is what *you* want, what *you* need." She paused, dragged in a quick breath, left him no room to interrupt. "*Damn* it, James, I'd understand if you had any intention of being an actual father to the twins, but you're just eager to shuffle them off somewhere, out of sight, out of mind!"

"Are you through?" James asked coldly.

"No," Tara replied, "I'm *not* through. I'm not sending Elle and Erin back to New York alone. If you want your daughters, bucko, you'll have to come and get them."

"'Bucko'?" James taunted.

Tara said nothing. She just stood there, seething, knuckles white where she gripped the receiver.

"You just love to make things difficult, don't you?" James said, after a long-suffering sigh. "The twins are perfectly capable of flying on their own—they've already proven that."

"I don't care," Tara said stubbornly. She'd spent most of their marriage doing just the opposite of "making things difficult." She'd been a fool.

"I could call the police," James

pointed out, but he didn't sound quite so confident as before.

"Go ahead," Tara challenged, imagining Boone coming to her door, in his capacity as sheriff, with some kind of interstate court order in his hand.

"You know I can't afford a scandal," James almost whined. "I'm a respected professional man, Tara. A top-flight surgeon, and in my business, reputation matters. *Be reasonable.*" He was definitely singing a different tune now, but Tara still wasn't inclined to dance to it.

"Then I guess you'll have to come out here to Montana and tell these children, face-to-face, that you don't really want to raise them, and you aren't about to let *me* do it, either, so you're sending them to boarding school."

Silence.

Tara heard the girls and Lucy moving around upstairs in their room.

She half expected James to hang up in her ear. Instead, he gave another sigh, this one ragged and genuinely weary. Tara didn't feel one bit sorry for him.

"*I* know what this is about," James said, in mock revelation. "You're thinking that if I come out there, you and I can get back together, patch things up. That I'd bring you back to New York and we'd all be one big happy family again."

Indignation surged through Tara, rendering her speechless for several long moments. That was the *last* thing she'd expected him to say—and the last thing she wanted.

"You are *so* wrong," she managed to say, mildly sick to her stomach.

"Am I?" James almost purred the words.

"Yes!"

He went quiet again, thinking. Then he said, "We did have some good times. Maybe we *could* work things out."

Was he being sarcastic? Surely James knew as well as she did that they were completely over.

"Tara?" he prompted, with a note of smugness, when she didn't reply right away.

Sometimes, a person had no choice but to fall back on a cliché. "Not if you were literally the last man on earth," she said. "Goodbye."

She hung up, paced the kitchen for a minute or so, trying to rein in her temper. What had she ever seen in her ex-husband, with his God-complex and his lack of concern for anyone but himself?

What kind of person didn't want to raise their own children?

Suddenly, she stopped in her tracks, and a chill went through her. *A person like Boone Taylor, that's who.*

Sure, Boone's boys were living with him now, but he'd been willing enough to farm them out with his sister after Corrie died—when they'd needed him most.

She stood at the sink, gazing at her own reflection, a gaunt ghost-version of herself, in the night-blackened glass. She'd fallen for the wrong man once, and now she'd done it again.

"Fool," she accused, turning away.

Boone hadn't slept the whole night, and now that sunup had rolled around, he knew he was going to pay the price. By the end of the day, he'd have to prop his eyelids open with matchsticks.

He made coffee and looked in on the

boys, saw that they were sleeping soundly.

Scamp, curled up between them, lifted his head to look at Boone, then quietly got up and jumped to the floor, tail wagging.

Boone grinned wanly, went back to the kitchen and poured coffee into a mug, even though the gizmo hadn't finished its chortling, steaming cycle. The stuff was half-again too strong, but he needed the caffeine, so he'd drink it, anyway.

He had some time before he had to get Griffin and Fletcher up, washed, fed and pointed in the right direction, and the restlessness that had kept him awake was still with him.

He went outside, stood on the sagging porch, gazed at the place where the new house would stand, ready to live in before the first snow, if luck was with him. He'd gotten the loan in place and hired a contractor, but after what had happened with Tara the day before, well, maybe he ought to put on the brakes.

He turned, walked toward the offshoot of the river, because he always did his best thinking anywhere near the water.

Scamp kept pace, prancing along beside Boone, pausing every now and then to sniff the ground.

Tara's house seemed to have an aura, with the sun rising behind it, spilling red-orange light over the land.

Boone's throat tightened, and he shoved a hand through his hair, confused about some things, and bone-sure of others. He bent to pick up a stick and toss it into the water and, to his delight, Scamp went right in after the twig and proudly brought it back, shaking himself off as he looked up at Boone. Boone laughed and bent to pat the dog's head, take the stick and throw it again.

Scamp rushed after it, splashing as he went.

Watching the dog, Boone didn't glance toward Tara's place again, but he could hear the chickens clucking, Lucy barking, Tara calling something to her.

It took a moment to register the note

of alarm in Tara's voice and, when he did, Boone looked up quickly, saw her coming toward him. She crossed the board bridge nearly at a run, and that was when he caught the expression on her face. Terror.

"The twins are gone!" she blurted out.

Boone frowned. "What?"

"They're not in their room," Tara gasped out, stumbling as she neared him, nearly falling before he caught hold of her arms and steadied her. "Boone, they've run away—they said they would—"

"Take a breath," Boone ordered, sounding calmer than he felt. Out of the corner of his eye, he saw Scamp drop the newly retrieved stick and wander off along the bank, nose to the ground.

Tara was trembling, and her face was pale. "They're *gone,*" she said, almost whimpering the words. "I looked in the garden, behind the barn—everywhere I could think of—"

"When did you see them last?" Boone asked, still grasping her arms. She looked frail enough to blow away with the first strong breeze.

"Last night," Tara answered, "after they'd gone to bed. I went upstairs to talk to them—they'd gotten some upsetting news—and everything seemed to be okay, after a while, anyway." Boone had called Tara right after and they'd talked on the phone, briefly and shyly, with too much still needing to be said. "But this morning—"

"Any idea where they might be headed?" Boone persisted. Kids didn't go missing in Parable County, it just didn't happen. But there was always a first time.

Tara shook her head, fighting tears, struggling so hard to keep her composure that Boone's heart broke for her.

"We'll find them," he told her. "Tara, I promise we'll find them."

She lifted her head to meet his gaze and in that moment he saw the contents of her heart right there in her beautiful eyes. She loved those children.

And she loved *him.* If it hadn't been for the circumstances, he'd have shouted hallelujah.

Scamp gave a single, sharp bark just then.

Frowning, Boone turned his head, squinting against the dazzle of a copper-penny sun, about to call the dog back to his side. He'd take Tara to the double-wide, make some calls, round up his deputies and Slade and Hutch to start searching for the twins.

A moment passed before Boone realized that that derelict old rowboat he'd always meant to haul off was gone. Scamp was standing in the muddy gouge on the bank. He barked again.

Boone clasped Tara's hand and bolted toward the spot, barely able to believe his eyes, even now. That boat had been a ruin when *he* was a kid, and there was no way it would stay afloat.

Lucy joined them, drawn by Scamp's barks, and sent up a worried whine.

Tara's grasp tightened around his hand. "Wasn't there a boat . . . ?"

Dread filled Boone as he shaded his eyes from the sun and looked hard toward the natural spillway where the branch and the main river connected. There was no sign of the twins *or* the boat, but his gut told him the impossible had happened—somehow, Elle and Erin pushed that warped and rotted wreck into the water and rowed it far enough to disappear.

He was betting they'd gone upstream, toward the river, since the split drained off into a pond about a quarter of a mile in the other direction. He let go of Tara's hand and bolted for the spillway.

CHAPTER FIFTEEN

Tara ran behind Boone, not quite catching up even though she was moving faster than she ever had before, even as a child. Her heart pounded and adrenaline raced through her system like a fast-acting drug, causing her head to reel, and the most elemental of fears thrummed inside her.

Boone rounded a bend up ahead, both dogs flashing at his heels like streaks of furry light, and, impossibly, Tara quickened her pace.

A boat, rickety and definitely not seaworthy. And in it her stepdaughters, the treasures of her soul, in obvious danger.

She heard a thin cry then, riding the wind, and stumbled, nearly fell, covering the rough ground, which had begun to tip and sway under her feet.

She kept running, blindly now, praying a one-word prayer under her breath, syncing it with her heartbeat. *Please—please—please . . .*

Boone shouted something just as Tara reached the scene, already kicking off his boots.

It was all surreal to her, like some horrible vision, a nightmare playing out in the bright, clean light of a Montana morning.

The concrete spillway resembled a small dam to Tara, though it must have been twelve feet high, and water thundered over its top, foamy white. Below it, in the midst of a whirlpool, a vortex, a black hole, Erin clung to what remained of the ancient rowboat, and to her sister, who looked as boneless as a rag doll.

Tara screamed.

Boone was already in the water, fighting his way through the noise and the foam and the parts of dead trees, swirling, caught at the edge of the whirlpool's orbit. For all his strength, he had to fight his way through.

Finally reaching the overturned boat, Boone curved an arm around Elle, held her firmly, tossed his dark head once to shake away the water and clear his vision. With his free hand, he gripped Erin's shoulder.

Tara, caught in some strange time freeze, broke free, ran down the bank.

"Stay where you are, Tara!" Boone yelled over the roar of the spillway. "My phone's on the ground somewhere—call 9-1-1. Now!"

Something in his tone reached past Tara's hysteria into the calm part of her mind, submerged until then. She searched the muddy grass, found his phone, flipped it open and made the call.

A woman named Becky told her to hang on; an ambulance was on its way.

Tara closed the phone, sank to her knees, watching as Boone spoke to Erin, his words lost in the din of the Big

Sky River, spilling into the churning pool. She nodded, her blond hair slicked back from her face, and when Boone turned, supporting a now-stirring Elle, keeping her head above the water, Erin let go of the remains of the rowboat. After an instant's hesitation, she flung her arms around Boone's neck and clung to him.

Slowly, Boone made his way back toward the bank, toward life and breath and safety. Once or twice, waking, terrified and confused, Elle struggled in his grasp, but he held her and, with just his legs and his left arm, battled the wild water that might so easily have taken them all under.

Tara was on her feet again when Boone reached out and grabbed hold of a clump of tree roots, looked up at her as she reached for Elle.

"Be careful," he said hoarsely. "I think she might have some broken bones."

Tara moved past her panic, shoving it into the background to be dealt with later, and pulled her half-conscious stepdaughter onto dry ground. The dogs, fitful, hovered nearby, giving the occasional yelp.

Boone hauled himself and Erin out of the water. A siren sounded in the near distance.

Tara knelt, sopping wet even though she hadn't gone in, held a shivering Erin in one arm and a moaning Elle in the other.

Boone's young sons appeared, still in their pajamas and barefoot, drawn by the shriek of the approaching ambulance. It came to a screeching halt up the hill, and two EMTs, a man and a woman, neither of whom Tara had ever seen before, hurried down the slope, gear in hand, sidestepping.

Boone was on his feet by then, breathing hard and fast and deep.

Explanations were made while the EMTs checked both Elle and Erin for injuries.

"Dad?" Tara heard one of Boone's boys say in a shaky voice.

Boone went to his sons, but his gaze was locked with Tara's.

Thank you wasn't enough, she thought, shaken, but that would have to be figured out later. Elle needed X-rays and both girls were in shock. Tara scrambled up the hill, her arm supporting a still-mobile Erin, though Elle was strapped to a stretcher by then.

She and Erin climbed into the back of the ambulance once Elle had been loaded inside and secured, and as the doors closed, Tara caught a glimpse of Boone Taylor, dripping wet, holding Fletcher in one arm while Griffin clung to his wet pant leg, wide-eyed with fear.

"It hurts," Elle whispered, "it hurts, it hurts . . ."

"I know," Tara whispered back, holding the child's hand, smoothing tendrils of soaked hair away from her forehead. "Hold on, sweetheart. Try to be strong. We'll be at the clinic in a few minutes."

Elle nodded, her face still ghastly pale. "Sorry . . ." she murmured, either fainting or falling asleep.

Tara wanted to scream again—*wake up, wake up*—but of course she didn't. There was plenty of fear to go around—it was courage that was most needed. She looked at sweet Erin, kneeling on the other side of the stretcher, meeting Tara's eyes.

"Are we going to be arrested?" she asked.

Tara made a sound, part laugh, part sob, so raw that it clawed painfully at her throat. "No, honey," she hastened to say. "Of course not."

Erin's expression was soft and unfocused—only then did Tara realize the girl had lost her glasses. "We looked at a map on the internet," she said, rotelike, staring off into an unseeable distance now. "We thought the river would take us far enough away that Dad couldn't find us and make us go to that school. . . ."

Tara's heart clenched as painfully as if a strong hand had reached into her chest and locked around it mercilessly. The plan had been foolish, of course, wildly improbable and, needless to say, dangerous. But the twins were only twelve years old, after all, and they must have been desperate.

The next hour or so passed in a colorful blur—Erin's wet clothes were stripped off and she was wrapped in warm blankets, while the initial medical exam and subsequent X-rays revealed a fracture in Elle's left forearm that would require minor surgery, as well as a cast. Because she, too, was suffering from shock, Elle had to be stabilized before the operation could take place, so she was blanketed, like her sister, and a mild painkiller was administered.

Boone arrived, his hair still wet but wearing dry clothes, and it was all Tara could do not to run to him.

"The boys?" she asked softly, when he stepped into the small room where Tara kept vigil with both her stepdaughters.

"They're at the office, with Becky and Scamp," Boone replied. "Lucy, too."

Tara felt a soft spilling sensation, balm to her fear-battered heart. He'd saved Elle's and Erin's lives, this man, risking his own in the process, and he'd even thought, in the aftermath, of Lucy's well-being.

Whatever his reasons for handing over his very young sons to his sister to look after following Corrie's death, Boone wasn't anything like James Lennox.

"Thank you," she said softly.

He cocked a weary grin at her, executed a half salute. “All in a day’s work,” he replied.

“Hardly,” she said.

Now that Elle and Erin were both resting comfortably, with a cheery young nurse to attend to them, Tara felt she could leave the room.

It was time to call James, not only because he had a right to know about the boating “accident,” but because his permission would be needed before Elle’s surgery could take place. Tara had no authority.

She and Boone stepped out into the corridor. Though referred to loosely as a hospital, the establishment was actually a clinic, exceptionally well equipped. Babies were delivered here, tonsils were removed, the odd appendectomy went down, but the seriously ill or injured, like Dawson McCullough, were always airlifted to a larger city with adequate facilities—Missoula, Boise, even Seattle.

It was one more thing to be grateful for, Tara thought distractedly. None of the E.R. staff had said anything about sending Elle away for treatment.

Boone grasped her shoulders there in the empty hallway and tilted his head to one side to look directly into Tara's face. "What about you?" he asked. "Are *you* okay, Tara?"

"I'm just fine," she told him, feeling a strange urge to kiss the cleft in Boone's chin, snuggle into his arms, cling a little. "Color me very, very grateful, though, Sheriff Taylor."

He chuckled, a reassuring sound, masculine and somehow soothing. "Is this the part where I say, 'Aw, shucks, ma'am, it weren't nothing'?"

"It *was* something, Boone. Without you, I wouldn't even have found the girls in time, let alone managed to swim through all those currents and get them both back to shore."

Clearly, Sheriff Boone Taylor was not very comfortable in the role of hero. The way he saw it, most likely, he'd done what anyone would do in the same situation. A crisis had arisen, and he'd handled it.

Tara sighed. "I'd better call their father," she said. "He's *not* going to be happy about this. Especially when he finds out they posted their big plan online beforehand—a lot of schools monitor things like that, especially with new applicants—and running away, successfully or not, ratchets up the legal-liability factor sky-high."

"I could call him for you," Boone offered solemnly. "Make it an official call."

Tara actually considered taking that out—she was still pretty shaken up herself, after all—but after a few moments of thought, she shook her head no. This was her responsibility, not Boone's.

Except she'd left her phone at home, too panicked after finding Erin and Elle missing from their room to remember the handy device. Luckily, she'd dressed as soon as she got out of bed, or she'd probably be standing here in her nightgown.

"Borrow your phone?" she asked.

Boone nodded, handed it to her.

She went outside, sat wearily on the rock surround of one of the clinic's flower beds and searched her memory for James's numbers—work, home, cell, etc. Nothing. She'd so rarely had reason to call her ex-husband.

In the end, she had to call Information, and the operator put her through to James's office, where an assistant picked up. Tara identified herself, gave a short, faltering version of what had happened and asked to be put through to James.

Dr. Lennox, the assistant explained coolly, was already in transit, on his way to Montana to "collect" his children. Did he have the proper contact numbers?

Tara dredged them up, her mind sluggish now.

James was on his way. Damn.

And when he got to Parable, there would be hell to pay. Once he learned the whole story, he'd be furious at Tara, accuse her of being irresponsible, probably remove his daughters from her company—permanently—as soon as they could travel. And since he was a doctor, that would probably be allowed to happen sooner rather than later.

He'd whisk Elle and Erin away for good, and she'd be very fortunate indeed if she saw them again before they turned eighteen and could legally make such decisions for themselves.

And it would be *six years* until the twins came of age. By then, they might have been poisoned against their erstwhile stepmother, or simply have lost interest, young women busy with beginnings, with wide circles of friends, college and careers to plan, attractive guys asking for dates.

Tara set the borrowed cell in her lap, rested her elbows on the still-damp, mud-streaked knees of her jeans, and covered her face with both hands.

Hours later, Boone and the boys stepped up onto Tara's porch. Griffin and Fletcher both held balloons and bouquets, bought at the supermarket in town. Their faces were scrubbed and their hair and clothes were clean. All without any help from Opal, Boone thought drily.

Tara answered their knock, looking harried and so beautiful that Boone wondered if he'd always been in love with her, long before they met, even before Corrie.

"Hello," she said, smiling at the boys.

"Can we see Elle and Erin?" Griffin asked earnestly. According to Boone's source—namely, Becky—both twins had been released after Elle's brief surgery and a little time in the recovery room.

Boone realized, albeit belatedly, that he should have insisted on waiting until tomorrow to pay a visit, instead of giving in to Griffin and Fletcher's nonstop campaign to do it now. Witnessing the tail end of the rescue operation down at the spillway that morning the way they had, the kids had been jumpy all day, unable to concentrate in day camp, full of questions when Boone arrived at the community center to pick them up.

So they'd stopped for the flowers and balloons, spruced up at home and practically *herded* him next door, like a pair of minute wranglers driving cattle to market.

"We'll come back if they're resting," Boone said awkwardly, feeling his neck redden around the collar of his crisp white shirt.

Tara's smile was as bedazzling as a Montana sunrise, and she pushed open the screen door, shaking her head as she did so. "Elle and Erin will be glad to have company," she said. "Come in, all of you."

Lucy, the golden retriever, greeted the ever-present Scamp with a little more interest than usual, and he seemed to be beside himself at the compliment.

"The girls are in the living room, watching TV," Tara said.

At this, the two boys rushed past her, balloons bobbing and bumping behind them, and the dogs, suddenly excited, leaped to join the noisy parade, barking gleefully.

Tara laughed at the ruckus, but her eyes were warm and solemn on Boone's face. "Come in," she repeated.

He couldn't help remembering the last time he'd stepped over this threshold—was it only yesterday?—drunk on Tara's kisses, her scent, the soft heat of her body.

Boone took off his hat and held it—subtly, he hoped—in front of his crotch. He had it bad, all right, but there was a lot to be settled, and nothing this important ought to be rushed. Just the same, it was all he could do not to ask her to marry him, right then and there.

"No sign of the ex yet?" Boone asked, following her through the house and into her kitchen, the heart of that old house.

The four kids were in the living room, all talking at once, while the dogs sang backup. The din was something to be relished as far as Boone was concerned—noise and children and dogs equaled life in his book.

Once inside the kitchen, Tara made a face and said, "No, but he'll be here anytime."

"Is there a plan?"

Tara trembled, sank into a chair at the table, as though her knees had gone weak. Did she still love this doctor-dude, Boone wondered? Or was she afraid of the man?

He sat down across from Tara, giving her space, and waited for her answer.

She shook her head again, the way she had at the front door when Boone had wanted to leave, come back later when things had calmed down a little.

Now, seeing her face, he was glad he hadn't gone.

"No plan," she said at last, after biting her lower lip for a few moments. “James called a little while ago, after his plane landed, and I told him what had happened.” She paused, swallowed, glanced nervously at the door, in case of eavesdroppers, then went on in a quiet voice. “Do you know what he said?” she asked.

Boone didn’t reply, figuring the question was rhetorical, since there was no way he could have known what Dr. James Lennox had to say.

Tara’s eyes filled with tears, but they were angry, defiant tears. “He said,” she whispered furiously, “that now everything was botched up because there’s some problem at the year-round boarding school he has picked out for the twins and he’s hitting a brick wall hiring a new nanny, too. Elle and Erin don’t have the best reputation in those circles, it seems. Now he’ll have to scramble to make other arrangements, and it’s all my fault.”

Boone cursed under his breath. “*That* was the man’s big concern?” he rasped. “That bringing the kids home and finding a sitter would disrupt *his* life?”

Tara nodded, swiping the moisture from her eyes with the backs of her hands. “He didn’t even ask how they were—if they were scared or in pain—not even *how close they came to drowning.* Instead, he yelled that he never should have let them come out to this ‘godforsaken wilderness’ in the first place—forgetting, of course, that it was his idea.”

“Sounds like he has quite a temper,” Boone said moderately, knowing he was on dangerous ground, given what he was about to ask. “Is he potentially violent, Tara? Would he hurt you or the girls?”

Tara immediately shook her head. “He’s not a monster, Boone,” she said, without a touch of defensiveness on her ex’s behalf. “But James *is* a selfish, egotistical, inconsiderate *jerk.*”

Boone grinned, partly because he was relieved. “Don’t hold back, now,” he teased. “Tell me what you really think.”

She smiled a tiny, fragile smile, ran a hand through her brown hair, which looked attractively rumpled. “Once upon a time," she responded, "I thought the same thing about you."

Something inside Boone took flight and soared, wheeling high overhead with the big sky for a backdrop. "And now?"

Her answer stunned him. "And now I love you," she said.

Boone went light-headed. He blinked, tugged at one ear, not trusting his own hearing. "Did you just say—?"

She laughed this time. "I just said that I love you," she confirmed.

"Since when?" Boone countered, remembering all the times she'd harangued him about his yard and his double-wide and his duty, as a public official, to set a good example for other home owners.

"I'm not sure," she answered, "but what happened this morning cleared up all my doubts."

Boone opened his mouth, closed it again. "I never expected to love another woman after Corrie," he heard himself say. "But I do believe I love you, Tara Kendall, chickens and all."

Her eyes lit up and she reached

across the table to squeeze his hand. Obviously, with all that was going on, the celebratory sex would have to wait awhile, but the promise of it was right there in the room with them, just the same.

"I have a confession to make," she said, after a short, pulsing silence that caused about a million nerves to batter Boone's skin from the inside.

"What?" He hardly dared to ask the question.

"I'm a fraud," she confided. "I've never killed a single chicken. Around here, they die of old age."

Boone took that in. Then he threw back his head and laughed, and it felt so damn good, leaching some of the tension from his neck and shoulders.

"When you asked me to donate some poultry for the fundraising over at Opal's church, I practically lost it, right then and there."

"I guess I didn't notice that you were upset," Boone noted mischievously, "what with your throwing yourself at me and all."

She blushed then, swatted at him.

Outside, the chickens put up a fuss, and Tara's expression changed instantly. "He's here," she said, pushing back her chair, shooting to her feet.

"Take it easy," Boone said, taking the time to enfold her in his arms, rest his chin on top of her head. "We'll deal with him together. You and me."

He felt her soften with relief. Then she lifted her chin, squared her shoulders and said, "Here goes."

Tara had been dreading James's arrival for most of the day, but now that Boone had her back, she felt braver.

Disgust twisted James's handsome face when the chickens clustered around his rental car, squawking and pecking at the tires. He rolled down the driver's side window and stuck his head out to holler, "Are these things dangerous?"

Tara, standing on the porch, stifled a laugh. Boone stood quietly behind her, as solid and strong as the Great Wall of China, and said nothing at all.

"No," Tara called back. "They're *chickens.*"

Looking doubtful, James pushed open his car door and stepped out gingerly onto the ground, wincing a little. Tara had always considered her ex-husband a very good-looking man, with his lean frame and sandy hair, but now, in proximity to Boone Taylor, he seemed ineffectual, almost effete.

Would *he* have jumped into the dangerous waters at the base of the spillway to save his daughters?

Probably, Tara reflected, because he *was* their father, after all. But she couldn't picture it. Conversely, the image of Boone fighting his way to Elle and Erin, rescuing them and then fighting his way *back,* would be engraved in her mind and on her heart forever.

Not surprisingly, Elle and Erin had heard the exchange and stepped out onto the porch. Elle's right arm was in a gleaming white cast, already emblazoned with Erin's and Griffin's autographs and a smiley face that was almost certainly Fletcher's.

"We don't want to go back with you," Elle said boldly.

Erin, standing shoulder to shoulder with her twin, nodded agreement.

"Well," James bit out, keeping his distance, "you've certainly ruined any chance of attending Briarwood."

"Good," Elle replied. "Because Erin and I want to stay here, with Tara."

James's gaze shifted to Boone, sized him up, swung back to Tara. He let out a long, exhausted sigh and shoved away some of the chickens with the side of one now-dusty oxford. "It's been a very long day," he said, no doubt thinking of his travel ordeal, rather than what the girls had been through. "I have a hotel room in town. Maybe we could talk all this over tomorrow?"

Tara felt a slight easing inside, the faintest flicker of hope.

"That sounds like a good idea," she said. James hadn't taken a single step toward his daughters. No hugs, no kisses, no declarations like "I love you" or "Thank God you're safe."

He'd had a long day.

As an afterthought, James took in Elle and Erin. "You're all right?" he asked lamely, the car door already open so he could make a speedy exit.

James was ever so good at exits. It was sticking around, sticking things out, that came hard to him.

"Yes," the twins replied.

James got back into his rental car, turned it slowly around, scattering chickens in all directions and raising a storm of good old country dust, and drove away.

Elle and Erin went back into the house, evidently uninterested.

So did Griffin and Fletcher and the two dogs.

Which left Tara and Boone and the chickens.

Boone turned to Tara, cupped her chin gently in one hand and lifted her face for his kiss. "Everything's going to be all right," he told her.

He was all man, she thought, as strong and solid as the mountains surrounding Parable on all sides, sheltering the little community from all kinds of storms and mishaps.

Tara nodded. "I believe you're right," she replied. "Not all the time, of course."

Boone laughed, kissed her forehead lightly. “Of course,” he agreed. “I’m not going anywhere, Tara. When you need me, I’ll be right here.”

She knew that was true—that Boone *would* be there for her, for Griffin and Fletcher, for any children they might have together.

“This will take time,” she told him.

“I know,” he said. “There’s a lot to figure out.”

A few minutes later, Boone had gathered his boys and Scamp and they’d all gotten into the police car—which had drawn a few curious glances from James during his brief visit—and headed for home.

Tara lingered on the porch for a few moments, her heart full of love for Boone, for his little boys and her stepdaughters and both the dogs. Impossibly, she felt an equal measure of sorrow, because James would probably take the girls away with him, and their absence would be a soul-wound, one she might never get over.

She went back into the house, found the girls in the living room with Lucy.

They'd turned off the TV, mercifully, and Elle was starting to fade from fatigue and pain, since her medications were wearing off.

"Will Dad let us stay?" Erin asked, her voice small and tremulous. She was wearing her spare glasses, but they were outdated and sat crookedly on her nose.

"I don't know," Tara admitted, because it was important to be honest. She sank into an armchair, sighed and swept up both girls in a pointed glance. "What you two did today was stupid," she added. "You could have been killed, both of you, and if you ever, *ever* do anything like that again, I'll—I'll—"

She'd *what?*

The girls were homeward bound, for all practical intents and purposes. In a day or two, they'd be out of her life, probably forever, and it wasn't as if she'd be able to ground them via email or text.

"I'll be very disappointed," Tara finally finished. "Because I love you, both of you, with my whole heart."

"But Daddy has all the power," Erin supplied wisely. Sadly.

Out of the mouths of babes.

"Yes," Tara answered. "He's calling the shots, and we have to accept that."

Elle's lower lip jutted out a little ways. "I wish we'd made it all the way to the river," she fussed. "By now, we'd probably be in Idaho *at least,* maybe even in Oregon."

Tara suppressed a smile even as she blinked back more tears. *Tears.* What good were they?

"Must I go over—*again*—the many dangers of running away?" she asked, sternly loving. "There are some really *bad* people out there, remember?"

It was a shame the world could be such a dangerous place, but the truth was the truth. All manner of creeps lurked in bus depots and in train stations, down-at-the-heels cafés and even shelters, waiting to take advantage of young, innocent girls hungry for what they perceived as kindness.

Instead of arguing, Elle and Erin joined Tara in the armchair, squeezing in on either side of her, snuggling close, reminding her of the way chicks nestled under the wings of hens, mistakenly believing that nothing could hurt them there.

She kissed Elle's temple and then Erin's.

"How about supper?" she asked gently.

Elle countered with an unrelated question. "You do like Boone Taylor, don't you? Like we said before?"

Tara sighed. "Yes," she said, resigned. "I like him."

Erin's eyes were big behind her extra glasses. "He's pretty strong," she said.

"And brave," Elle capitulated.

"Griffin and Fletcher are lucky he's their dad," Erin added.

Tara merely nodded, too choked up to reply.

The whole thing was none of his business, Boone concluded, but he knew James and Tara were facing each other across a back table at the Butter Biscuit Café that very morning, and it made him uneasy.

To make matters worse, Treat Mc-

Quillan, now Parable's official chief of police, was hanging around Boone's office, prattling on about how there'd be some changes around this town now that he was in charge.

In charge.

Boone let that one pass, since he was mainly concerned with Tara and her meeting with her ex-husband. If the man had a shred of decency in him, he'd let Tara raise his daughters, since he clearly didn't want the job himself, and go on with his life. The problem was, Lennox didn't strike Boone as the honorable type.

Still, if he was as self-serving as he seemed, the good doctor might see granting Tara legal guardianship of the twins as a plus, since he'd be free to do whatever he damn well pleased. But there was a hitch: Tara had clearly wounded Lennox's masculine pride at some point, and he enjoyed spiting her.

"Are you listening to me?" former deputy McQuillan demanded, stepping into Boone's personal space and thereby risking a mouth full of knuckles.

"Actually," Boone answered, "no. I'm

not. Most of what you say goes in one ear and out the other—or haven't you noticed that before?"

"I'm entitled to respect!" McQuillan flared, going red around the jowls.

"That's where we disagree," Boone said quietly. "Respect is *earned,* and nobody—but nobody—is 'entitled' to it, including you."

Treat looked apoplectic for a moment, then he turned on one heel, spitting mad, and stormed out of the office, slamming the door behind him. Both Becky and the dog jumped at the sound.

"That went well," Becky said sweetly.

"Isn't it time for your coffee break or something?" Boone retorted.

She made a big drama of looking at her watch, one of those small, old-fashioned ones with the stretchy band she'd probably had since she was twelve. "Darned if it isn't," she sang out. She stood up behind her desk, reached for her purse and pranced toward the door. "See you when I see you," she said, and disappeared.

Boone growled under his breath, dragging his gaze over the empty cells on the other side of the room. With McQuillan policing the town, they'd probably be full by nightfall, holding dangerous nursing-home escapees who'd pinched a banana over at the supermarket, or Boy Scouts caught crossing against the one traffic light in the whole town.

Scamp looked up at him, gave a sympathetic whimper and wagged his tail once.

The door opened again and Boone turned, expecting to see McQuillan, wanting to rant some more, or Mayor Hale with another demand for Hutch Carmody's arrest.

But it was Tara standing there, her face glowing. She clutched a paper in her hand, some sort of document, and waved it like a flag of triumph.

"James is going to let the girls stay with me—indefinitely!" she crowed. "Maggie Landers happened to be in the café at the same time we were, and she drew up a preliminary custody agreement then and there!"

If Tara was happy, Boone was happy.

He crossed to her, lifted her by the

waist and spun her around in a laughing circle. “How did that happen?” he asked, setting her down but still holding her close against him.

“I was right about the social-media thing. The school isn’t going to take Elle and Erin because they’re afraid they’ll run away again.” She paused, sobered a little. “They’re probably right about that, I’m afraid.”

“But the bottom line is the twins are staying right here in Parable,” Boone supplied.

Tara nodded happily. “Indefinitely,” she said, tearing up a little.

And then he kissed her.

She melted against him. “I’ve never made love in a jail cell,” she crooned after the kiss.

Boone laughed. “I’d call that a good thing,” he said. “And I don’t want to be a wet blanket or anything, but this isn’t going to be your first time.”

Tara pouted prettily. “Don’t you want me?”

“Like a brush fire wants dry grass,” Boone answered huskily, “but it’ll have to wait.”

There was no telling how long the wait would be, since they'd agreed that lovemaking was out when the kids were around, which was pretty much all the time, at least until after they were married. And Boone was partial to beds when it came to sex, though a grassy meadow or the backseat of a car—a private car, not his cruiser—would probably fit the bill, too.

"Slow and steady," Boone murmured, kissing Tara's nose. "That's how we're going to play this, lady."

Tara twinkled up at him, her arms around his neck, her hips grinding slightly against him.

No hat was going to cover *this* hard-on.

"That's how I like it," she teased, her tone sultry, her scent making him lightheaded. "Slow and steady."

"Then I'm your man," Boone told her.

She smiled and kissed him, quickly but with sizzle. "Keep that in mind," she answered. "At least for the next fifty years or so."

EPILOGUE

Concert Night

Come Saturday afternoon, as he made a few rounds in his cruiser before turning his badge over to Slade Barlow for the night, Boone could have sworn he felt a sort of thrumming in the air, the pre-echo of music, heavy on the bass, even though Casey's benefit concert wasn't scheduled to start until 9:00 p.m. He supposed it was excitement and anticipation; Parable was already filling up with folks from out of town, including some news crews, and the stores and cafés were doing a lively business.

Pulling into the parking lot at the courthouse, with Scamp at his side, Boone met Treat McQuillan in his rattletrap interim patrol car, salvaged from a scrap outfit, by the looks of it.

They stopped, side by side, to nod curtly at each other.

McQuillan looked agitated, so Boone sighed and rolled down his window.

"You can't deputize Hutch Carmody!" blurted the new chief of police, tiny eyes bulging. That nasty temper of his had to be hard on veins and arteries; one of these days, the man was going to blow a gasket. "He's practically a suspect!"

In point of fact, Boone *hadn't* deputized his old friend, but suspected, after a quick glance around the lot, where he spotted Hutch's shiny truck, that Hutch had gone ahead and appointed *himself* to the position.

Which was fine with Boone—and even finer if it got under McQuillan's lazy hide, as seemed to be the case.

"Hutch isn't a *suspect*," Boone replied reasonably. *He's definitely guilty.*

Saw him tear down that damnable water tower with my own eyes.

"I'm warning you, Boone—I'll nail those guys. That water tower was an historical treasure."

"It was a death trap," Boone countered, rolling up his window again. This conversation was over.

McQuillan sped off, muffler rattling, probably on his way to bust choir-practice attendees on a charge of unlawful assembly.

Shaking his head, Boone parked in the usual spot, unbuckled his seat belt and got out of the cruiser, Scamp jumping out after him. These days, the critter went by the name Deputy Dog around Parable, riding shotgun most of the time and hanging out in the office with Boone.

Inside, Boone and the dog followed the corridor to his office door, which was slightly open. Stepping through, he spotted Slade right away, trying to work the new coffeemaker, a contraption Becky had purchased on QVC and expected to charge to the county. Boone had paid for the gadget himself.

"Afternoon," Slade said in that laid-back drawl of his. "Feels weird to be back here—déjà vu all over again, to quote Yogi Berra."

Boone answered with a nod of acknowledgment and swung his gaze toward Becky's desk. Sure enough, Hutch was sitting behind it, with his booted feet propped on the surface, old-West style. Looked like a scene out of that 1950s movie *Rio Bravo.*

"Make yourself at home," Boone said drily.

"Don't mind if I do," Hutch replied with a grin. He settled back in his chair, cupped his hands behind his blond head. "Tough job," he added as a good-natured gibe.

Boone batted the proverbial ball right back over the net. "Compared to what you normally do," he quipped, "I suppose it is."

Although Hutch worked Whisper Creek Ranch, his home-place, and could cowboy with the best of them, he had a lot of hired help and a net worth sizable enough to bail out the banking sector all over again.

"My brother here," Hutch drawled,

gesturing toward Slade, "is acting sheriff. And he's already signed me on to help keep the peace."

"Right," Boone said, finally letting loose with a chuckle; he was wound up tight, not because of the concert, though he was looking forward to hearing Casey sing and watching one of her legendary performances, but because afterward he and Tara were spending the night together, alone. All the kids would be at Casey's place for the minishow and the sleepover.

"Patsy McCullough's back home," Slade commented, finally extracting a cup of coffee from the machine. "She and the girl, anyhow. Dawson's still in the hospital, of course, but he's doing real well, already getting in some physical therapy and grousing because he can't attend the concert tonight."

Boone grinned. He'd gotten the news earlier, and driven by Patsy's place to have a look at the brand-new wheelchair ramp in front of her small house. "I love this town," he said.

"Me, too," Hutch agreed wryly. "Except when I hate it."

Slade chuckled at that, and so did Boone.

The regular deputies arrived, and Slade took charge with no trouble at all.

Boone headed for the community center with Scamp, leaving the squad car for Slade and taking his old beater of a truck, and picked up Griffin and Fletcher. In a few hours, Opal would collect them and take them, along with Elle and Erin, to Casey's place. Along with her churchgoing posse, Opal would serve as a chaperone.

She's the one I should have deputized, Boone thought with another grin.

"You're not taking this truck on your date with Ms. Kendall, are you?" Griffin immediately asked, once he and his brother were planted on the bench seat, cheek by jowl. There was no backseat, like in Hutch's and Slade's fancy extended-cab rigs, so the boosters were wedged in, and the dog had to ride on the floorboard.

"She said we could call her Tara," Fletcher interjected. They'd spent a lot of time together over the past few days, since James Lennox's dramatic departure for New York, and Tara had won his sons' hearts as surely as she had his.

Griffin gave his brother an impatient glance. "This thing might fall apart before you even get to the fairgrounds," he complained to Boone.

Boone smiled, ran his knuckles lightly over the kid's crew cut. "Don't worry about it, Romeo," he replied. "We'll probably take her car."

"Who's Romeo?" Fletcher wanted to know.

"Never mind," Boone answered.

And so it went.

At home, the boys rushed to gather up their new sleeping bags and other overnight gear, piling it all carefully next to the kitchen door as though they might have to make a break for it. Once the collecting was done, Griffin went outside with Scamp, and Boone had a rare moment alone with his younger son.

"Hey, buddy," he said. "You gonna be all right away from home for a whole night and everything?"

Fletcher squared his shoulders. "I'm

not a baby, Dad," he reminded Boone. "I even stopped wetting the bed."

"You sure did," Boone agreed. He hadn't had to throw sheets into the washer and dryer for a while now. "I'm proud of you."

"Can we go see Aunt Molly and Uncle Bob?"

Boone crouched, so he and the boy were eye to eye. "Sure," he said gently. "As soon as they're ready for company. Uncle Bob's still in rehab right now, so he's pretty busy."

Fletcher nodded solemnly, and Boone ached for him, wondering if he was still homesick for Molly and her family.

"Are you going to marry Tara?"

The question, earnest and hopeful, knocked Boone back on his figurative heels. "I hope so," he answered. "It'll be a while, though."

Fletcher broke into a grin. "Can we live in her house, instead of this one?"

Boone laughed and squeezed the boy's shoulder as he stood up straight again. "We're still figuring that out," he replied. In fact, he and Tara had discussed future living arrangements and agreed that building a whole separate house didn't make sense, since they had a perfectly good one already.

Full circle, Boone had thought. He'd begun his life in Tara's farmhouse, he and Molly growing up there with their mom and dad, and it looked as though he'd live out the rest of his days under the same roof.

Once, not so long ago, the idea, while appealing, would have chafed his pride. Now, if it meant being with Tara, he'd have set up housekeeping in her chicken coop.

Anyway, instead of a house, they planned on putting up a good barn, getting horses and riding gear for the whole crew.

Outside, a car horn tooted, and Fletcher practically vibrated with excitement.

Boone went out, hauling some of the boys' gear, and grinned at Opal, who was just getting out of her station wagon. There was something different about her, he thought, but he couldn't quite put his finger on it. Same straitlaced dress, practical shoes, outdated hairdo.

It was the *glow,* he realized suddenly. The woman was lit up from the inside, as if she'd swallowed a harvest moon whole.

Griffin and Fletcher got busy loading their stuff into the back of the station wagon while Boone stood in the tall grass, facing Opal, and tilted his head to one side, grinning.

"What's different about you?" he asked forthrightly.

Opal seemed to preen for a moment, her smile full of mischief and spirit, and then she simply lifted her left hand, showing off the respectable diamond glittering on her ring finger.

"The Reverend proposed," she said, and then she actually blushed.

Boone was pleased. "When's the wedding?" he asked.

Opal executed a mock glare that failed to lessen the twinkle in her dark eyes. Leaning in a little, her voice low so the boys wouldn't overhear, she replied, "After I've got you and Tara married up proper, that's when."

He laughed. "Your mission in life, I presume?" he teased.

"Joslyn and Slade and Hutch and Kendra finally got it right," Opal declared, as though still winded by her matchmaking efforts. "Once you and Tara tie the knot, I can retire and just be a minister's wife."

"What about all the other loners in Parable County?" Boone asked, touched as well as amused. "Don't you have to fix up a few other couples?"

Opal looked thoughtful. "Well," she said, in all seriousness, "I might have to step in with Casey Elder and Walker Parrish, so maybe I'll just be *semi*retired. But everybody else is on their own, 'cause I'm going to be real busy lovin' my husband."

Boone kissed her forehead. "Congratulations," he said. "The Reverend Dr. Walter Beaumont is one lucky man."

"And he sure can catch fish," Opal confirmed, turning to make sure the boys were ready to roll and leaving Boone standing there baffled. *He sure can catch fish?*

They drove off then, the boys waving,

Opal honking and Scamp barking a farewell.

Boone watched them until they turned onto the county road, then went back into the double-wide, Scamp keeping spritely pace, to get ready for his hot date.

Tara felt as giddy as a high school girl about to attend her first prom, and she changed clothes three times before settling on black jeans, a blue silk shirt and boots.

By the time Boone knocked at her front door, she was downright jittery and very glad Opal had already picked up Elle and Erin for the big night at Casey's since they would surely have teased her.

Tara almost tripped coming down the stairs, and when she opened the door, her heart swelled with love. Boone looked cowboy-handsome, standing there in his crisply pressed white Western shirt, creased jeans and shiny boots. He held his hat in one hand and regarded her almost shyly.

"Ready?" he asked.

"Ready," she managed to say.

He'd brought Scamp over to keep Lucy company while they were out, and the two dogs sniffed noses and went amiably off toward the kitchen, their owners forgotten.

"You look beautiful," Boone said with gruff sincerity.

So do you, Tara wanted to say. She let her eyes make the statement and said, "Thank you," instead.

She got her purse and stepped onto the porch, locking up the house behind her. "I hope I'm not underdressed," she fretted, as Boone took her arm in a gentlemanly hold, escorting her toward the front gate.

"I actually prefer you underdressed," Boone said. "Make that *un*dressed, but you look way beyond good right now, lady."

The rusted-out truck, parked where the chickens normally roamed, looked especially bad sitting forlornly in the gathering dusk. Like the double-wide, it seemed to be disintegrating before his eyes.

Boone felt a twinge of embarrassment. *I'll get a new rig,* he promised himself. *Tomorrow, damn it.*

"I guess we could take your SUV," he said, glancing down at Tara. She sparkled brighter than Opal's new engagement ring.

And she looked up at him, smiled. "Let's take yours. I'm trying to live down my city-slicker reputation."

Boone laughed, loving her even more than he had a minute before, and helped her into the old wreck, glad he'd wiped down the seats and vacuumed the floorboards. "If word gets out that your chickens are practically house pets," he joked, once he was behind the wheel, "you might be stuck with the label for life."

She reached over, patted his blue-jeaned thigh. "Surely my secret is safe with you," she said, smiling conspiratorially.

"I don't know," Boone replied. "I *am* fond of fried chicken."

She made a face, but it was obvious she knew he was teasing.

The parking lot out at the fairgrounds,

where the rodeo was held every summer, was jammed with cars and pickups, news vans and even a few semitrucks. Casey's fans came from all walks of life, and judging by the varying license plates, some of them were willing to go the distance.

Boone parked the truck and helped Tara out. He bought tickets, even though Casey had offered him free seats, because the cause was a good one. They made their way through the excited crowds and managed to find seats.

The special stage set up in the middle of the arena flashed with colored lights, but only the instruments were visible, which added to the excitement of the many, many waiting fans.

High school kids hawked souvenir T-shirts and glossy programs—all profits going to the fund for the McCullough family, like the ticket sales—and Boone bought two of each. It was goofy, he supposed, but he liked the idea of him and Tara going around town in matching T-shirts. *Going steady,* he thought, amused.

Finally, the band members took the

stage, and the lights went crazy, as did the audience. The keyboard man sounded a familiar chord, everything went dark, and when the lights came up again, Casey stood front and center, resplendent in a rhinestone-studded white pantsuit and matching boots, a guitar slung over her shoulder. Lighters flickered all over the bleachers, and the foot-stomping and shouting was deafening.

Once the audience settled down a little, Casey made a little speech about how welcome she and her family felt in Parable, and how glad they were to be a part of such a fine community, a place with a heart. She reminded them that every nickel raised that night would go to Dawson McCullough, his mom and his sister—Patsy and her daughter had seats near the stage, and she asked them to stand—and cheers erupted again. Tears ran down Patsy's smiling face, while Casey acknowledged the applause humbly, and the lead guitar player launched into a familiar refrain.

The concert was on.

Casey Elder rocked the Parable

County Fairgrounds that night, performing for nearly two hours before bringing everybody to their feet with a stirring rendition of "God Bless America."

Hokey, maybe, Boone thought. But he sang along loudly, like everybody else in the bleachers.

Wrapping it up, Casey thanked everybody for coming and promised to autograph programs over at the Boot Scoot Tavern later on, where there would be lots of dancing and more opportunities to contribute to the fund.

Boone turned to Tara as people streamed past all around them, racing for the exits. He sure hoped Slade and the deputies were ready for the onslaught.

"Feel like dancing?" he asked.

Tara leaned forward, touching her lips to his chin. "No," she said. "I feel like making love."

Boone felt a rush of joy and no small anticipation. He'd carry his hat to the truck, he decided, instead of wearing it on his head.

"Then let's get out of here," he said, squeezing her hand.

* * *

Tara was high on music, high on love, and when Boone carried her up the front steps and over her threshold like a bride, she reveled in it.

Lucy and Scamp barely greeted them, there in the darkened entryway, before wandering away again, patently disinterested in the oddity of human beings already kicking off boots and peeling off their clothes.

"I can't wait," Tara said, "not even until we're upstairs—"

Boone arched his eyebrows comically, closed his hands over her bare breasts, right there in the foyer, and eased her back against the wall.

He kissed her endlessly, it seemed to her, taking his time before moving on to her neck, her shoulders, her collarbones, her belly, then going back to her mouth again, all the while plying her gently with his fingers.

After what seemed like an eternity, he knelt, running his lips over her thighs, even her knees, and finally—finally—he took her into his mouth.

Tara cried out softly, already in an anguish of welcoming pleasure, and perspiration broke out all over her body. She writhed as he enjoyed her, bringing her to the brink, withdrawing, taking her to new heights but not quite *there.*

She whimpered, wanting Boone to hurry and, conversely, praying that he'd take his time, prolong the almost unbearably delicious sensation of climbing, climbing toward ecstasy.

Boone enjoyed her at his leisure, brought her to several knee-melting climaxes before he finally stood up again, holding her upright, his hands at her waist, and pressed against her.

"No condom this time," he warned, nibbling at her right earlobe even as he prepared her for more loving with his fingers. "If there's a baby, there's a baby. Agreed?"

"No condom," she moaned, nodding, jubilant with need, every nerve singing under her skin, her heart skittering, her breath so rapid and so shallow that she was afraid she might hyperventilate.

Boone lifted Tara off her bare feet, and she wrapped her legs tightly around his waist. He looked deep into her eyes, paused for a long moment, and then he entered her, hard and fast, and she welcomed him with a low, frantic croon, her back pressed against the wall. The ferocity of it, the boldness of making love in her entryway, for pity's sake, took away her breath.

Her body seized with one climax and then another. She moaned Boone's name, groped for his mouth with her own, flying higher and then higher still.

She waited for his control to break, but it was a long time before he came, with a thrust so hard it sent her spinning into yet another release, sent her spiraling into a vortex of sensations, not just between her legs, but in her mind and spirit, too.

Boone had not just *taken* Tara; he'd laid permanent claim to her. She was his woman, now and forever, fused to him in ways that seemed almost sacred. Boone's eruption was a magnificent hardening of his entire body, and he groaned her name as he flexed against her, over and over.

Exhausted, murmuring, they sank to their knees and then lay on the hooked rug, legs entwined, fighting to breathe, as if they were shipwreck survivors, clinging together on a flimsy raft.

Gradually, they recovered, though they remained where they were.

"I can't believe you just had me against a wall," Tara said, very glad that he had, as small aftershocks moved through her like a festive trail of descending fireworks against a dark sky. It was so deliciously decadent.

"I can be pretty inventive," Boone told her, nibbling at her neck.

And he proceeded to prove it by having her again, this time on the floor.

Eventually, they'd made it as far as Tara's bed.

She lay sleeping now, her lashes like dark feathers against her cheeks, her breathing slow and deep and even, her lips forming a little smile as she dreamed.

Boone was content just to look at her, for the time being, anyhow. Physically, and in a lot of other ways, too, he couldn't get enough of Tara Kendall.

She was so beautiful. So smart and so strong and so passionate.

Why in hell had it taken him so long to realize she was the woman for him?

Because he'd been holding on to a memory, that was why. Holding on to Corrie, and everything they were supposed to have had, as though by resisting he could bring her back.

It struck him now that Corrie would be happy for him, happy that her boys were going to have a mother again. Had he been holding her back somehow, mourning so hard for so long?

In that moment, he let go, once and for all, and in the next, he felt a strange, soft parting, and he knew Corrie had finally been set free, and moved on.

Tears burned the backs of his eyes. *Goodbye,* he said silently.

Tara stirred a little.

Miracle of miracles, she *loved him.* And that was the greatest gift she could have given him, even if they lived and loved into their old age, surrounded by children and grandchildren and great-grandchildren.

And he loved her, no doubt about it, more with every passing day, every beat of his heart, every drawn breath.

Presently, she opened her eyes, all fluttery and disoriented for a moment.

"Yep," Boone said, grinning. "It's true. You've been making love to a redneck sheriff with a double-wide for most of the night. And in some mighty scandalous places, too."

She grinned back, purring a little in sultry contentment, and punched him lightly in one shoulder, and her eyes glowed, warming him through and through. "It just so happens that I love my 'redneck sheriff' with all my heart," she told him. "And when it comes to scandalous places to have sex, I have a few ideas of my own."

"That's good," Boone said in a voice rumbly with emotions he couldn't quite contain. Didn't *need* to contain, because he could tell this woman anything, let her see into his very soul. "Because I'm pretty crazy about a certain pseudo chicken rancher myself."

She touched a finger to the tip of his nose, sending a thrill through him as easily as that. "Remember your promise," she said.

"You can take it to the bank," Boone

told her. "Along with every other promise I ever make." A pause, during which they both choked up. Then, "When are we getting married?" he asked. "Only being able to make love when none of the kids are around is going to be tough."

That was part of the agreement, until they were husband and wife.

"You'll just have to improvise, Boone Taylor. It would be absolutely *indecent* to have a wedding in less than six months." She smiled a sexy smile. "In the meantime, I think we ought to get in as much practice as we can."

Boone sighed. "All right," he agreed. "Six months."

She kissed him, snuggling close. "I'll make it up to you," she promised.

* * * * *